An
Unsuitable Attachment

By the same author
Already published:

Excellent Women
Jane and Prudence
Less than Angels
A Glass of Blessings
Quartet in Autumn
The Sweet Dove Died
A Few Green Leaves

Forthcoming:
Some Tame Gazelle
No Fond Return of Love

An
Unsuitable Attachment

Barbara Pym

E. P. Dutton · New York

Published 1982 by Macmillan London Limited
London and Basingstoke

Published in the United States by
E. P. Dutton, Inc.
2 Park Avenue
New York, N.Y. 10016

Library of Congress Catalog Card Number: 82 -7 07 41

ISBN: 0-525-24117-5

10   9   8   7   6   5   4   3   2   1

First Edition

LITERARY EXECUTOR'S NOTE

In various conversations I had, over the years, with Barbara Pym about *An Unsuitable Attachment*, she spoke of ways in which she intended to 'improve' (her word) it. Some cuts have been made along the lines she had been considering – though nothing, of course, has been added.

A few short passages which have dated in a way that she would have found unacceptable have also been deleted.

The original, full text is now lodged with the Bodleian Library, Oxford, along with her other manuscripts.

H.H.

1

They are watching me, thought Rupert Stonebird, as he saw the two women walking rather too slowly down the road. But no doubt I am watching them too, he decided, for as an anthropologist he knew that men and women may observe each other as warily as wild animals hidden in long grass.

The situation had nothing particularly unusual about it – an unmarried man visiting the house he had just bought and wondering where he should put his furniture, and two women – sisters, perhaps – betraying a very natural interest in the man or the house or both. One day, he thought, we shall probably know each other, and for that reason he turned away from the window, not feeling quite equal to meeting the unashamed curiosity of their glances as they came nearer. But now the taller one, who looked older, was gazing rather ostentatiously away. The smaller one seemed to find it necessary to raise her voice, so that Rupert heard a sentence of their conversation before they passed out of earshot.

'The vicar's wife and her sister – isn't that *just* what we look like,' said Penelope Grandison, 'and laden with parcels too. *Not* the kind of people who have everything sent.'

'We've been shopping,' said Sophia Ainger, 'so of course we're laden.' She spoke rather absently for she was remembering a vase of stiff-looking artificial flowers of an unknown species, seen fleetingly in a funeral director's window, which now overlaid her memory of the bright Kensington shops and brought her back to the reality of her life in North London. The afternoon's shopping had been arranged to console her sister Penelope, who at twenty-five was still young enough to suffer disappointments in love as commonly as colds or headaches. On this occasion it was to be hoped that humiliation and hurt pride had been assuaged by a new pair of shoes and a many-stranded jet necklace – like early travellers taking presents to the natives, Sophia felt.

'Men seem to prefer young girls of eighteen,' said Penelope gloomily, 'and *then* where are you.'

'But there have always been girls of eighteen, even in my day,' Sophia protested.

'Well you just married the curate, so it was all right. One wouldn't expect a *clergyman* to be interested in young girls of eighteen.'

'I don't see why not – after all I was only just twenty-one when I married Mark.'

'How old would you say that man standing in the window of that house was?' asked Penelope tentatively.

'Oh, in his thirties probably. I didn't see him very clearly,' Sophia added. Yet she had retained an impression of somebody so ordinary-looking that his very lack of distinction was in itself reassuring. She hoped that if he was a churchgoer – which was unlikely these days – he would not recognise her as the vicar's wife. He had probably not even noticed her, a tall, rather too thin woman of thirty odd, with dark auburn hair. Penelope, with her brighter red hair and rather flamboyant appearance, was much more distinctive.

'I suppose Mark will call on him as he's living in the parish?' Penelope suggested hopefully.

14

'He will do what he ought to do – you can depend on that.'

'It's a comfort when people do what they ought to do. Not like *him*,' said Penelope bitterly.

'Never mind, Penny. He wasn't good enough for you, anyway,' said Sophia.

'But men and women never do match each other in that kind of way – that's life.'

'No, women are usually too good for men, but Mark is much too good for me,' said Sophia. 'Do you know, he told me not to worry about supper tonight but to enjoy my afternoon out. He said he'd get something.'

Penelope did not answer. Her brother-in-law, with his remote good looks, never seemed quite real to her. She found it difficult to imagine him getting something for supper.

'FRYING TONIGHT. ROCK SALMON – SKATE – PLAICE.' Mark Ainger read from the roughly chalked-up notice in the steamy window. Which would Sophia prefer? he asked himself. And which would tempt Faustina's delicate appetite? Rock salmon – that had a noble sound about it, though he believed it was actually inferior to real salmon. Skate – he imagined that was one of those flat bony fish, with the teeth showing in a sardonic grin. Only plaice was familar to him, so he supposed it had better be that. Plaice, then, and two helpings – better make it three if Faustina was to be included – perhaps 'portions' was the word – and some chips. He must get this right, not make a fool of himself by stumbling over the words, not using the correct terminology or not knowing which fish he wanted.

Turning down the collar of his raincoat and arranging it to expose his clerical collar – for he was not ashamed of his calling – Mark entered the shop.

'Three portions of plaice and some chips, please,' he

said firmly in his pleasant baritone voice.

'Mind, Father, it's hot – have you got something to put it in?'

Mark lifted up his zip-fastened bag and the fragrant, greasy, newspaper-wrapped bundle was placed carefully inside it. Good-nights were exchanged and he left the shop with a feeling of satisfaction, as if a rather difficult task had been successfully accomplished.

This was the very fringe of his parish, that part that would never become residentially 'desirable' because it was too near the railway, and many of the big gaunt houses had been taken over by families of West Indians. Mark had been visiting, trying to establish some kind of contact with his exotic parishioners and hoping to discover likely boys and men to sing in the choir and serve at the altar. He had received several enthusiastic offers, though he wondered how many of them would really turn up in church. As he walked away from the house, Mark had remembered that it was along this street, with its brightly – almost garishly – painted houses that Sophia had once seen a cluster of what she took to be exotic tropical fruits in one of the windows, only to realise that they were tomatoes put there to ripen. 'Love apples,' she had said to Mark, and the words 'love apple' had somehow given a name to the district, strange and different as it was from the rest of the parish which lay over the other side of the main road, far from the railway line.

Here the houses were less colourful, drably respectable but hardly elegant. On the extreme eastern boundary of the parish, however, where the church and vicarage were rather oddly placed, a number of small terrace houses had been bought up by speculative builders, gutted, modernised, and sold at high prices to people who wanted small houses that were almost in town but could not afford the more fashionable districts of Islington, St John's Wood or Hampstead. It was in one of these that Sophia and Penelope had seen the stranger.

Afterwards he went by way of St Basil's Terrace, looking as Sophia had done earlier at the newly done up houses with their prettily painted front doors and rather self-conscious window-boxes and bay trees in tubs, when a woman's voice called out behind him, 'Good evening vicar – been getting fish for pussy?'

When he turned round, rather startled, the voice went on, 'Oh, *I* know what you've got in the bag – you can't hide anything from me!'

'No, Sister Dew, I don't suppose I can,' said Mark in a resigned tone. All the same he did not feel inclined to reveal that the fish was not only for Faustina – who was never called 'pussy' – but also for his and his wife's supper.

'How you do love pussy,' Sister Dew went on. 'Only the other day I was at the vicarage, seeing Mrs Ainger about my stall at the bazaar – I'm doing the fancy work this year, you know – and there was pussy, bold as brass, if you please, walking into the lounge as if she owned it.'

But she does, Mark thought, though he said nothing.

'"Oh, Mrs Ainger", I said, "you wouldn't want pussy going in your lounge, would you."' Sister Dew smiled up at Mark, for she was a little dumpy woman. Her prominent blue eyes, seeming to bulge with curiosity, met Mark's eyes, which were also blue, but with that remote expression sometimes found in the eyes of sailors or explorers. Although invariably kind and courteous he had the air of seeming not to be particularly interested in human beings – a somewhat doubtful quality in a parish priest, though it had its advantages.

'You'll find pussy going on the beds next,' Sister Dew went on. 'On the beds and in the lounge – you couldn't have that.'

Mark's smile did not reveal that Faustina naturally went on the beds as well as in the lounge. He was wondering if, strictly speaking, a vicarage could be said to have a lounge – he would have thought not. Sister Dew was a tedious little woman but she must be listened to because of all his parishioners she was the one most likely to take offence. She was a retired hospital nurse and Mark had often wondered why her noble profession, so intimately connected with the great events of life, should have made her so petty-minded. Perhaps it was their very greatness that made her so – one couldn't be noble all the time.

'How pretty those houses are,' said Mark, feeling that he ought to stay and talk to her a little longer. He was hungry and conscious of the delicious greasy bundle in his bag, but he believed fish and chips were usually heated up in the oven anyway, so they wouldn't spoil.

'Yes, and nice people coming to live in them.' She lowered her voice. 'I've heard this one we're standing by has been bought by a television producer. Associated Rediffusion,' she added reverently.

Mark puzzled over the words, but they meant nothing to him.

'And there's Miss Broome opposite, with the mauve front door – she's sweet, I think. Just the kind of person we want at St Basil's.'

Mark's face brightened for he remembered who Miss Broome was – a nice-looking youngish woman who had been to church the last two or three Sundays.

'Her mother was a canon's widow,' said Sister Dew, in her reverent Associated Rediffusion voice.

'So her father must have been a canon,' said Mark, though he felt that for some reason it was the canon's widow who cut more ice here. Since Miss Broome's parents were both dead, it could never be known how it had been in life.

'She's a librarian or something like that,' Sister Dew went on. 'And that lovely fur coat! Chinchilla, I *would* have said, but I suppose it couldn't be. Grey squirrel, more likely, though one doesn't see that much nowadays. Well, I mustn't keep you, vicar, or pussy will have something to say, won't she.'

Sister Dew scuttled off to her own house, which was at the as yet unfashionable end of the terrace, and Mark hurried along the short distance to the vicarage. Beyond it lay the Victorian Gothic church and some large houses of the same period, now mostly turned into flats.

Sophia was in the kitchen, laying the table for supper.

'What is chinchilla?' Mark asked, as he handed over the fish and chips.

'Why, a kind of fur, pale grey and very expensive – worn mostly by wealthy Edwardian ladies with a bunch of Parma violets and perhaps a toque.'

'Ah yes, the kind of hat your mother used to wear.'

'Why do you want to know about chinchilla? I can't believe you've come across any in Love Apple Road this afternoon.'

'It's the kind of fur Sister Dew thought Miss Broome's coat might be – but apparently it would be too expensive even for a canon's daughter.'

'Oh yes – but how well it would suit Ianthe Broome – she's just the type for chinchilla.'

'And so are you, darling,' said Mark. 'And all I bring you is fish and chips.'

Sophia had, in a sense, married beneath her, for although Mark came of a good clerical family he was without private means. Sophia's mother spoke in hushed tones of her son-in-law's parish – much too near the Harrow Road and *North* Kensington to be the kind of district one liked to think of one's daughter living in, though of course a vicarage was different. The clergy had to go to these rather dreadful places, but it was a pity

Mark couldn't have got something 'better', like a Knightsbridge or *South* Kensington church, or even a good country living.

'I love fish and chips,' said Sophia warmly, 'and I think they're ready now.'

No sooner had the dish been taken from the oven than a tortoiseshell cat entered the room, and leapt, via Mark's knee, on to the table.

'You wouldn't want pussy on the table, as Sister Dew might say,' said Mark, making a feeble attempt to remove her.

'*No*, Faustina,' said Sophie more sternly. 'We do *not* leap on to the table for our food. We take it from our dish in the proper place.'

'But there is nothing in the dish,' Mark pointed out.

'No, but we must be patient,' said Sophia, helping the cat first. 'Whatever would Daisy and Edwin Pettigrew say if they could see such behaviour!'

The Pettigrews, brother and sister, lived next door to the vicarage. Edwin was a veterinary surgeon and Daisy looked after the animals who were sometimes boarded with them.

'Well, one naturally expects a cattery to be more austere,' said Mark. 'It must be like animals leading a monastic life.'

When they had washed up they went into the sitting room – neither 'lounge' nor 'drawing room' seemed right to describe it – and listened to a concert on the wireless, for they had no television set and no grateful parishioners had yet clubbed together to provide one. Mark thought out his letter for the October number of the parish magazine, while Sophia sorted out a basket of quinces which her mother had sent up from the country.

'I shall make jelly,' she said, 'and keep some on a dish here – they smell so delicious.' She sighed, not wanting to add that they reminded her of her childhood home in case Mark should be hurt. In these less gracious sur-roundings she had tried to recapture the atmosphere of her mother's house with bowls of quinces, the fragrance of well polished furniture, and the special Earl Grey tea, but she often realised how different it really was. The vicarage had been built to match the church and the style of the rooms had not yet, and perhaps never would, become fashionable again.

'How was Penelope?' Mark asked.

'Oh, much as usual. I helped her to choose a dress. And she was going for an interview for a new job tomorrow.' Sophia did not mention the unsuccessful love affair. Mark could not really enter into such things.

'I suppose her autumn social life will be starting,' he said absently, 'and I suppose the note of my October magazine letter ought to be something about the autumn and winter social activities,' he went on, taking up his pen again. 'And perhaps a welcome to the strangers in our midst?'

'Yes, that would be most appropriate,' said Sophia. She suspected that Mark was thinking of the West Indians who had come to live in the parish and of course that was very right. But *she* was thinking more of Ianthe Broome and the man she and Penelope had seen that afternoon, and wondering what they would be like. There was always that slight excitement and uncertainty about living in a London parish – one never knew who might turn up in church on Sunday.

2

Daisy Pettigrew changed her reading for her long distance glasses, so that she could see the vicarage garden more clearly. Sitting in her window, she commanded a good view of the vicarage garden and of the 'object' whose identity had been puzzling her for some days now. It looked like – and surely it was – a statue of the Virgin Mary, and before long, no doubt, it would find its way into the church among all the other statues, though why it was now in the garden puzzled her a little. Grey stone and blue drapery, she thought, the whole thing rather shabby, not brightly painted like the other statues, but still a popish image.

As she watched, Daisy saw Sophia come out into the garden with Faustina in her arms. The cat looked like some great noble bird, a hawk or even an eagle, the golden streak down her nose giving the effect of a beak. She struggled from Sophia's embrace and jumped down among the windfall apples, rolled one over with her paw, then turned and stalked indifferently away among the Michaelmas daisies. Sophia went back into the house and came out again with a bowl of washing, from which she shook out a large Union Jack. This she draped over the line, pinning it with a row of clothes pegs.

Wherever did she find that, Daisy wondered, that symbol of Empire. What rare objects, what richness, the attic of a vicarage must hold! Probably not many in this neighbourhood or, for that matter, in any other would have a Union Jack on their clothes line. Of course one didn't say Empire now, but Commonwealth – common weal, weal and woe ... Daisy's thoughts wandered inconsequentially. Then she saw Sophia go over to the statue of the Virgin Mary. Was she about to make some obeisance to it? Daisy leaned forward, at once horrified and fascinated. But no, she was removing the blue drapery, and now, with that gone, what had seemed to be a popish image turned out to be merely a tree stump with a blue cloth spread over it to dry. The shape and folds of the cloth had suggested a draped figure.

Sophia now picked up Faustina again and went back into the house with her. She makes too much of that cat, Daisy thought, for a young woman that is. It was a pity she had no children. . . .

Somewhere downstairs a clock struck a quarter to nine. Daisy left her position in the window and hurried down to get ready for the morning surgery. This was likely to be crowded, for her brother had a large number of patients, many of whom came in taxis and private cars from the more fashionable districts farther afield. Going into the big general waiting room, Daisy no longer noticed the many photographs of grateful animals and their owners which decorated the walls, most of them signed with fulsome messages indicating every degree of gratitude. Some who went to the surgery thought that Daisy looked like an animal herself, moving sometimes like a slow marmalade cat, other times like a bustling sheep dog – for she was a woman of moods – and seeming to combine the best and worst qualities of each. She was sandy-haired and rather fat and usually wore blue or grey tweeds, though with the passage of years she had become comfortably indifferent to dress.

She went over to the round table in the middle of the

room, moved *The Field* and *Country Life* into slightly different positions, concealed the one ashtray to discourage smoking, and went down the passage to see if her brother was ready. This passage or corridor was carpeted in moss green, now faded and stained in places from water and the urine of nervous animals, so that it looked more like some natural substance, moss or close-cut turf, than man-made carpet. At the end of the passage was a stained-glass window with a design of tulips, and on the left the door leading to the surgery.

Edwin Pettigrew was, like his sister, of sandy colouring, a kindly-looking man more interested in animals than in human beings, though he was an expert at calming and reassuring the agitated and often hysterical women who brought their animals to see him. He had not been able to deal so skilfully with his own wife, however, that relationship needing more of himself than he could spare from the animals, and she had left him many years ago.

'All ready, Daisy?' he asked, looking over the top of his spectacles.

A loud cry was heard coming from somewhere underneath them.

'They want their breakfast,' said Daisy. 'I must go to them.' She descended to the basement where the boarding cats were housed and began to prepare their breakfast. Cries rose on all sides of her as she filled the dishes, but she worked on steadily oblivious, like some eccentric female St Francis, brooding a little about the image seen in the vicarage garden, which, although it had turned out to be only an old cloth flung over a tree stump, was an indication of the way things might go. Not that she had anything against the vicar personally, though it had been hard to forgive his refusal of her request for an 'Animals' Sunday' to which people might bring their pets to be blessed. She glanced round at the

24

cats to see how much food would be needed. Their cries rose louder and more urgent now in their primitive longing for meat. They were great and splendid creatures, perhaps hardly in need of any blessing from man or God, she thought defiantly, and it was wonderful to be able to satisfy their hunger with raw meat, a real privilege. One did not get the same feeling opening tins of cat food, admirable though it was in many ways.

Now they were all feeding, and she stood back, watching them with love. Then she moved over to the basement window and contemplated the pairs of legs striding along the pavement to work. One pair – those of Ianthe Broome – interested her particularly. They wore ladylike stockings with seams, in a colour described in Marshall's hosiery sale as 'medium beige', and ended in brown court shoes of good leather with a sensible heel. Daisy wondered where the canon's daughter was going.

Ianthe always hurried past the vet's house, fearful of seeing or hearing something dreadful. The basement cattery seemed to her a sinister place, though she knew that the animals were most lovingly tended by Miss Pettigrew. They had got into conversation one evening when Ianthe was coming back from the library where she worked, and it had reassured her – coming as a stranger to this rather doubtful neighbourhood – to meet somebody whom her mother would have described as a 'gentlewoman'.

Ianthe was the only child of elderly parents, who seemed to be a whole generation removed from those of her contemporaries. When her father died it had been necessary for her to do some kind of work and the training in librarianship had seemed the most suitable. Working among books was, on the face of it, a ladylike occupation, Mrs Broome had thought, and one that

25

would bring her daughter into contact with a refined, intellectual type of person. She had never seen Ianthe handing out books to the ill-mannered grubby students and cranks of all ages who frequented the library of political and sociological books where she worked.

On the crowded train a man gave up his seat to Ianthe and she accepted it gracefully. She expected courtesy from men and often received it. It was as if they realised that she was not for the rough and tumble of this world, like the aggressive women with shaggy hair styles who pushed their way through life thrusting their hard shopping baskets at defenceless men. The man who had offered the seat had seen Ianthe as a tall fragile-looking woman in a pretty blue hat that matched her eyes. He might also have noticed that her dark hair was touched with grey and that although she was not exactly smart there was a kind of elegance about her. She saw herself perhaps as an Elizabeth Bowen heroine – for one did not openly identify oneself with Jane Austen's heroines – and *To The North* was her favourite novel. Even her little house was somehow in keeping with this picture, although it was definitely not St John's Wood and there was no delicate wrought iron balcony with steps leading down to the green garden. Yet her small garden *was* green, if only because of much rain and leaves rather than flowers, and there was a little mossy stone cherub left behind by the previous owner. It was so much more congenial than the flat near Victoria – unsuitably dominated by Westminster Cathedral – where she had lived with her mother. Ianthe arrived at the library five minutes before she need have done. Mervyn Cantrell, the librarian, was unpacking his lunch. He was a tall thin irritable-looking man in his early forties, who had the idea that he could not 'take' restaurant food, at least of the kind served in the restaurants where the rest of the staff had their midday meal – luncheon was hardly the

26

word for it – and therefore always brought a packed meal with him. Today it was a cold fish mayonnaise with lettuce and french dressing in a little bottle, brown rolls, and a special goatsmilk cheese obtainable only at one particular shop in Soho.

'Good morning, Miss Broome,' he said, for they were not always 'Ianthe' and 'Mervyn' to each other and the early morning was usually a very formal time, 'I hope you're getting settled into your new house.'

'Yes, thank you – my furniture seems to fit in very well.'

'You've got some nice things, haven't you.' There was a tinge of envy in his tone, for his humdrum childhood home in Croydon had not provided him with the kind of 'things' his taste now craved.

'Well, family things, you know – but one gets attached to them.' Mervyn had visited the flat once for tea on a Sunday afternoon when her mother was still alive, but the occasion had not been very successful. Mrs Broome had not thought much of Croydon as was evident from her patronising manner.

'I remember you had a lovely Pembroke table – I coveted *that*.' He laughed, not very mirthfully. 'And those dining-room chairs – Hepplewhite, aren't they?'

'Yes, I believe so,' said Ianthe uncertainly. She found the conversation embarrassing and wondered if the time had come when she could no longer avoid asking him to come and see her new house.

'Surely you must know if they are,' he said testily.

'You must come and see for yourself when I've got things a bit tidier,' she said, trying not to be irritated. Poor Mervyn, she knew that she ought to feel sorry for him, living with his disagreeable old mother – at least, this was how she appeared in Ianthe's imagination – disappointed at not having got a job in one of the University libraries, unable to find staff accurate enough to

27

appreciate the niceties of setting out a bibliographical entry correctly, with it seemed few friends of either sex, unable to eat restaurant food – really, the list seemed endless when one thought about it.

'I shall be sorting out some of the applications for Miss Grimes's job this morning,' Mervyn said. 'She's really getting past her work and it'll be a relief when she goes. What we need is a younger person.'

Ianthe sighed, perhaps foreseeing the day when both of them would be replaced by younger persons.

'A young *man*, I think,' he went on, holding up a letter. 'This one sounds quite promising, but of course I must see him first – one can't always tell from the application,' he added primly.

'No, he might be *quite* unsuitable,' Ianthe agreed, half hoping that he would be. She would have preferred a woman of her own age and background. She did not like men very much, except for the clergy, and found younger women rather alarming. Miss Grimes, with whom she had worked for several years, was hardly the most congenial of companions but at least she was familiar.

This morning she was dusting books in the reading room, which was so far empty of readers.

'And how's his nibs this morning?' she grunted in her slightly Cockney voice. It was this voice and expressions like 'his nibs' which jarred on Ianthe. Indeed, Miss Grimes was sometimes altogether jarring. She was a squat, dusty-looking woman on the threshold of sixty, who had been taken on in the library during the war and whom Mervyn had tried unsuccessfully to dislodge ever since he had become librarian. But now the passage of the years was doing it for him. 'Time like an ever-rolling stream', Mervyn had said, 'bears even Miss Grimes away.' But Ianthe did not like jokes about hymns.

'I'll help you with the books,' she said.

'It's not your day, is it, dear?'

'No, but they've got to be done, and Shirley's making the tea.' Ianthe had not told her mother that she sometimes had to dust the books in the library.

Later when she was drinking her tea Mervyn came into the room with a card in his hand.

Ianthe realised from his triumphant expression that he had caught her out in a mistake and waited with resignation to hear what it was.

'*Government in Zazzau*,' he declared. 'The place of publication is London, *not* Oxford. It was published *by* the Oxford University Press *for* the International African Institute – do you see?' From behind his back he now produced the book itself, open at the title page.

'Of course – how stupid of me. I'm so sorry, I'm afraid I do make mistakes sometimes.'

'But there is no need to make *that* kind of mistake,' he said rather obscurely and left the room with a springy step.

So Ianthe's day passed, punctuated by cups of tea and a lunch of welsh rarebit and trifle at a café run by gentlewomen. It was not much different from other days. At five minutes to five, Shirley, the typist who had been helping Ianthe to file some cards, covered up her typewriter, put on the black imitation leather coat she had just bought, and hurried away singing. Ianthe herself stayed until nearly six o' clock to avoid the rush-hour crowds. She was still not completely used to the journey northwards to the small empty house, when for so long she had gone southwards to the big flat near Westminster Cathedral, where her mother had waited, eager to hear every detail of her day.

As she walked from the Underground to St Basil's Terrace Ianthe noticed that curtains had appeared in the windows of the house nearly opposite to hers where the new arrival had moved in. Perhaps they might become friends, she thought doubtfully, or at least neighbours, passing the time of day if they met in the road.

It was sad coming back alone to an empty house, Ianthe thought, but how much worse if it had been a single furnished room, like poor Miss Grimes. Ianthe had always wanted a house of her own and as soon as she had shut the door behind her she forgot the lonely home-coming in the pleasure she still felt at seeing her furniture and possessions in their new setting. Here were the Hepplewhite chairs and the Pembroke table, coveted by Mervyn Cantrell, portraits of her grandparents and of her father in cope and biretta, the corner cupboard with the lustre jugs collected by her mother, the old silky Bokhara rugs on the polished parquet floor of the sitting room, the familiar books in the white-painted bookshelves, and the china ornaments she remembered from childhood.

Ianthe was not the type to pour herself a glass of sherry or gin as soon as she got home after a day's work, nor yet to make a cup of tea. One did not make tea at half-past six in the evening like the 'working classes', as her mother would have called them. Instead she set about cooking herself a suitable supper in the almost too perfect little kitchen. The grill was heated for a chop, tomatoes were cut up, and a small packet of frozen peas tipped out of its wrapping into a saucepan. 'We have come to this,' her mother used to say, 'eating frozen vegetables like *Americans*.' She had been deeply conscious of her position as a canon's widow. Frozen vegetables were, somehow, a lowering of standards, but they were quick and convenient and really fresher than anything one could get in the London shops.

When the meal was ready Ianthe ate it in the dining room, which opened on to the garden now piled with drifts of sycamore leaves. While she ate she read, another thing her mother would have disapproved of, but her 'book' was the parish magazine and somehow that made it better. It gave her a comfortable glow to think of the church, and the life that went on around it, dear and familiar and with the same basic pattern everywhere. During their years in London together Ianthe and her mother had not attached themselves to one church, Mrs Broome liking to hear a good preacher and fine music. Sometimes they had to attend the fashionable church in Mayfair where Canon Broome's brother-in-law was rector. Now that she was free to choose, Ianthe looked forward to going to the same church every Sunday and finding her place in the congregation. Indeed, one of the reasons why she had liked this house was because it was near St Basil's which appeared to be a 'suitable' church for her.

She was just about to make some coffee, when the front door bell rang. She went into the hall a little nervously, her eye on the chain which could be hooked across the door to guard against burglars, but it seemed silly to put it up. Opening the door a crack she saw a man in a clerical collar and a woman beside him. The vicar and his wife, of course.

'We do hope you've finished your supper – dinner,' said Sophia, uncertain what form Ianthe's evening meal might have taken.

'And that you aren't in the middle of watching your favourite television programme,' said Mark conscientiously, for his parochial visiting now made this question automatic.

'I *have* finished my supper and I *haven't* got a television set,' said Ianthe, smiling. 'How nice of you to come.'

In the hall Sophia looked around her with unconcealed curiosity. It had been of course her suggestion that Mark's pastoral visit should be no longer delayed. 'And she may be lonely,' Sophia had added, 'wanting to meet people of her own kind, if we can be called that.'

'Those were painted by my grandmother,' said Ianthe, seeing that Sophia was examining the water-colours of Italian scenes which hung in the hall. 'People seemed to stay abroad so much longer in those days and to have time to do things like that.'

'Yes, they were leisured days,' said Mark a little uncomfortably, feeling that he should say that things were 'better' now when great coachloads of people could whirl round the Italian lakes in an eight-day tour. But he found himself unable to say it, especially not to this so very obvious gentlewoman. A friend for Sophia? he wondered, following the ladies into the sitting room. He always felt slightly guilty that there were so few suitable for this role in the parish.

Now Sophia was interested in the furniture and objects, and it was not until they had finished their coffee that the talk turned to parish matters.

'We are having our Harvest Thanksgiving next week,' said Mark, glancing without much hope towards the little leaf-filled garden.

'Oh, then I must bring some flowers or fruit,' said Ianthe. 'I know how difficult it is in London – I suppose tropical fruits would be allowed?'

'Certainly – they're really most appropriate here,' said Mark.

> 'What though the spicy breezes
> Blow soft o'er Ceylon's isle,'

Sophia quoted. 'How one longs for the days of Bishop Heber sometimes!' It was an inconsequential remark but she hoped it might lead to some interesting revelation on Ianthe's part, that Bishop Heber had been an ancestor or that she loved Victorian poetry, for, looking at the bookshelves, she was sure that she did.

But Ianthe seemed not to know how to answer Sophia's remark and soon they were on to another topic

– the strangers in the parish and whether it was likely that they would come to church.

'Well, you come,' said Sophia, 'and last Sunday I noticed the man who lives opposite you sitting at the back.'

'You mean the television producer?' asked Ianthe, puzzled. 'That seems rather unlikely doesn't it?'

Ah, but he isn't – he's not in television at all. Sister Dew had it all wrong. His name's Rupert Stonebird and he's an anthropologist.'

'Darling, how do you know this?' asked Mark, but without much surprise, for Sophia knew many things.

'Stonebird,' said Ianthe. 'What an interesting name. It sounds like a character in fiction. And you say he's an anthropologist.'

'Yes, Daisy Pettigrew told me. I suppose he goes around measuring skulls and that kind of thing.'

'Measuring skulls – *here*?' said Mark solemnly. 'Whatever would he want to do that for?'

The three of them dissolved into laughter at the idea of it, and Ianthe went to make some more coffee.

3

'Measuring skulls and that kind of thing. . . .' Rupert
Stonebird would have sighed inwardly, for he was used
to this particular joke, but explained politely – if anyone
was still listening – that he was actually a lecturer in *social*
anthropology, which was concerned with the behaviour
of men in society rather than with the size and shape of
their skulls. But probably by this time nobody would
still have been listening. People were not really very
interested in what one did, and a quick classification was
all that was needed to distinguish an academic type from
a farmer or stockbroker.

Rupert was a quiet sort of person who disliked
pushing himself forward and was therefore well fitted to
observe the behaviour of others. Nevertheless, now that
he had come to live in this new house he was aware that
he would probably be an object of interest to his neighbours. He was thirty-six years old and not yet married,
mainly because his trips to Africa – where most of his
work had been done – had not left him much time to find
a suitable wife, though others in similar positions
seemed to have achieved wives and marriages, whether
suitable or not. He was quite good-looking, of medium
height with dark hair and brown eyes. He wore glasses
for reading.

His coming to live in this particular house had been
preceded by a change in his life which he was finding a

little difficult to accept. For it had been on a cold Sunday evening in the spring, after he had been looking over the house with the idea of buying it, that he had happened out of curiosity to 'pop in', as fashionable Anglo-Catholics said, to Solemn Evensong and Benediction at St Basil's at the end of the road. The service was no novelty to him for his father had been a High Anglican vicar in another part of London and Rupert had not lost his boyhood faith until his first year at Oxford – late really, he had thought, for a clergyman's son. And now, eighteen years afterwards, in a poorly attended North London church of hideous architecture and amid clouds of strong incense, he seemed to have regained that faith. It had been an uncomfortable and disturbing sensation and he was still wondering whether it hadn't been only the incense, the spring evening, and nostalgia for his boyhood. He had almost considered not buying the house, but it was what he wanted, and how was he to know that things would be any different in another district?

So far he had attended Mass at St Basil's only once, sitting at the back and hurrying out after the service before anyone could speak to him. He had not been to any of the social functions advertised – it would have seemed like living his life backwards to enter voluntarily a church hall full of women and cups of tea – he could see his mother at the urn and himself as a boy handing round those very cups. He did not think that anyone at St Basil's had even noticed him so far.

He could not know that Sophia was taking a keen interest in him and had even been considering him – provided he were not divorced or otherwise unsuitable – as a husband for her sister. The next time he went to church she waylaid him after the evening service, and tried to persuade him to enter the hall, where – as he had guessed – a cup of tea was about to be made. He had murmured some excuse but had been unable to refuse an invitation to supper at the vicarage during the coming week.

'My sister will be there and perhaps one or two of our parishioners, so I hope it won't be too dull for you,' Sophia said.

'Oh, I'm sure it won't be,' said Rupert politely.

'You won't expect anything too elaborate – I mean, in the way of food,' said Sophia in her most sensible tone.

'Well, I was brought up in a vicarage myself and know how things are or can be,' he said confusedly. He wondered if he had sounded discourteous, though 'things' could have a wider meaning than just food. 'One does not go out for a meal just for the food,' he added, hardly improving the situation.

Sophia laughed. She was at once amused and happy at his vicarage connections which seemed to bode well.

'You're a clergyman's son, then?' she asked.

'Yes.'

'Oh, how splendid!' Sophia's face seemed to light up and her tone to brighten. *Most* unlikely that he would be divorced, she thought, taking this naive and optimistic view of the sons of the clergy. But he did go to church, so perhaps she was right. She decided not to probe any more deeply for the moment.

Sophia then invited Ianthe Broome and Edwin Pettigrew, thinking that they might 'do' for each other, at least as partners for the evening. Then it seemed unkind to leave Daisy out, so she was invited too. A woman of Daisy's age would hardly expect to have a man invited for her, Sophia decided. And anyway an extra woman was useful when it came to bringing things from the kitchen and clearing dishes.

Sometime before the guests were due to arrive, Mark went down to the cellar to bring up the wine. He peered in the half darkness at the metal rack in which two bottles, the remains of an Easter present from Sophia's mother, sat in lonely dignity for each was a good wine of its kind.

'Red or white, darling?' he called, seeing that there was one of each.

'Red, I think,' said Sophia. 'It's a sort of casserole or beef stew we're having.'

Mark picked up the dark-looking bottle to read the label.

'This seems to be port,' he said, 'so it will have to be the white. Oh, but *this* is the Niersteiner, the last bottle, and it wouldn't go very well with beef.' He had been saving it for Sophia's birthday.

'Well, let them drink beer or cider,' said Sophia. 'Neither Edwin nor Daisy drinks much and I don't suppose Ianthe Broome does.'

'So it's only Mr Stonebird we're considering – as a clergyman's son and an anthropologist he might drink a great deal.'

'Is his name really that?' said Penelope, who had just come into the kitchen. 'He sounds quite interesting.'

'Yes, I think he may be,' said Sophia. 'He's about thirty-five – dark and not bad looking.'

'And not married?'

'No, I don't think so. He seems to be living alone in one of the little houses in St Basil's Terrace.'

'Are you sure he isn't living with his mother?'

'I haven't *seen* a mother but I suppose there could be one in the background.' Sophia looked worried for a moment. 'I suppose I ought to have made more enquiries when I was inviting him – I mean, it would seem discourteous to ignore her, if she exists. But he didn't mention her.'

'Then perhaps we can assume that she doesn't exist,' said Penelope. 'But of course there may be other ties.' She had now reached the age when one starts looking for a husband rather more systematically than one does at nineteen or even at twenty-one.

At that moment the front door bell rang and Sophia went to answer it. Penelope could hear a woman's voice talking to her sister in the hall. Who could *this* be? she wondered rather crossly, not having realised that there was to be another woman there. Then she realised that it must be Ianthe Broome, the canon's daughter they were always talking about, and perhaps in some way a kind of 'rival' for the affections of a man she had not yet seen. Even Penelope realised that it was a somewhat farcical situation.

But she was reassured when Ianthe came into the room, and her observant eye took in every detail of Ianthe's ladylike but hardly fashionable appearance – the hair smooth and neat, gathered into a little roll at the back – the dress of a rather uninteresting shade of blue, with the skirt a good two inches too long by Penelope's standards – the stockings with seams, and the shoes with sensible heels and rounded toes. The jewellery, consisting of a small aquamarine and pearl pendant on a gold chain, and a gold bracelet with a turquoise clasp, was obviously real.

'This is my sister Penelope,' said Sophia. 'Penny, this is Miss Broome – or perhaps we may call you Ianthe? It's such a pretty name.'

'Please do,' said Ianthe, who was temporarily a little bewildered at Penelope's appearance and unconventional clothes.

Conversation between strange women at the beginning of a party is often strained and this occasion proved to be no exception.

After a pause Penelope said, 'I hear you've just come to live in one of those little houses in St Basil's Terrace – they look so pretty.'

'Yes, I'm very pleased with mine,' said Ianthe.

'She has it most elegantly furnished,' said Sophia enthusiastically.

'It's really no credit to me,' said Ianthe. 'All the furniture came from my old home – I was lucky to have it.'

'I think I can hear Edwin and Daisy at the door,' said Sophia in a relieved tone, going out into the hall. 'Oh, and Mr Stonebird too. Now we're all here.'

Rupert Stonebird entered the room a little shyly. He had changed into a dark suit as a kind of protective colouring, so that he could sit quietly observing rather than being observed. He had noticed Ianthe coming out of her house and now saw her as a woman of about his own age, nicely dressed, worthy no doubt, quite pretty but not particularly interesting. The sisters – Sophia and Penelope – made a stronger impression. Sophia, with her long neck and auburn hair, looked like a figure in a minor Pre-Raphaelite painting, her velvet dress a deep peacock blue. But there were hollows in her cheeks and she was too thin for beauty. Penelope had the same colouring and generally romantic air, but was shorter and dumpier with rather fat legs. She wore a black sacklike dress, a large silver medallion on a chain, black nylon stockings and flat-heeled shoes. Her hair was dressed in a 'beehive' style, which was now collapsing at one side. The Pre-Raphaelite beatnik, Rupert thought, wondering if anybody had ever called her that.

'Mark is in his study,' Sophia explained. 'A young couple called about putting up their banns and he has to talk to them, but he won't be long. Shall we have a glass of sherry? And now Faustina is with us – come along, darling.'

Faustina walked slowly into the room and Daisy Pettigrew stooped to pick her up. The cat crouched uneasily in her arms, then uttered a curious low cry and struggled free.

Penelope turned away from the little scene, to avoid

the inevitable explanations and interpretations of Faustina's behaviour and found herself facing Rupert Stonebird. She had been disappointed in her first sight of him, but she gave him an amused little smile, hoping that he was not one who doted on cats.

'Have you any animals?' she asked.

'No, I haven't really got round to it,' he said, frowning a little, as if he ought to have done.

'I suppose studying the human animal is enough for you,' said Penelope.

'Yes, it does take up most of my time – that and moving into a new house.' Rupert was surprised that Penelope appeared to know what he did, with no jokes about measuring skulls. It was rather a relief.

'Shall we go into the dining room?' said Sophia. 'I think everything's ready now.'

'Beer or cider?' asked Mark, a shade unconfidently.

After they had been served, Rupert found himself under fire again.

'I hear that you have worked in *Africa*,' said Daisy, fixing him with an accusing stare.

'Yes, my field work has been in Africa, mostly,' he said patiently.

'What work did you do, exactly?' she continued.

'Oh, nothing much, really,' he said feebly. The eyes of four respectable women, bright with friendly interest, were looking eagerly towards him and somehow he found himself unable to explain that he had been making a study of extra-marital relations, detached and scientific though this had of course been. 'I mean it was merely a study of kinship,' he added, seeing before him now the outraged faces of his colleagues at his letting the side down by describing such work as 'nothing much, really'.

'A very complicated subject, I imagine,' said Edwin Pettigrew.

'I hoped that perhaps you had been doing something for the *welfare* of these poor peoples,' persisted Daisy.

Rupert hesitated, unwilling to admit that anthropologists did no good, yet for the moment unable to think of a positive example that would convince her.

'Are you settling down well in your house?' she asked, feeling that a change of subject was now called for.

'Quite well, thank you, though as the weather gets colder, heating becomes rather a problem,' he said.

The conversation now became highly technical, touching on the advantages of electric and paraffin convector heaters, oil fired central heating, open fires, boilers, and the like.

Penelope felt rather bored and irritated and began to speculate on whether Rupert had a car and would offer to run her home. She laid great stress on these little courtesies, the formal acts of politeness that women in their emancipated state seemed to be in danger of losing.

They rose from the table with Daisy stressing the need for a heater that could not be knocked over by cats. 'The man who can invent *that* will make a fortune,' she declared.

Once in the drawing room the party seemed to divide, Ianthe talking to Edwin Pettigrew about dogs, Mark rather nobly taking on Daisy, and Sophia and Penelope plying Rupert with questions about himself, his life, and his work, probing to find out without actually asking whether he had a mother, wife, fiancée, or 'friend' in the background.

'I did wonder,' said Sophia at last in desperation, 'whether I had committed a grave social error in asking you to dinner alone when you may very well have a mother, wife or fiancée who should have been invited too.'

Rupert laughed. 'I can assure you that I have none of

those – er – appendages.'

'Then you are without female dependants,' said Sophia, almost like a chairman summing up at a meeting.

'Well, I have a sister,' he admitted.

'A sister?' But that was nothing.

'Yes, married and living in Woking.'

'Ah yes, Woking,' said Sophia thoughtfully. 'There's a mosque there, I believe.'

'A mosque?' Rupert sounded surprised, as he had every right to.

'It's funny how one associates places with irrelevant things,' said Penelope, who had been listening to Sophia's probings with a kind of fascinated horror.

At that moment the telephone rang in the hall. The call was for Edwin Pettigrew, who seemed to be expecting it.

'A very nervous poodle having her first puppies,' he explained. 'I thought it would be some time tonight.'

'I really ought to be going,' said Penelope, 'what with having a long journey and work tomorrow.' She waited, but without much hope, for Rupert to offer to run her home in the car they did not know he possessed.

'Oh, darling, I thought you'd stay the night,' said Sophia. 'You know you can if you want to.'

'Well, if you must go I'll run you back in the car,' said Mark, much to Penelope's disappointment.

'And Ianthe and Mr Stonebird' – 'Rupert' did not quite come out – 'live so near that I dare say they can escort each other,' said Sophia. She had sensed her sister's disappointment but realised that nothing could be done about it. And if she flung Rupert and Ianthe together they would probably take a dislike to each other.

They walked away from the vicarage in silence.

'I hear that you are a canon's daughter – and I am an

archdeacon's son,' said Rupert lightly, trying to make conversation. 'So we must have something in common.' His tone faltered a little and he stared in front of him into the darkness.

'Yes, a vicarage upbringing, I suppose,' said Ianthe. 'But somehow that can lead people into such different paths.'

'Yes, sons of the clergy often go to the bad, and daughters too. At least, one hears of it occasionally,' he added hastily, afraid that Ianthe might misunderstand him.

She did not answer him because at that moment they came to her house. There was a light in the hall and Rupert commented on this.

'I always leave the hall light on when I go out,' Ianthe explained. 'I feel it discourages burglars and it seems more welcoming when one comes back to an empty house.'

Oh, this coming back to an empty house, Rupert thought, when he had seen her safely up to her door. People – though perhaps it was only women – seemed to make so much of it. As if life itself were not as empty as the house one was coming back to. And now he too was returning to an empty house. Groping for the light switch, whose position he had not yet memorised perfectly, he saw the evening's post still lying on the table in the hall where he had put it before he came out. There was a fat envelope, probably the proofs of an article he had written for an anthropological journal. There would be time to look at it before he went to bed.

Rupert opened the envelope and unfolded the bundle of galleys. 'SOME ASPECTS OF EXTRA-MARITAL RELATIONS AMONG THE NGUMU', he read. Not strikingly original as anthropological titles go, but it looked well with his name set out underneath it in italic capitals. The sketch map and kinship diagrams had come out well, also, and the French summary, with its cosy phrase 'chez les Ngumu', seemed adequate. How many offprints did he want – would the usual twenty-five free ones be enough? asked the letter accompanying the proof. Better make it fifty, he thought, seeing himself distributing them like Christmas cards. Then he remembered the eager questioning eyes of the four women he had met that evening – it would hardly be suitable for *them*. And his colleagues would have read it in the journal anyway. It seemed that he was like the poet with his nosegay of visionary flowers:

'That I might there present it – O! to whom?'

All the same, he thought, better make it fifty. When he was an old man the younger generation might clamour for it.

4

'Miss Broome, this is John Challow.'

Ianthe looked up from her work to see Mervyn Cantrell standing at her elbow, with a tall, dark young man of about thirty hovering deferentially a pace or two behind him.

'How do you do, Miss Broome?' he said. 'I must say all this is rather terrifying for me – these card indexes and things – or should one say indices? – I never know.' He laughed, a rather confident, charming laugh.

'How do you do?' Ianthe murmured, not quite knowing what to say.

'I thought it would be best if Mr Challow were to help you for a bit, Miss Broome,' said Mervyn, 'while he's getting settled down, that is.'

'Why, of course,' said Ianthe politely, wondering what she was going to do with him, and wishing, as she had before, that Mervyn had engaged a comfortable middle-aged woman to fill Miss Grimes's place.

'I'll leave you to it then,' said Mervyn. 'Just ask Miss Broome anything you don't understand and she'll explain it.'

Left by themselves Ianthe and John made a wary appraisal of each other. She saw a young, rather handsome man, whose brown eyes looked at her in a way she found slightly disturbing, though this was not the kind of thing she would have admitted to anybody but

45

herself. He saw a rather pretty woman, not very young, with an air of good breeding that somehow attracted him. A woman rather shy of men, whose eyes did not quite meet his when he looked at her.

'Fancy me working in a library again,' he said, one hand resting idly on a card index.

'Why, haven't you been doing this sort of work?' Ianthe asked.

'No, I've been freelancing the last couple of years.'

'Oh, I didn't know one could do that in libraries.' She looked puzzled. 'You mean part-time work?'

'No, not in libraries. You might be rather shocked if I told you.'

'Shocked? Do you think so?' Ianthe smiled uneasily, feeling that some kind of guessing game was being played between them and that she ought to play her part by making a suggestion as to what the work could have been. 'People do so many unusual things nowadays,' she said lamely.

'Well, this was film work, actually – crowd work and that sort of thing. Dancing in a night club scene at eight o'clock in the morning – TV commercials too, sometimes.' John smiled and glanced quickly at Ianthe, as if to see how she was taking it.

'How interesting,' she said brightly, 'and what a change from this sort of work. What made you decide to come back to this?'

'Well, film work's very precarious, of course – so I thought I'd better get a steady job for a bit, especially when my money ran out.'

Ianthe's smile was becoming a little forced now. She was just trying to think what she could say to bring John back to the subject of the library and its workings when Shirley came in with two cups of tea.

'Well, I can't say that I've really earned this,' said John, taking a cup, 'but perhaps I can be forgiven my first day. Is it China tea?'

'China tea? No, I don't think so, but it certainly does look rather weak.'

'I should imagine *you* would like China tea?' he said, looking at her intently.

'I do, very much,' Ianthe admitted, 'but somehow it doesn't seem to go with work. Now, shall I show you what I'm doing here?'

For a few minutes she explained the system on which the cards were arranged, then let him try to select some for a bibliography she was compiling on nutrition in underdeveloped countries.

'Nutrition,' John said, after he had been working for a short time. 'That doesn't really sound like food, does it. At least not the kind of food one would like to eat. By the way, what does one do about lunch? Are there any good places round here – not too expensive of course?'

'Well, there's Lyons and the ABC and a coffee bar, where Shirley sometimes goes, and various pubs, of course.'

'Where do *you* go?'

Ianthe hesitated. Today she had brought sandwiches, as she wanted to spend her lunch hour writing personal letters, but she felt reluctant to reveal to this young man the name of the little restaurant near Westminster Abbey, run by gentlewomen, where she often lunched. 'I quite often bring sandwiches,' she said. 'But I believe the pub on the corner's quite good.'

'I can't imagine you in a pub,' said John, 'or Mr Cantrell, for that matter.'

'No, he usually brings his own lunch and eats it here.'

For some reason Ianthe felt tired by so much talking and was glad when half-past twelve came and John suggested tentatively that he might go out. Left to herself she unpacked her sandwiches and got out her writing things. She was absorbed in a letter when Mervyn Cantrell came into the room.

'Oh good, you haven't finished your lunch yet,' he said. 'I've just been brewing some coffee – I expect you'd like a cup. What's in your sandwiches?' he asked cosily, lifting the corner of one. 'Cold meat,' he declared, sounding disappointed. 'That's not very interesting.'

'No. I just had a bit of my Sunday joint left over,' said Ianthe apologetically.

'Have you ever tried a cold egg-and-breadcrumbed veal cutlet eaten in the fingers – holding it by the bone of course?'

'And with a paper frill?' asked Ianthe. 'It sounds lovely, but somehow I never seem to have time to make things like that and as you know I usually go to the Humming Bird for lunch.'

'I can't bear those two who run it – English gentlewomen with a vengeance, I always think – the kind that have made England what she is.'

'I think Mrs Harper and Miss Burge do a very good job under rather difficult conditions, said Ianthe, 'after all the whole place is very small and the kitchen especially so.'

'Quite. And who but two women like that would be pigheaded enough to try and run a restaurant there?'

'Miss Burge's brother was an admiral, and Mrs Harper is the widow of a cathedral organist. I can't remember *which* cathedral.' Ianthe frowned, trying to recall the name.

'You imply that she is used to producing a four-course dinner on a primus in the organ loft,' said Mervyn, then, losing interest in the subject, he went on 'How do you think John Challow's shaping?'

Ianthe hesitated. She certainly had not thought of him as 'shaping' at all in any direction. 'It's rather early to tell,' she said. 'I suppose he's used to this kind of work and will be able to do it once he gets into our ways.'

'Our ways – and what ways they are!' Mervyn sighed and prepared to go back to his work. 'Perhaps he isn't quite what we've been used to, but I thought we might give him a trial. All the other applicants seemed so highly qualified, I thought they'd probably turn up their noses at what – between ourselves, Ianthe – is really rather a stooge's job. Besides, one gets so tired of willing gentlewomen of uncertain age,' he laughed rather cruelly, 'just when we'd succeeded in getting rid of old Grimes too.'

Ianthe said nothing. She felt guilty that she had not yet been to visit Miss Grimes in her bed-sitting room somewhere off the Finchley Road, really within easy distance of where she lived, so there was really no excuse. She made a resolution to go before Christmas.

When John returned from lunch – very punctually, just before half-past one – Ianthe found herself studying him and taking in the details of his appearance. She could find no fault with his dark grey suit, red patterned tie and white shirt. Only his shoes seemed to be a little too pointed – not quite what men one knew would wear. He was less talkative now and settled down to work quietly, only occasionally asking her a question about what he was doing.

When tea was brought he took out a book he had been reading over his lunch. It turned out to be – most improbably, Ianthe thought – a paperback selection of the poems of Tennyson.

'You read poetry?' she asked rather formally.

'Oh, yes – do you?'

'Yes,' she said hesitantly, wishing that now she had not commented on the book, for one did not talk about poetry with chance acquaintances. It was a precious thing to be kept to oneself. She felt she did not know

49

where to begin with Tennyson, imagining him plodding through *In Memoriam*, though perhaps *Maud* was
more likely. Then she remembered that it was only a
selection of the poems he had been reading and she did
not need to speculate further, for – much to her surprise
– he began to read

> 'Now lies the earth all Danäe to the stars
> And all my heart lies open unto thee . . .

I like that,' he said. 'How do you pronounce Danäe, by
the way?'

'I don't know,' she said in confusion, for she felt his
eyes upon her.

'Anyway,' he said, closing the book, 'I suppose I'd
better get on with my work now or I'll get the sack. But
you wouldn't tell Mr Cantrell, would you.'

Ianthe bent her head over her work and said nothing.
This was not at all what she had imagined when Miss
Grimes left. It would be better, she felt, if John were to
work with Shirley, the typist, as he was only going to
do odd jobs. He might even be a suitable 'boy friend' for
her. She would mention it tactfully to Mervyn some
time. Altogether she was rather relieved when it was
time to go home.

'I hope there's a post office still open,' said John, as he
got up to go.

'They stay open quite late,' said Ianthe.

'I'll need to draw something to keep me going till pay-
day,' he said, taking a post office savings book from an
inner pocket.

Somehow the sight of this touched Ianthe, who had
never herself been in the position of having to wait till
pay-day. There must be many people who knew this
state of financial insecurity but she found that she did
not want to think about them. She looked forward
rather selfishly to a quiet evening at home surrounded

by familiar objects, perhaps reading or listening to a concert on the wireless. Her first impulse, therefore, when she saw the vicar's sister-in-law, Penelope, walking from the underground station just in front of her was to hurry past and pretend she hadn't seen her. But her natural good manners got the better of her and she found herself saying 'good evening' and reminding Penelope that they had met at the vicarage.

'Yes, of course I remember,' said Penelope. 'You live in one of those sweet little houses, like Mr Something-bird the anthropologist.'

'Mr Stonebird,' said Ianthe seriously, as if Penelope had really forgotten his name.

Penelope laughed. 'Does he take an active part in the life of the parish? Will he be at this meeting tonight?'

'Oh, of course – the meeting to discuss the Christmas bazaar,' said Ianthe, remembering now that it would have been impossible for her to have had the quiet evening she had planned. 'I shouldn't think he'll be there. Men don't usually take much part in these things,' she added, more from experience than from cynicism. 'And are you coming to help?'

'Well, Sophia likes me to, you know. But most of these good people are a dead loss when it comes to plan-ning anything unusual or amusing,' said Penelope fiercely. She was hoping very much that Rupert Stone-bird would be there. Surely it was his duty to be? she told herself, not realising that at that very moment he was sitting listening to a paper being read at a learned society, his mind occupied with a particularly tricky question he intended to ask when the speaker sat down.

'I shall see you later then,' said Ianthe, when they reached her house. 'Eight o'clock, isn't it?'

Penelope went hopefully into the vicarage where she found Sophia smiling over a letter which had just come by the evening post.

'Isn't it splendid,' she said, waving the letter at Penelope, 'Mother has persuaded Lady Selvedge to come and open our bazaar. That ought to draw people – the title, you know.'

'But Sophia, would people *here* care about that sort of thing?' said Penelope doubtfully. 'Now if it were Lady——' she named a titled person at that time popular on television – 'it might make a difference. But who *is* Lady Selvedge, after all?' she asked on a note of challenge.

'The former wife of Sir Humphrey Selvedge – his relict, but not his widow, I suppose you might say. Oh dear,' Sophia looked depressed, 'perhaps it *isn't* so splendid after all. Sir Humphrey was unfaithful and she had to divorce him – at least she did divorce him so that he could marry again, I believe.'

'But *she* hasn't remarried?' asked Mark anxiously.

'No. One hopes that her principles wouldn't allow it.'

'I don't suppose for a moment that anyone has asked her,' said Penelope. 'She's pretty dreary, as far as I remember.'

'Penny, we do *not* look upon divorce and remarriage in that way,' said Mark sternly, but – Sophia thought – rather in the tone he used when Faustina jumped on to the table and began licking the butter dish. 'I'm sure that Lady Selvedge is a woman of the highest principles.'

'You've met her, dear,' said Sophia. 'She was at that cocktail party the Sheldonians gave – don't you remember? – when we were staying with Mother the summer before last.'

'Well, I suppose I must have met her, then, if you say so, but somehow I can't remember anything about her.'

'No, I don't suppose you do,' said Sophia soothingly. 'And in any case high principles aren't the kind of things one notices at a cocktail party – or perhaps only in a negative way, as when somebody drinks tomato juice rather than gin.'

'And that might be only because of her figure,' said Penelope.

But Mark had now become absorbed in an idea for a sermon that had suddenly come to him. He was quite a forceful preacher, too intelligent for the majority of his congregation, so that the rather dry instructive sermons to which he inclined personally had to be diluted and sweetened to suit their taste. Mark usually achieved this by thinking out an arresting beginning, nearly always of the same type, asking his congregation to imagine themselves standing gazing at the Pyramids or the Acropolis or even the New York skyline, hardly realising, until Sophia pointed it out to him, that these sights would be unfamiliar to the majority of his hearers. But now these beginnings had become something of a joke between them and the congregation had learned to accept them with amused tolerance. They always made Sophia think how much more Mark would be appreciated in a different sort of parish, though she never said anything about it now. If he felt that his work lay here, it was not for her to question his decision, but she sometimes wished that something might happen to make him change his mind.

'People seem to be coming to the door,' said Penelope. She saw with disappointment that Rupert Stonebird was not among the little group that Sophia was now bringing into the room. Ianthe Broome, Daisy Pettigrew, Sister Dew and one or two others whose names she could never remember, now sat down round the table and began to discuss the final arrangements for the bazaar, which had always been exactly the same and always would be, except that from one year to another a pint more or less milk might be ordered for the teas.

Penelope's way home took her along St Basil's Terrace, or if it had not done she would have arranged her journey to include it, even if it had meant a slight detour. In the weeks that had passed since she had met Rupert Stonebird at the vicarage her interest in him had deepened, mainly because she had not seen him again and had therefore been able to build up a more satisfactory picture of him than if she had been able to check with reality. It was therefore important and exciting to notice that there was a light in a ground-floor window of his house and that, by a fortunate piece of carelessness on somebody's part, the curtains had not been drawn.

Walking as slowly as she dared, Penelope was able to see that there were two figures in the room – Rupert himself and a woman, not very tall and wearing a dark, tweedy-looking suit. It was difficult to see exactly what she looked like, for she and Rupert were bending down over a table examining something together. The room looked like the dining room; a sideboard with some bottles and a bowl of fruit on it was visible, and Penelope was now able to see that the remains of a kind of meal – a loaf of bread, a hunk of orange-coloured cheese and two glasses – were set out on one half of the table. Altogether it was a little disturbing – the man, the woman, the Omar Khayyam-like details – or like a Victorian problem picture in the Royal Academy. What exactly had they been – or were they now – doing?

Penelope walked slowly away from the house, then pretended to be looking at an empty house which was to be sold two doors away from where Rupert lived. As she did so she was conscious of voices by his front gate. Rupert's visitor, whoever she had been, was now leaving and he was giving her instructions how to get somewhere.

'Goodbye, Esther,' he called out, 'and many thanks for bringing them.'

Penelope walked on, thinking, 'Esther', some glamorous Jewess, no doubt. And *what* had she been bringing?

The footsteps behind her seemed to be hurrying, almost as if they were trying to catch her up.

'I suppose I *can* get a bus for Baker Street somewhere here?' said a rather gruff voice, addressing Penelope.

Penelope turned round. 'Oh yes, I'll show you.' She smiled for the woman was short and dumpy, with roughly-cut grey hair – in her middle fifties, at least. So it was all right. The appearance of her 'rival' so encouraged Penelope that it was as if Rupert himself had come out of his house and made her a declaration of love.

5

Lady Selvedge and Mrs Grandison arrived at Victoria Station on the day of the bazaar shortly after noon, and proceeded to look for a place where they might have lunch, or luncheon, as they called it. Mrs Grandison had promised her daughter that they would not inflict themselves on her for a meal – realising that Lady Selvedge might well be something of an infliction – and had assumed that from Victoria they would take a taxi to some Soho restaurant or perhaps Simpsons in the Strand. Indeed, during the train journey she had been weighing in her mind the advantages of an Italian dish – 'something with *funghi*' – as against sole in an exquisite sauce or a cut off a splendid classic sirloin. She was therefore a little disconcerted to find when they left the station that instead of waiting for a taxi Lady Selvedge began to stride away in the direction of Victoria Street, saying 'I know just the place for us to get a snack. There's a very good tea-shop just near here.'

'Don't you think,' Mrs Grandison suggested, 'that we need a little more than just a snack? After all we have a long and tiring afternoon ahead of us?' But of course, as she now remembered, Lady Selvedge had the reputation of being mean.

'Oh, you can get quite substantial dishes here,' she said. 'I used the word "snack" figuratively.'

Mrs Grandison followed her apprehensively into one

of those ubiquitous tea-shops which cater for the multitudes of office workers and others who want a cheap meal at any time of the day, and which, excellent though they are, can hardly be compared with the restaurants Mrs Grandison had been hoping to lunch in.

Fortunately, as it was still only a quarter past twelve, there was no queue and Lady Selvedge and Mrs Grandison were able to walk straight up to the counter and take their trays.

'Do not handle food you do not intend to consume', Lady Selvedge read loudly from a printed notice. 'That seems most sensible and hygienic, don't you think so, Dorothy?'

Mrs Grandison could not but agree with her.

'I will have steak pudding and *mashed* potatoes,' said Lady Selvedge. 'And do I see *greens* there? I will have some of those.'

Mrs Grandison chose ham and salad, thinking sadly of the splendid sirloin, for she had decided that it would have been that if she had been given the choice.

They found a table for four occupied by one young man, and arranged their food around them. Perhaps they looked a little incongruous sitting in their smart hats and fur coats, talking more loudly than anybody else. Lady Selvedge was a tall, pale-faced woman, with a camel-like caste to her features – perhaps a Hapsburg lip if one took a more kindly view. Because of her husband's matrimonial adventures and the fact that she was by no means the only Lady Selvedge she was usually known as Lady (Muriel) Selvedge. The parentheses gave her a sense of not existing, un-being perhaps was not too strong a word. She would have preferred Muriel, Lady Selvedge, with its dowager-like dignity. Sometimes people addressed letters mistakenly to Lady Muriel Selvedge, and on these occasions she imagined herself as the daughter of an earl, a marquess, or even a duke, comfortably unmarried.

Mrs Grandison, the mother of Sophia and Penelope, had the remains of her daughters' Pre-Raphaelite beauty, now much faded and overlaid with some other quality, which had made her the President of the Women's Institute in the village where she lived but which did not seem to be quite Pre-Raphaelite.

Lady Selvedge ate quickly, commenting on the excellence and cheapness of the food as she did so. 'Luncheon for only three and ninepence,' she declared, reaching out towards a miniature steamed pudding and drawing it towards her, 'excellent!'

At this point the young man, who had been reading a folded newspaper, looked up and said in a slightly truculent voice, 'Excuse me, madam, but that's *my* pudding you're about to eat.'

'Oh no, this is mine,' said Lady Selvedge firmly, making a shielding movement with her hands round the pudding in its little dish.

'I think the young man is right,' said Mrs Grandison. 'I don't remember seeing you take a pudding. The dishes get rather confused when they're all together on the table,' she added, trying to put things right.

'Oh well then, I suppose it is not mine,' said Lady Selvedge grudgingly pushing the pudding back towards the young man, who then proceeded to eat it in a kind of defiant confusion.

'Those sort of people eat far too much *starch*,' said Lady Selvedge to Mrs Grandison in an audible whisper. 'Meat pie, chips, roll and butter, and now this stodgy pudding. A dish of *greens* would be much better for you,' she said, raising her voice and turning towards the young man.

'If you'll pardon me, madam, I think you're – bloody – interfering,' he stammered, flushing scarlet from the – surely unaccustomed – boldness and violence of his

58

language. Then, gulping down the remains of his cup of tea, he got up and left the table.

This would *not* have happened in Simpsons, thought Mrs Grandison grimly. She had been a fool to let Muriel choose a place to have lunch and would take good care that it did not happen again.

'There will be time for us to have a look round Westminster Abbey,' said Lady Selvedge, not in the least disturbed by the upsetting little incident of the pudding. 'I always like to have a good look round the Abbey.'

We dare not *ask* for the grace of humility, but perhaps we don't need to when it is so often thrust upon us, thought Sophia, beating together eggs and sugar for a sponge cake, knowing that her cake would not rise as high as Sister Dew's. When she took it from the oven she was pleased with it, but later, placing it on the trestle table in the hall where refreshments were to be served, she saw that Sister Dew's was higher.

'So you've made one of *your* sponges,' said the latter in a patronising tone. 'It looks quite nice.'

'But yours is much better, Sister Dew,' said Sophia nobly. 'I don't know how you do it.'

'Oh, I'm sure *she's* got a light hand with pastry,' said Sister Dew. 'I suppose one is born with a light hand in these things.'

'Yes, I suppose so,' Sophia agreed. 'Miss Broome has promised to make some sausage rolls.'

'Oh, I'm sure, *she's* got a light hand with pastry,' said Sister Dew eagerly. 'I hope I get a chance to taste one of her sausage rolls.'

'Yes – is that her coming now? I thought I saw somebody pass the window,' said Sophia. Her tone was a little agitated for she had also just seen Faustina mount the refreshment table and pick her way delicately among the dishes of the cakes and savouries, sniffing the air,

59

ready to pause and pounce when she came upon something that took her fancy.

Luckily Sister Dew allowed herself to be distracted and opened the door for Ianthe and her covered dish.

'Now here's Miss Broome with her sausage rolls,' she said fulsomely. 'They do look good, I must say. But they're not for Pussy,' she added, with a disapproving look at Faustina now held firmly in Sophia's arms.

'I hope they're all right,' said Ianthe. 'It's quite a long time since I made any. How this reminds me of old times,' she sighed, looking round at the hall with its decorated stalls and paper chains and lanterns hanging from the rafters. 'What time is the bazaar to be opened?'

'Half-past two,' said Sophia. 'I wonder if Mr Stonebird will come?'

'I didn't see any sign of him when I passed his house,' said Ianthe. 'Not that I looked, really.'

'But you might have seen signs,' Sophia reassured her.

'Yes, one might, though I'm not sure quite what. Is your sister coming this afternoon?'

'Yes, she's promised to help with the teas and refreshments.'

At that moment Penelope appeared, bringing with her a breath of Chelsea – or was there, Sophia wondered, some newer and more fashionable district it might have been, such as Islington, Earls Court or Camden Town? Sophia wished her sister had not been wearing tartan trews, but it would never do to say anything. And what *did* one wear at these parish functions? Poor though the district was, old Saturday morning clothes would not do – one must be seen to have made an effort. Sophia herself was wearing a green jersey suit and a small hat, but she felt that she did not look so absolutely right as Ianthe, whose plain blue woollen dress was set off by a feather-trimmed hat which had just the right touch of slightly dowdy elegance – if there could be such a thing. Her long training in church circles was evident too in her ease of manner with the other parish women, which contrasted with Penelope's slightly defiant air resulting from shyness and uncertainty.

Penelope wished now that she had worn a dress or suit instead of the elegant tartan trews, but they had seemed the only way to make Rupert Stonebird notice her. Standing behind the refreshment table, though, she now realised that only her upper half was visible. And anyway he had not yet arrived. He would probably slip in at the last minute, just as a matter of duty.

We should have taken a taxi, thought Mrs Grandison unhappily as she and Lady Selvedge, jostled by crowds, hurried down the passage leading to the northbound Bakerloo trains. She should have insisted, have pretended that Sophia's part of London was inaccessible by public transport, and of course, when one came to think of it, there *was* quite a long walk from the station. Mrs Grandison's pointed Italian-style shoes were already beginning to pinch her left foot. Lady Selvedge, she now realised to her surprise, was wearing low-heeled walking shoes, not really quite the thing with her elaborately draped velvet toque but eminently sensible.

'This is the train,' she declared. 'Come along, Dorothy, or we shan't get a seat.'

A great many people seemed to be crowding in, presumably returning home for their Saturday half day. Was it right, Mrs Grandison asked herself, that she should stand while men sat? But the question was academic, for there was nothing she could do about it. This was no way for the opener of a bazaar and the guest of honour to arrive, she thought indignantly. Perhaps they would be able to get a taxi at the station.

But it was not the kind of station that has taxis waiting

61

outside it, and the two ladies were forced to walk through the crowded streets, now full of people doing their weekend shopping.

'So many *black* people,' said Lady Selvedge in her penetrating voice. 'And do I see *yams* on that stall? I don't think the vicarage can be *here* – Dorothy, are you *sure* we're going in the right direction?'

'I have always been by car or taxi before,' said Mrs Grandison shortly. 'Of course the streets near a station are always sordid. Think of Victoria.'

'Well, Buckingham Palace is near Victoria,' said Lady Selvedge unhelpfully. 'And so are some of the best parts of Belgravia – not to mention Westminster Cathedral.'

'That's a Roman Catholic cathedral,' snapped Mrs Grandison, whose feet were now hurting considerably, 'so I see no reason why we should mention it. If only Mark could have got a living in a better district, she thought, as she had so often thought before. 'My son-in-law was offered the living of St Ermin's when it fell vacant recently,' she said, 'but he felt there would be more scope here.'

'*Scope?*' echoed Lady Selvedge as if the word were unfamiliar to her. 'Ah, *scope*, I see what you mean. Yes, scope is a great thing where the clergy are concerned.'

'This part of the district is becoming quite fashionable,' said Mrs Grandison as they approached the terrace where Ianthe Broome and Rupert Stonebird lived. 'Such pretty little houses – and there is St Basil's spire,' she added encouragingly.

'Ah, yes – you see, it hasn't been such a long walk after all,' said Lady Selvedge. 'I always believe in saving a taxi fare where possible.'

'Sophia will be waiting for us at the vicarage,' said Mrs Grandison. 'I expect you would like to go upstairs to tidy yourself before the opening.'

'Tidy myself?' Lady Selvedge raised a hand to her

elaborate hat. 'Oh, I doubt if that will be necessary. Ah, my dear,' she said, seeing Sophia at the front door, 'Here we are, you see, safe and sound.'

'How nice to see you. I take it you've had lunch?' It would be disastrous if they had not, Sophia thought.

'Yes, thank you, an excellent meal and only three and ninepence.'

Where could they have lunched? Sophia wondered. 'Perhaps you'd like to sit down and rest for a while?' she suggested.

'Rest? Oh no, thank you.'

Then what were they to do? Sophia wondered.

'*I* should like to go upstairs,' said her mother plaintively and left them.

'Do you know, I thought I saw *yams* on one of the vegetable stalls as we were coming along,' said Lady Selvedge. 'It reminded me of our time in Nigeria. Humphrey was there, you know.'

When Mrs Grandison had rejoined them it was still not quite half-past two, but Mark came in to say that as everybody was already waiting in the hall and it would be difficult to restrain them from buying things much longer, the bazaar might as well be opened immediately.

Lady Selvedge allowed herself to be led on to the platform and was introduced in a short speech by Mark, who found himself unable to think of very much to say about her, confused as he was by the talk of 'high principles', cocktail parties, and her former husband's misdeeds which he remembered having with Sophia and Penelope. It was obviously good of her to have given up an afternoon – perhaps a precious afternoon in these days when all time was precious –'to come from afar to open the bazaar'. Here Mark stopped, dismayed at finding himself breaking into rhyme. There was some laughter and he took the opportunity to sit down. Lady Selvedge then rose and made her little speech – the one she always made on these occasions, for the 'cause', whether Church, Conservative Party or District Nursing Association, was always a good one and it was safe to urge her hearers to spend just a little more than they thought they could afford, however relative the amount might be. Penelope had taken note of the two quite personable-looking men who had just come into the hall and were standing looking about them with some bewilderment, as if uncertain what they ought to do. Then, to her surpise and annoyance, she saw that they were greeting Ianthe Broome with every appearance of being old friends.

'Why, Mervyn, and Mr Challow, too,' said Ianthe, who had experienced a shock of dismay mingled with pleasure on seeing them, 'how did *you* know about St Basil's bazaar?'

'Oh, you let slip a word about it,' said Mervyn, 'something about making two dozen sausage rolls, so we thought we'd come along.'

'Shall we buy something off your stall, Ianthe?' John asked.

'Yes, of course you must,' she said quickly, a little taken aback by his use of her Christian name. 'I'm not sure that there are many things suitable for men, though,' she added, looking helplessly at the aprons, bed jackets and hand-knitted babies' woollens.

'I'll have this mauve bed jacket for Mother,' said Mervyn. 'It'll be just the job.'

'This blue one's pretty. It would suit *you*,' John said, lowering his voice and looking at Ianthe intently. 'That's swansdown round the neck, isn't it, that soft fluffy stuff.'

Ianthe turned away, slightly embarrassed, and began wrapping up the purchase. Sister Dew, who was also helping at the stall, said gushingly, 'Well, Miss Broome, you *are* a good saleswoman – another bedjacket gone already! Now who wants a nice apron or a baby's romper suit? Haven't you got a little nephew or niece?' she asked, thrusting a small knitted garment at Mervyn. But at that moment Lady Selvedge and Mrs Grandison were seen approaching the stall and Sister Dew quickly switched her attention to them. Both bought a gratifyingly large number of things before passing on to the next stall, where Miss Pettigrew sat behind pyramids of tinned food, most of which, on closer inspection, proved to be for cats.

'We hoped we might get a peep at your house,' said Mervyn to Ianthe.

'Oh yes, of course,' said Ianthe. 'It will be a good chance for you to see it later on – a cup of tea or a glass of sherry – I should be so pleased.'

'I'm dying to see where you live,' said John.

'Perhaps we should pass on to the home-made cakes,' said Mervyn. 'I should like to buy a sponge before they all go.'

Whoever *can* they be? Sophia wondered. They did not seem quite the sort of men one imagined Ianthe knowing as friends, though she had certainly greeted them cordially enough. Perhaps they were former choirmen or servers from her father's old parish – that might be the answer. Sophia could imagine them in cassocks, doing something with candles or incense. Having, as she thought, placed them, she turned her attention to her own stall. Mark was approaching with an elderly clergyman, Father Anstruther, a former vicar, who had on his retirement bought a house just on the boundary of the parish, rather tactlessly, some thought, but as he was a celibate there was no wife to poke her nose into parish affairs which was something to be thankful for.

'Ah, Mrs Ainger, you see before you the dog returning to his vomit,' he said cheerfully, greeting Sophia.

Not the happiest of phrases, she thought, though one

could see what he meant.

'You know we're always glad to see you,' she said, not quite insincerely for he was a source of amusement in many ways and quite willing to take Sunday duties when Mark was on holiday.

'We always had a big crowd here in the old days,' said Father Anstruther, glancing round the hall, which certainly might have been fuller. 'People came from miles around.' He shook his head, then took a plate and wandered off to choose cakes for his tea. 'Fairies,' he murmured, 'who *was* it now who used to make such deliciously light fairies?'

'Why, Father, it was Mother,' said Sister Dew oddly. 'You always did say that her fairies were the lightest you ever tasted.'

Mark and Sophia drew away together, feeling themselves to be excluded. 'Old times and fairy cakes,' Sophia whispered, 'we can't compete.'

'A bond of fairies,' said Mark. 'Obviously a title for something. And people came from miles around, did they – well, things aren't quite what they were thirty years ago.'

'No, darling, but Mother and Lady Selvedge have come from quite a long way – miles, really – and those two young men talking to Ianthe are strangers, and I dare say Mr Stonebird will look in,' said Sophia comfortingly. 'Penelope will be so disappointed if he doesn't.'

'Why, does she like him particularly?'

Sophia sighed but did not answer, for on such an occasion as this there wasn't really time to go into whether Penelope particularly liked Rupert Stonebird or not or to embark on the sort of explanation that a man couldn't be expected to understand.

If I were to go in *now*, thought Rupert, I should attract

far more attention that if I'd gone earlier. The whole thing must be nearly over – hardly anything on the stalls – nothing to eat – people looking surreptitiously at their watches wondering if they were at all justified in slipping away home. Perhaps, though, he might stroll out in the direction of the church hall, to see if people were coming out, then he would feel that he had made some kind of an effort. If he met anyone he could say, with perfect truthfulness, that he had been absorbed in correcting students' essays and had not realised the time until it was after five o'clock. It was disquieting, though, the way he seemed to have to make these excuses to himself, as if his conscience which he had, so he thought at the age of sixteen, successfully buried, had suddenly reawakened to plague him, not about the fundamentals of belief and morality but about such comparative trivialities as whether or not one should attend the church bazaar. Was it to be like this from now onwards? he wondered apprehensively.

He opened his front door, walked out and crossed the road. He had nearly reached the church when he saw a group of people approaching him. Miss Broome – Ianthe – the vicar's sister-in-law – Prudence, Jenny, was it? – or one of those fashionable names that often seemed so unsuitable for their bearers – and two men whom he had not seen before. It must obviously be too late to go to the bazaar now, he thought with relief as he came face to face with the group, but he found himself trotting out the excuse about correcting papers and not noticing the time before anyone had had the chance to comment on his non-attendance.

'We did rather wonder what had happened to you,' said Ianthe.

Only somebody as naive and unworldly as Ianthe could have come out with such a disconcertingly honest statement, thought Penelope, who had of course wondered even more.

'Ianthe has invited us in to have a glass of sherry,' she said, hoping that Ianthe would invite Rupert too.

'Yes – would you like to join us? It isn't worth your while going to the hall now. They were packing up the stalls when we left,' said Ianthe. 'Oh, I'm sorry, you don't know Mervyn Cantrell and John Challow, do you. We all work together.'

'Well, I'm only a sort of stooge,' said John. 'Mervyn and Ianthe are the clever ones.'

They turned towards Ianthe's gate and went into the house. It was pleasantly warm in the little hall, Rupert thought, noticing the red glow of a paraffin heater, almost like a sanctuary lamp or the lamp that was said to have burnt clear in Tullia's tomb, for close on fifteen hundred years. He must set about getting something like that himself. There was a coal fire in the sitting room and when Ianthe had drawn the curtains to shut out the November evening everybody agreed with John when he exclaimed how 'cosy' it was. Really there was no other word for it, though only he or Mervyn could have said it.

'And there's that lovely Pembroke table,' said Mervyn, bending down to examine it.

John and Rupert sat down rather stiffly, not quite liking to roam about the room appraising the furniture and objects, as Mervyn was doing.

Ianthe and Penelope went upstairs to take off their coats. Penelope was interested to see Ianthe's bedroom, which was at the back of the house, looking over the garden. Here as in the rest of the house, the furniture was good and well cared for. The hangings were rather chintzy and old-fashioned. The dressing table held only a silver-backed brush, comb and mirror and two trinket boxes, with an old-fashioned flowered china tree for holding rings placed in one corner. No cosmetics of any kind were visible. The bed looked neat, smooth and austere, and the books on the table beside it had dark sober covers and were obviously devotional books and anthologies of poetry. It was a typical English gentlewoman's bedroom, Penelope thought, in boringly good taste. There was something chilling and virginal about it.

'Oh, you've got a little statue or something in your garden,' she said, going over to the window. 'It's too dark now to see exactly what it is but it looks rather sweet.'

'Yes, it's a kind of cherub. It was here when I came,' said Ianthe.

'Perhaps it's significant or prophetic,' said Penelope.

'Yes, perhaps. I hope it means that I'm going to settle down happily in this house.'

Penelope hadn't exactly meant that. She had been thinking of the three men downstairs, though perhaps one could hardly count John as being in the running. Perhaps one could hardly count Mervyn either, which left only Rupert. And *that,* of course, was unthinkable. Yet they did live near to each other, so there might be danger.

'Your sister and brother-in-law have been so kind to me,' Ianthe went on. 'I really feel at home in the parish.'

'I know Sophia is glad to have you here,' said Penelope. 'She meets so few people of her own sort. If only Mark had taken St Ermin's when it was offered to him.'

'Would she have been happier, do you think? I mean, if her husband had taken the living only for *her* sake?' Ianthe asked.

'No, of course you're right. I suppose a wife should consider her husband's work before her own happiness,' Penelope agreed, for like many modern young women she had the right old-fashioned ideas about men and their work.

'Well, we must be getting downstairs or those poor men will think they're never going to get that glass of sherry,' said Ianthe more lightly.

She really is perfect in this setting, Rupert thought, as she came into the room. Surely Landor's lines about Ianthe ought to have come into his head if he could have remembered them.

'Let me do that for you,' he said, for it did not seem fitting for her to be pouring out drinks.

'I'm afraid sherry is all I have,' she apologised. 'I hope everybody likes it.'

John, who had hoped there might be some gin, jumped up and began to hand round glasses. 'What shall we drink to?' he asked, when everybody had been served.

There was a moment's silence – perhaps of embarrassment, as if too much of an 'occasion' were being made of it.

A rather strange collection of men and women, thought Rupert with an anthropologist's detachment, none of whom really know each other but between whom waves and currents of feeling are already beginning to pass. What, indeed, could they drink to?

Then Mervyn came to the rescue. 'Why, to the success of St Basil's bazaar,' he said. 'That's surely the obvious toast.'

6

As Christmas approached and the weather became colder, Faustina assumed her pear-shaped winter body and spent the evenings curled up in her basket by the boiler in the kitchen, while Sophia stirred various mixtures stiff with fruit and nuts and laced with brandy.

A week before Christmas she was icing the cake one evening when Mark came in with a letter in his hand.

'I've been thinking,' he said, 'we ought to ask Ianthe Broome's uncle to preach some time. I'd thought of a course of Lenten addresses.'

'A course?' said Sophia. 'Isn't that rather rash? We don't know what he's like yet – wouldn't it be better to ask him for an odd Sunday first before we let ourselves in for a *course* of sermons?'

'I should imagine he must be all right,' said Mark.

'You mean because he's Ianthe's uncle?' said Sophia. 'And because he's a canon's brother-in-law? How far can the influence of a canon be expected to extend?'

'Well, I've written the letter now,' said Mark. 'And if he isn't much good it will be all the better for us. I never see why people should expect *interesting* preachers in Lent.'

'No, of course – humble fare with no meat and sermons of the same kind,' said Sophia.

'Ought Faustina to be licking out that bowl?' asked Mark.

'Yes, there's a bit of almond paste in it and she likes that. I'm just going to give her some milk.'

'Is this all you're putting on the Christmas cake this year?' asked Mark, picking up a rather battered-looking plaster Father Christmas.

'Yes, I forgot to buy new decorations.'

'People have robins and holly and Yule legs,' said Mark. 'I'm sure Sister Dew does.'

'No doubt – and we have our old solitary Father Christmas left over from several years ago.' Sophia placed him in the middle of the cake which was covered with white icing forked up into ridges.

'He looks like King Lear in the snow, deserted by his daughters,' said Mark. 'But many old people are lonely and neglected at Christmas, so our cake decoration won't be so inappropriate after all. It should put us in mind of the old people in our own parish.'

'Daisy Pettigrew is doing her usual food parcel scheme for the old age pensioners,' Sophia reminded him.

'Yes, and their cats will be looked after too – one only hopes Daisy won't put in more food for them than for the humans.'

Faustina looked up from her saucer, her dark face made all the more reproachful by its beard of milk.

In the library where Ianthe worked the approach of Christmas had made itself felt, though it would be too much to say that any particularly Christmas spirit or noticeable increase of goodwill could be discerned, even though Shirley had hung up a few coloured paper chains.

On the last day before the holiday Mervyn seemed more irritable than usual.

'Mother is a Spiritualist, you know,' he said to Ianthe, 'and somehow that doesn't seem to make our Christmas a particularly jolly one.'

'I suppose preoccupation with those who have – er – died isn't quite in accordance with the spirit of Christmas,' said Ianthe tentatively.

'No – and our relations and friends who have passed over seem to be a particularly dreary bunch. Perhaps it's the fault of the medium – she's a Miss Stylish and lives in Balham, *not* very promising, you'll agree,' said Mervyn sourly.

Ianthe never knew how to talk to him when he was in this sort of mood. She felt she could have done better than she did with her next remark.

'Balham,' she said, thoughtful yet desperate, 'that's on the Northern Line, isn't it.'

'Yes, my dear. It's black on the Underground map, so very suitable, I always think. Picture us arriving there on Boxing Day in time for tea by public transport, of course.'

Then, before Ianthe could comment further, he switched in his usual way to another subject.

'Now here's something wrong *again*,' he said, taking up a card. 'London colon – *not* semi-colon and *not* comma. I should have thought it wasn't too difficult for other people to get the details right occasionally. That doesn't seem too much to ask, does it? I can't see to *everything* myself.'

Ianthe and John were silent, feeling that no adequate answer could be made. In any case it was Shirley who had typed the card and she was in a higher or lower world that cared nothing for such trivia.

Just before five o'clock Mervyn came up to Ianthe carrying a wrapped bottle with a Christmas label tied round the neck. She produced from her shopping bag the box of crystallized fruits she had bought for him, and a mutual exchange took place.

'This is Madeira,' said Mervyn. 'It seems a suitable

present for a respectable unmarried lady who might be visited by the clergy.'

Ianthe murmured her thanks.

'*I* don't think of Ianthe like that,' said John. '"A respectable unmarried lady" – that makes her sound old and dull.'

'Well, I am that,' said Ianthe, with the uncomfortable feeling that she was being a little coy.

'You're old compared with John,' said Mervyn a little too sharply.

'Yes, of course – quite a lot older,' said Ianthe, surprised at his tone.

'What does age matter,' said John gallantly.

'In some cases it does,' said Mervyn and then went out of the room.

'Oh dear,' said Ianthe. 'He's in a funny mood today, and I don't feel I've thanked him properly for his Christmas present.'

She was able to do this when he came back after having given Shirley her present.

'Three pairs of seamless mesh nylons in a shade called "Incatan",' he declared. 'How many of these girls who wear this colour have ever heard of the Incas of Peru?'

John looked at Ianthe and winked, a curiously old-fashioned gesture that made her want to laugh. Mervyn had his back to them and was getting a bottle of sherry and some glasses out of his private cupboard.

'A little drink before Christmas,' he announced.

After one glass Ianthe said she must go, as she had decided to visit Miss Grimes on the way home. She had bought some cigarettes for John and was wondering when she could give them to him. She had put on her hat and coat and was about to leave when he came up to her with two bunches of violets, so that she was able to press the cigarettes into his hand while taking the flowers from him.

Ianthe hurried down the library steps holding the flowers to her face. Their cold fresh scent and passionate yet mourning purple roused in her a feeling she could not explain. It was with a slight shock of coming back to reality that she remembered her resolution to visit Miss Grimes on her way home that evening, as part of her contribution to Christmas goodwill, a sort of 'good turn' done to somebody for whom one felt no affection. To love one's neighbour, she thought as she trudged resolutely up the Finchley Road, must surely often be an effort of the will rather than a pleasurable upsurging of emotion.

She had decided to take food rather than flowers. Old people liked little delicacies and Miss Grimes probably couldn't afford to buy all she wanted. A tin of short-bread, a box of chocolates and a jar of chicken breasts in aspic had seemed suitable. She hoped Miss Grimes wouldn't think them too extravagant.

The house where Miss Grimes had a room was in a side road, tall and of red brick, with many little cards by as many bells. It made Ianthe uncomfortable to think of so many people living alone. Should she offer to have Miss Grimes in her house? she wondered in a rush of wild impractical nobility. *That* would be true Christian charity of a kind that very few can bring themselves to practise.

Miss Grimes answered the bell quickly, for her room was on the ground floor. It was a large, almost gracious, room with a high ceiling and long windows hung with faded blue brocade curtains. There were some rather good pieces of furniture and china. Why, she had seen better days, thought Ianthe in surprise, for the Miss Grimes she had known in the library, with her raffish appearance and slight Cockney accent, had not sugges-ted anything like this.

'I always wanted to have nice things,' she explained,

seeing Ianthe's interested looks, 'so I collected these over the years.'

'Oh, I thought they might have been in your family.'

'Oh no, dear,' Miss Grimes laughed. 'I've always rather liked the idea of being a "distressed gentle-woman" – it's got a nice old-world sound about it. And people think more of you if you have nice things – as if you'd once had a "beautiful home",' she gave the words a slightly scornful emphasis that made Ianthe feel uncomfortable.

'I've brought you a few things,' she began, taking up her basket.

'So I can see, dear. What's this ah, bottle – violets,' she scrabbled with her not quite clean hands in the basket and took out Mervyn's bottle and John's violets. 'Oh, it *is* good of you, dear, it really is.'

Ianthe opened her mouth to speak but she could not bring herself to explain that these were her own Christmas presents. It served her right for thinking too much of the violets; not caring much for drink, she did not mind losing the Madeira.

'And there's some shortbread and chocolates and a jar of chicken breasts,' she said, taking them out of the basket and putting them on the table.

'Oh my – what a feast,' said Miss Grimes, tearing the wrapping paper off the bottle. 'Madeira. "Have some Madeira, m'dear" – I'll keep this for Christmas if you don't mind. But now you must have a drink with me. I find this Spanish Burgundy – Vino Tinto they call it – not bad. Reminds me of holidays on the Costa Brava.'

Ianthe remembered that Miss Grimes had been to Spain for her holiday one year, but she supposed that she must have bought the wine specially when Ianthe had said she was coming to see her. It was rather touching, especially when one realised that she had practically no money but her old age pension.

'I get a bottle of this every week,' Miss Grimes went on. 'It's six-and-six – quite cheap really. You want to warm it a bit, though.' She laughed and took a gulp of wine. 'We had one of those social workers come round a few weeks ago – she was doing a sort of survey of old age pensioners – some idea that they could live on twenty-five shillings a week for food. She asked me to join in like a kind of guinea pig and keep a weekly budget. She was a bit surprised about the wine – told me I'd be better off spending the money on haricot beans and lentils. They'd got it all worked out what we ought to eat – would you believe it!'

Ianthe took a rather prim sip of wine. She had not imagined Miss Grimes spending six-and-six a week on drink and might well have taken the attitude of the officious social worker. There was something slightly shocking about an old woman drinking wine alone in a bed-sitting room. Haricot beans and lentils – or chicken breasts in aspic if they could be afforded – were really much more suitable.

'Now tell me the library gossip,' said Miss Grimes. 'What's this new young man like? More to our Mervyn's taste than a girl, I shouldn't wonder.' She gave Ianthe a sly look.

Really, she wasn't a very nice old woman, thought Ianthe, beginning to feel indignant that Miss Grimes wasn't conforming more to type.

'He's very pleasant,' she said, but somehow she did not want to talk about John.

'He might do for you – it's not too late,' said Miss Grimes jovially.

'Oh, but he's younger than I am,' said Ianthe, and then found herself flushing with annoyance at having taken Miss Grimes's joke seriously.

'Well, you're not on the shelf yet, even if you are a librarian.'

Ianthe felt obliged to laugh at this and after telling Miss Grimes about some of the everyday happenings at the library, she got up to go. She was relieved to be out in the cool night air, but the journey home was an awkward one and she felt a little sorry for herself as she waited for her second bus. She had set out with the idea of doing good by visiting poor lonely Miss Grimes but she did not seem to have achieved anything much. Miss Grimes had certainly been glad of the presents but she had not really seemed as destitute and lonely as Ianthe had expected – perhaps secretly even hoped – and she found herself resenting the way she had taken the violets.

How tired and drab she looks, thought Rupert Stonebird, walking up the road behind her. By no means 'lightly advancing thro' her star-trimm'd crowd' – he had even gone so far as to look up Landor's lines about Ianthe – but perhaps women couldn't be expected always to live up to what poets wrote about them. He turned into his house, thankful not to have had to make conversation with her.

More Christmas cards lay on the mat in the hall. The first one he opened – an obviously carefully chosen new-old Victorian snow scene – was signed 'Penelope'. He stared at the signature, wondering who could have sent it? One of his students, perhaps. Then he remembered that the vicar's sister-in-law was called Penelope – but why should she send him a card? It must be somebody he had forgotten.

The next card, signed 'Esther', showed an African carving of startling unsuitability and crudeness. On the back was printed 'Proceeds from the sale of this card will be given to the Fund for Needy and Indigent Anthropologists (FUNIA).' Really, he thought in disgust, must they even cash in on Christmas? Then he remembered with a sinking heart that he had rashly accepted an invitation to spend the holiday with a colleague and his wife who had, as they put it, 'taken pity on your loneliness at this so-called festive season'. They were agnostics – perhaps even old-fashioned Rationalists – and had a family of young children. No doubt he would be woken up in good time to go to church.

7

Penelope found Christmas disappointing. Not that it ever really came up to her expectations, but this year – spending it at the vicarage with Mark and Sophia and her mother – she had hoped for at least a glimpse of Rupert Stonebird. It had been a blow to learn that he had gone away to spend Christmas with 'friends in the country', and she imagined him surrounded by fascinating girls all more attractive than herself. Rupert had not specified what the 'friends' consisted of, so nobody could have known about the anthropological colleague and his wife and their children aged seven, five, and three, or pictured Rupert going to church alone on Christmas morning, helping to wash up after the adequate but plain Christmas dinner, spending the evening talking shop, and retiring early to his hard uncomfortable bed. He came back to London on Boxing Day evening, but the vicarage party went to the theatre that night and asked Ianthe Broome to join them. So nobody saw Rupert return to his house, or standing in his overcoat in the unheated hall, opening late Christmas cards, then going from room to room switching on electric fires.

The New Year came and with it a kind of hope, though of what Penelope was not sure. She was invited to a few parties, kissed good-night outside her door in South Kensington, taken out to lunch by a young man training to be a chartered accountant, and to an Italian film by another who was 'in the City'; she was beginning to forget about Rupert when one evening towards the end of January she was later than usual leaving Toogood and Shelve, the publishers, where she worked as secretary to Mr Shelve. An elderly female novelist had come in at a quarter to six and Penelope had found herself trying to explain why her latest novel had not been reviewed in the *Sunday Telegraph*, why it had not been advertised more widely, why copies had not been displayed on the bookstall of a friend's local station, why it had not yet been reprinted. It was perhaps fortunate for both of them that Mr Toogood was in America and Mr Shelve was at home in Haslemere with influenza, but publishers had to go to America and they were also as likely as anyone else to catch influenza, Penelope explained.

'This would *not* have happened with Mr Chatto or Mr Windus,' said the female novelist, as Penelope at last managed to get her out of the building. 'I shall go to the Army and Navy Stores,' she announced. 'They are sure to have copies of my book *there*.'

Penelope thought it wiser not to point out that the Stores would certainly be closed by the time she got there, but felt she had done enough in showing her which bus to take.

She had come rather out of her way and now walked back along a square where a learned society had its premises. In the days when she had first known him she had wondered idly whether she might see Rupert round here, 'going in' or 'coming out', though she was not clear when this might be expected or even what he might have been doing. This evening, however, she was surprised and excited to notice that the great carved door was wide open and that groups of people were coming out.

An elderly man with a white pointed beard was being shepherded into a chauffeur-driven car by the short rough-haired woman in a thick tweed suit, who had been at Rupert's house that evening in the autumn; a little man carrying two heavy-looking suitcases was hurrying away as if to catch a train; a group of younger men and women was standing on the pavement, talking and laughing.

'Well, Rupert, back to your solitary meal in your neo-Edwardian house rather too far west of St John's Wood,' said a voice near Penelope. 'And I must away to my Green Line bus – Lydia will be keeping something hot for me.'

Penelope dared not stop or turn her head, for she realised that Rupert must be close behind her. It was fortunate that at that moment the handle of her basket, insecurely mended, should suddenly give way, scattering the contents over the pavement – a library book, some oranges, and a rather shamefully adolescent bag of liquorice all-sorts.

'Let me help you – why, it's Father Ainger's wife's sister.' Rupert looked at Penelope seriously, concentrating on the relationship as an anthropologist should.

'Yes, Sophia is my sister. We met at dinner at the vicarage and at Miss Broome's house after the bazaar,' said Penelope firmly reminding him.

'Were you on your way to the vicarage now?'

Penelope hesitated, hardly remembering where she had been going. Home, she supposed, to wash her hair and do her nails – to have what her contemporaries called 'an early night'. On the other hand, she *could* have been going to see Sophia. Where was *he* going? That was the point.

'Would you like to have a drink with me?' Rupert asked, without waiting for her answer. 'That is, if you have no immediate engagement.'

Penelope could not help smiling at the formality of his words. 'That would be very nice,' she said.

They walked along together, neither quite knowing what to say, until they reached the pub, which was full and rather cosy. When they were settled down with their drinks she asked him about the learned society. Somebody had been reading a paper there, which apparently happened quite often, Penelope learned, and they usually finished at about this time. So there might be an advantage in working late and coming home a rather roundabout way, she reflected.

Now that she saw Rupert again he was rather less interesting than she had remembered — a little older, slightly inhibited in his conversation, and unresponsive to her semi-flirtatious looks and remarks in a way that puzzled her. It must be something to do with being an anthropologist, she decided. It seemed a dark mysterious sort of profession, perhaps in a way not quite manly, or not manly in the way she was used to. Her young men hitherto had been in the City, or in advertising, chartered accountancy, or even television. They took her to the sort of restaurants she could mention without shame next day when her colleagues at work asked 'Where did he take you?' And now here was Rupert, asking her if she was hungry and would she like a sandwich. He had suddenly realised that he hadn't had any lunch.

'No thank you,' said Penelope, feeling that he could hardly sit there eating a sandwich unless she did too.

But her life had been, though in different ways, as narrow and sheltered as Ianthe's. Men could and did eat sandwiches while their female companions ate nothing. Rupert went to the bar and came back with more drinks for them both and a thick and delicious-looking ham sandwich for himself.

Penelope poured tonic into her gin and looked away

from him.

Rupert, devouring his sandwich with enjoyment, looked at her. Her beautiful red hair was arranged in its usual chaotic beehive, but there was something strange about her eyes which had a curious bruised look about them. Perhaps it was just purple eye-shadow lavishly applied, he decided eventually. She was wearing a navy blue duffel coat with a tartan-lined hood, black stockings and pointed shoes with very high heels. As he had remembered, there was something slightly comic about her appearance.

The pub suddenly seemed to empty. Crowds of people went out and a young clergyman came in and ordered a pint of bitter. He seemed to be on good terms with the people behind the bar. He was handsome in a blonde rugger-blue sort of way.

'Curate having a drink,' said Penelope rather scornfully. 'Bringing the church to the people.'

'Yes, I suppose it's a good thing when they can do that,' said Rupert, seeming not to notice the scorn in her voice. 'I should think your brother-in-law gets on well with people,' he added formally.

'Mark? Oh yes, he does, but only because he feels he ought to. Really he's a very remote sort of person. He hardly even notices those endless cups of tea.'

Rupert smiled. 'Yes, it's a pity – I mean, the endless cups of tea. I grew away from the Church being a clergyman's son, of course, and now that I've come back to it I find it the same only more so – fewer people and even more cups of tea.'

'There should be more people and lots of wine,' said Penelope impetuously.

'Yes, but just imagine the practical difficulties. And of course the outward trappings. . . .' He paused.

'Don't affect the inward truth, do you mean?' Penelope asked. She was beginning to feel very hungry, hardly strong enough for a serious talk about religion. She found his 'return to the Church' peculiarly disconcerting, almost as if he might be going to become a clergyman himself. And when one came to think of it he did look a little like a clergyman in his dark grey suit, especially when he wore his spectacles.

'Have you ever been married?' she asked, boldly changing the subject.

'No – that hasn't come my way – marriage,' he said rather oddly, as if it were the sort of thing about which one had no conscious choice.

'But other things – oh, lots of other things, I'm sure,' went on Penelope, now a little desperate.

He smiled. 'There *are* other things, after all. What was it Dr Johnson said – "Love is only one of many passions and it has no great influence on the sum of life".'

He finished his drink, drained it, Penelope thought, 'with an air of finality', like a character in a novel. Soon he would get up and say he must be going.

'I suppose as an anthropologist you look on everything with detachment,' she said.

'Not quite *everything*.' He smiled – enigmatically, surely.

'Do you like your house?' she asked. 'Are you happy in it?'

'Yes – and I have good neighbours which is pleasant.'

Penelope supposed he must mean Ianthe Broome and Sophia and Mark.

'Do you know, one of them brought me an oxtail the other evening?'

'An *oxtail*?' Penelope saw it being carried in the hand, stiff and furry at one end like a kind of African fly switch. 'Whatever for?'

'To eat – it was in a basin.'

'Oh, I see – cooked. But surely not a *whole* oxtail?'

'Well, I don't know – it lasted me two meals. I

suppose it must have been a portion,' he said uncertain-ly, feeling that the word was wrong.

'Fancy that.' A mixture of scorn and jealousy made Penelope also express herself uncharacteristically.

'I thought it was very kind,' Rupert went on. 'It's such a bore cooking when one's alone.'

How naïve he was, thought Penelope, trying to see Ianthe bearing a portion of oxtail up to his door. But somehow it was difficult – impossible really – to imagine her doing anything with oxtails.

'Do you live far from here?' Rupert was asking.

'No, I can get a bus to South Kensington.'

'Then I shall get a train in the opposite direction,' he said, thinking that there was something sad about it, especially now that she was thanking him politely for the drinks. It might be amusing to run across her some time. No doubt he would see her at the vicarage.

Penelope went to the top deck of the bus and lit a ciga-rette. The 'evening', if such it could be called, had not been exactly successful, though one obviously shouldn't expect too much of a chance meeting. It was something that it had happened at all.

The conversation about oxtail had made her realise how hungry she was and she stopped at a delicatessen shop on the way home and bought a pizza. She inserted her key as quietly as possible in the front door of the house where she had a room and crept upstairs. A strong smell of coffee emanating from the basement reminded her that Mrs Crouching, her landlady, was having one of her monthly 'evenings' – mild social occasions when she and her friends met to talk over important topics of the day. Race relations seemed almost cosy discussed at this distance from Notting Hill or Brixton, Penelope thought scornfully. But that had been last month. Tonight it might be the Common Market or the future of space travel.

As Penelope mounted further to the third floor where she and the other lodger had their rooms, she was relieved to hear the limpid notes of a recorder playing 'Brother James's Air'. This meant that Jocasta was unlikely to come bouncing out and invite her in to listen to a Mahler symphony on her record player. It also meant that the bathroom would be free for her to wash her hair. But before that she would make a cup of tea and read for a bit.

It was a pretty room, with pale green walls and a chintzy covered divan, piled with rose-coloured velvet cushions. Penelope lay among them, eating the cold leathery pizza – surely not quite as it was meant to be? – and drinking sweet tea. Because she had felt it might be vaguely suitable she had chosen to read a volume of Donne –

> Whoever guesses, thinks or dreams he knows
> Who is my mistress, wither by this curse...

Why should the book have opened at that poem? All the same he *had* been rather cagey about Ianthe Broome, not saying who it was that had brought the oxtail. I must be subtler than that, Penelope thought – just bringing food won't be enough.

'Reading, were you?' Rupert picked up the book which lay on the little table by the fire. It turned out to be the poems of Tennyson, bound in green morocco. Could she really have been reading *that*? he wondered, looking around for the novel stuffed behind a cushion.

'Yes, but I was just going to make some coffee,' said Ianthe. 'Would you like some?'

How convenient women were, Rupert thought, accepting her offer, the way they were always 'just going' to make coffee or tea or perhaps had just roasted a joint in the oven or made a cheese soufflé.

'I didn't think people read Tennyson nowadays,' he said, 'but then of course you aren't just "people".'

Ianthe flushed and busied herself with the coffee tray. She had not exactly been reading Tennyson but had remembered John quoting one of his poems during the first days of their acquaintance.

> Now lies the earth all Danäe to the stars
> And all my heart lies open unto thee. . . .

She was ashamed to think that Rupert might have discovered her looking it up.

How comfortable it is here, he thought. Much better than sitting in pubs with young girls or even drinking with one's colleagues, the hastily snatched pint of bitter before they caught their trains home to their wives. There was a delicious smell wafting from a pink hyacinth which was growing in a glass on the table at his side. It seemed typical of Ianthe, the slightly schoolmistressy touch of growing the bulb in water so that its white Medusa-like roots were visible. One could almost imagine her saying 'Now, girls,' and explaining about osmosis or whatever the process was called. What an admirable person she was!

'I'm thinking of giving a small dinner party in the spring,' he said. 'My daily woman has offered to cook the meal. I do hope you will be able to come. The other guests will just be two of my colleagues and their wives, to whom I owe hospitality' – the way he said it made them sound utterly negligible, almost beneath contempt.

Ianthe looked up at him and smiled. 'That would be very nice,' she said. 'I should like to come.'

Looking at her Rupert remembered his colleagues and their wives. A vague idea formed in his mind – not that he loved her but that he would like to see her always in his house, like some suitable decoration or finishing touch.

'My dining room faces north and is difficult to heat,' he said rather briskly. 'I've been looking at some of those paraffin convector heaters. What do you think of them?'

Had she ever loved or been loved? he wondered. Perhaps living with her widowed mother had limited her opportunities.

> A maid whom there were none to praise
> And very few to love. . . .

Where had that fragment of Wordsworth come from? It must have been seeing her reading Tennyson that had dredged up an old forgotten quotation. He scarcely heard her soft voice going on about paraffin heaters and electrical wall fans. He only became as it were conscious again when he realised that she was on to another topic. Apparently there was talk of a party from the parish going to Rome after Easter. Would he be joining it?

Then he remembered that he had a conference in Perugia over Easter. He could certainly arrange to come on to Rome afterwards though he did not think he had quite enough courage to join the parish party. Rome for Rupert meant the Vatican Library, the Museo Preistorico Luigi Pigorini, and restaurants in Trastevere, but azaleas were massed on the Spanish Steps at Easter and he could see that this might be the ideal setting for Ianthe.

'The vicar and his wife, of course,' she was saying, 'and I expect Penelope will come too. It should be lovely.'

Yes, he might have an amusing time with the two women, he thought suddenly, in the nicest possible way. Who knew what might come of it?

8

Ianthe was disconcerted, even a little shocked, to see the bottles of milk still standing outside the door of her uncle's Mayfair rectory when she arrived there to luncheon on Quinquagesima Sunday. It looked as if nobody had been to church that morning and she even began to wonder whether there would be any lunch. Then she realised that her uncle would have entered the church through a side door connecting with the vestry, while her aunt, who enjoyed rather poor health, would not have set foot outside even to take in the milk. She was not sure what their present domestic arrangements were and whether there was some splendid woman in the kitchen who had perhaps failed in her duty on this occasion.

Ianthe picked up a bottle in each hand, then had to put one of them down to ring the front door bell. It seemed a long time before anyone answered and she felt rather stupid standing there with the bottles. Eventually it was the Reverend Randolph Burdon himself who came to the door, looking a little surprised, as if he had expected somebody else. He was a tall stout man with a florid complexion, who looked well in vestments seen from a distance. Close to he was somewhat overwhelming and earthy, the priest of a pagan cult rather than an Anglican rector of the twentieth century. Appropriately enough he was holding a bottle of wine with the corkscrew already inserted.

'An unfair exchange,' he said, taking the milk bottles from Ianthe. 'You will find your aunt in the drawing room.' He put the milk bottles down on a small table in the hall, where they were to remain until Ianthe left, and as far as she knew, for ever after.

'Ah, my dear,' said the languid voice.

'How are you, Aunt Bertha?' said Ianthe, bending to kiss her aunt's pale powdery cheek. She then wished that she had greeted her with less solicitude for she would now have to hear how her aunt was.

Fortunately a gong sounded at that moment and Bertha sprang up with surprising alacrity and led the way to the dining room, where Randolph was already at the sideboard carving the meat.

He seemed to be in a gloomy yet exultant mood at the approach of Lent.

'You know that I have been asked to give a course of sermons at St Basil's? I shall want your advice about that.'

'*My* advice?' said Ianthe.

'Yes, as to the type of thing required.'

'But you must know that, surely, with all your experience,' Ianthe protested, knowing that her uncle was quite a celebrated preacher.

'My dear, this is a fashionable London parish, so called,' said Randolph. He carved the saddle of mutton savagely, as if he were rending his parishioners. 'What hope is there for them this Lent? I suppose they can give up drinking *cocktails*.'

Ianthe thought the word 'cocktails' a little old-fashioned, and so evidently did her aunt, who protested that everyone drank whisky or gin and tonic now.

'Somebody has got to minister to the rich,' she added complacently. She was often thankful that her husband had not felt the call to serve in a slum parish or on a new

91

housing estate. Life in a Mayfair rectory suited her very well and she had private means. It had always seemed so hard, that saying about the rich man and the kingdom of heaven.

'I suppose St Basil's is a poor parish?' Randolph asked in an almost hopeful tone.

'Yes,' said Ianthe. 'The congregation tends to be a poor one and there are quite a number of coloured people living in the district.'

Randolph sighed. 'If only I had that opportunity – such a rewarding experience working among people of that type.'

'But they are much more naturally religious than we are,' said Ianthe. 'It is the white people who are the heathen.'

'No, dear, you must be mistaken,' said Bertha in a pained tone.

'Ah well, it was not meant that I should work in such a parish,' said Randolph. 'Bertha's health wouldn't have stood any district but W1 or SW1. Anything near the Harrow Road, or the canal, or Kensal Green cemetery had to be avoided at all costs. My particular cross is to be a "fashionable preacher", as they say. Bertha is quite right when she says that somebody must minister to the rich.'

'Of course,' said Ianthe. 'And you have some very nice people in your congregation,' she added consolingly.

'Yes, both my church wardens are titled men,' said Randolph simply. He stood with the carving implements poised over the ruined saddle. 'Let me give you some more mutton, my dear.'

'No, thank you, uncle – I've had plenty.'

'You aren't a great meat-eater, are you, dear,' said Bertha, 'so the approach of Lent won't be so much of a hardship for you.'

Ianthe murmured noncommitally.

'I *have* to eat meat, unfortunately – doctor's orders,' Bertha went on. 'He has forbidden me to fast or even keep the days of abstinence. "You are not to *think* of making do with a collation on Ash Wednesday", he said to me. "You must have a full meal *with meat*".'

'I don't think it does one any harm to fast a little – if one is in good health,' Ianthe added hastily.

'I hope you will savour the Lenten fare, as I call it, that is being offered in this church,' said Randolph. 'We're trying lunch hour services with a short address this year. They have them at St Ermin's, of course, and I know Ossie Thames used to get quite a lot of office workers when he had them at St Luke's. I've got quite an interesting lot of preachers.'

Ianthe said she would try to come, though it seemed as if Wednesdays in Lent were going to be almost too devotional with her uncle's course of sermons at St Basil's in the evenings. She felt she would have to attend those.

'Try and bring some of your fellow workers with you,' said Randolph.

'Yes, perhaps I will,' said Ianthe.

When Ash Wednesday arrived, however, she found herself going alone to the service. She knew that Mervyn Cantrell was an agnostic, though on this particular day, as he pointed out to her, his packed lunch consisted of tuna fish sandwiches and hard boiled eggs in deference, as it were, to the beliefs of others. Ianthe did not think of asking John to accompany her, because it was difficult to imagine him in a church. Then, too, she had felt rather shy of him since Christmas when he had given her the violets and had tried not to encourage his obvious interest in her. She often found herself making excuses to avoid him though in some ways she was interested in him, even attracted to him. But he was younger than she was and so very much not the type of person she was used to meeting. Ianthe was not as yet bold enough to break away from her upbringing and background, and while she did not often think of herself as marrying now, she still hoped, perhaps even expected, that somebody 'suitable' would turn up one day. Somebody who combined the qualities of Rupert and John, if such a person could be imagined.

Today John had gone out to lunch before her and she ate her sandwiches quickly, then started out on the brisk quarter of an hour's walk to her uncle's church. When she got there she found that it was rather full, but being a regular churchgoer she did not mind going up to the front where there were plenty of empty pews.

She had never particularly liked the church as a building – there was a coldness and lack of 'atmosphere' about it that had nothing to do, she felt sure, with the wealthy congregation. Some of them indeed seemed to be at the service, looking somehow different from the 'office workers' for whom the services had been arranged. Poor things, with their cocktails, Ianthe thought, remembering her uncle's scorn, some of their faces under the elegant hats and above the fur coats were kindly, even noble. She was sure that they were thoroughly nice, good people.

The organ started to play and Ianthe's attention was diverted by the entry of the preacher, so that she did not notice John walking quietly up the aisle and slipping into the pew behind her. The service began with a prayer, then there was a hymn, and then the address. It was of a suitable Ash Wednesday character and left the congregation feeling sober and a little cast down. It was not until the last hymn that Ianthe happened to turn her head slightly and not so much see him as become conscious that he was sitting behind her and presumably had been throughout the service. Understandably, therefore, her last prayer was a little self-conscious. She knelt longer than she would normally have done, not out of devotion but to give him time to get away. Yet she was not surprised to find him waiting for her outside the church, apparently absorbed in the design of an iron pineapple on the railings.

'Why hullo, John – have *you* been in church?' It was all she could think of to say. They were now walking along together as it was too cold to stand about.

'That fur collar suits you,' he said.

'It's nice and warm on a day like this,' said Ianthe apologetically, feeling herself like one of the rich members of her uncle's congregation. John's overcoat of a thin material in the rather common 'Italian' style did not look very warm, she thought with a pang.

They walked in silence for a few minutes. One could hardly assume that he had *not* gone to church out of piety and because it was Ash Wednesday, Ianthe thought, but it was rather puzzling and disturbing to think that she couldn't even attend to her devotions in peace.

'We must hurry or we shall be late back,' she said rather distantly.

'I'm sure Mervyn won't mind us being a few minutes late, and for such a good cause,' said John earnestly.

'I didn't know you went to church regularly,' said Ianthe.

'Well, I haven't done up to now.' He put his hand under her elbow as they crossed the road. 'I really only went today because of you. I'm afraid I followed you.'

'But that isn't the right reason for going,' she protested.

'Haven't you ever done such a thing?' He smiled down at her and Ianthe found herself noting, quite irrelevantly, that he was taller than Rupert Stonebird.

'Only when I was a schoolgirl,' she admitted. 'You shouldn't have followed me. If you'd wanted to go to church you could have gone to St Ermin's which is much nearer. You must pass the poster announcing their Lent services every time you go to your bus stop.'

'Yes I do, but I wanted to be where *you* were,' he said simply.

Ianthe was touched and flattered in spite of herself. This ridiculous young man, she told herself. And yet why shouldn't he be fond of her. He could be . . . well, a younger brother. Having, as she thought, settled their relationship satisfactorily, Ianthe was then conscious that he was looking at her in a way that did not seem quite what she thought of as brotherly, though she had never had any brothers of her own to make the comparison with.

'Oh there you are, you two,' said Mervyn irritably. He held an open book in his hand. 'I can't have all my staff out to lunch at the same time.'

'I'm sorry,' said Ianthe. 'We've been to church.'

'That doesn't impress me. A friend of mine knew a clergyman who used to have *bouillabaisse* flown over specially from Marseilles every Ash Wednesday. I don't call *that* self denial.'

'Well, we didn't have anything like that,' John protested, and Ianthe, remembering her uninteresting cheese sandwich, also felt that Mervyn was being a little unjust.

'Is there something wrong with that book you're holding?' John asked,.

Mervyn did not answer but thrust the book towards him. The pages appeared to be stained with gravy or some kind of reddish sauce.

'However can that have happened?' asked John. 'I thought people weren't allowed to take books out of the library.'

'Normally they aren't,' said Mervyn with a baleful glance at Ianthe. 'But the staff sometimes use their discretion.'

'Oh dear – was it somebody I gave permission to?' asked Ianthe.

'It was.'

'And he seemed such a nice young man,' said Ianthe helplessly, for by what standards was one to judge the kind of person who might be allowed to take a book out of the library if not by the usual ones of manner, speech, dress, and general demeanour?

'"Nice" he may be but his taste for Brand's A1 Sauce – or is it HP?' – Mervyn examined the page more closely – 'does seem to be excessive. Why is it, I wonder, that when books have things spilt on them it is always bottled sauce or gravy of the thickest and most repellent kind rather than something utterly exquisite and delicious?'

'I suppose because the people who read sociological and political books don't eat exquisite and delicious food,' said Ianthe sensibly.

'Of course,' said Mervyn thoughtfully, 'it could just be a genuine tomato sauce from a dish of spaghetti or ravioli. Yet it is difficult to imagine anyone reading Talcott Parsons and manipulating spaghetti at the same time.' He closed it up, obviously delighted to have found a reasonable explanation.

'I'm glad the young man's name is cleared,' said Ianthe.

'She rather likes good-looking young men,' said Mervyn rather spitefully, turning to John. 'I once caught her letting one eat his sandwiches in the library which, as you know, is *strictly* forbidden.'

'It was such a cold day,' said Ianthe, 'and you're not allowed to eat in the Public Record Office, so I thought just for once. . . .' She stopped, feeling that too much attention was being drawn to her and that they ought to be getting on with their work, especially as the Ash Wednesday service had made them late coming back from lunch.

During the afternoon she worked hard and realised almost with dismay that she was going home not to a comfortable evening by the fire but to yet another Lenten service at which her uncle was to be the preacher.

It was a relief to see Sophia standing in the window of the vicarage drawing room and beckoning her to come in. Ianthe was sure it must mean that her uncle had been unable to come – for some comparatively harmless reason – and that there was to be no service that evening.

But Sophia had something else to tell her.

'I feel I *must* show somebody the parcel I've just had,' she said, greeting Ianthe on the doorstep. 'I was so astonished that I've been waiting until people started to come to church so that I could show somebody and you're the first and most suitable. Come and see.'

Ianthe went into the drawing room which was in considerable disorder. Clothes were strewn on the sofa and chairs and Faustina was dragging a silver lamé belt along the carpet.

'Look!' said Sophia, with a gesture. 'Clothes – and from Lady Selvedge.'

'How generous of her! I suppose she knew you'd planned to have that big jumble sale after Easter.'

'But they're not jumble – they're for me! Look at this suit – it's a real Paris model with a mink collar.'

'Yes, so it is,' said Ianthe, stroking the fur. 'Did she *say* they were for you?'

'Yes, she wrote a little note. I suppose Mother had been telling her what a poor parish this is and what a pity Mark hadn't taken a more wealthy living. If only the clothes had been plainer and more suitable for the vicar's wife of such a poor parish,' Sophia lamented, holding up the lamé cocktail dress whose belt Faustina had now taken out into the hall. 'When should I ever wear *this*?'

Ianthe looked at it doubtfully.

'Yes, it is rather elaborate, isn't it, with that sequin trimming at the neck. Still you're about the same height, and they're obviously such *good* clothes.'

'Yes, like those wardrobes of titled ladies one used to see advertised,' Sophia agreed. 'Worn only once, or suddenly going abroad. I used to wonder about them. Perhaps somebody decided to enter a religious order just after she'd bought a whole new wardrobe. . . . I shall have to wear them obviously – it will teach me a rather curious and special kind of humility. People will think I've been terribly extravagant and I shan't be able to defend myself.'

'What will your husband think?' Ianthe asked tentatively.

'Mark? Oh, he probably won't notice. He is not of this world, you know, in some ways we're so far apart. I'm the sort of person who wants to do everything for the people I love and he is the sort of person who's self-sufficient, or seems to be. . . .' she paused. 'Then there's Faustina.'

Faustina? Ianthe was puzzled for a moment. Oh the cat, she thought but, perhaps wisely, didn't say it. Instead she remarked that cats were usually considered to be particularly self-sufficient sort of animals.

'But they aren't always,' said Sophia. 'I feel sometimes that I can't reach Faustina as I've reached other cats. And somehow it's the same with Mark.'

'Oh dear,' Ianthe heard herself saying, feebly, she felt, but it was difficult to know how best to express her sympathy. She felt she wanted to shut herself away from life if this was what it was like. Yet Sophia was not usually the kind of person to say disturbing things. Wives shouldn't talk thus about their husbands, she thought resentfully, especially when they were clergy wives. Nor could one really compare a sacred and honourable estate like marriage to a relationship with a cat.

'I think I'll go into church,' Ianthe went on. 'It must be nearly time for the service to start.'

'Yes,' said Sophia, meekly now, 'it is time.' She bundled the clothes onto a chair, leaving Faustina burrowing into the middle of them. She sat humbly in the cold church, making some effort to get into the right mood for the service. God is content with little, she told herself, but sometimes we have so little that it is hardly worth the offering.

9

In February or March, when spring was waiting to burst out but the trees were still leafless and the earth grey and cold, Sophia used sometimes to pretend that she was in Italy – not necessarily in a beautiful or famous part but perhaps in some obscure little town in the Alban Hills or a dusty coastal village between Naples and Sorrento. Sometimes she walked in imagination in a Roman suburb, passing tall old houses with balconies and secret leafy gardens glimpsed through a gate in the wall. She would even extend her fancy into the shops she visited, seeing them as markets where she could choose a fish by the brightness of its eye, a chicken by its stiff yellow claws and plump breast, or pick out tangerines with the leaves still on them. If only one could apply the same tests to people, she thought, and of course in a way one did; but as life went on this kind of choice came to be a luxury – one took what came one's way. If the fish was fresh it was because it had been deep frozen within minutes of being caught and packed up to be bought by her goodness only knew how many months later for Mark's Lenten supper. He ate it cheerfully enough or sometimes abstractedly.

Mark came home one evening to find Edwin Pettigrew, the vet, drinking tea in the kitchen with Sophia.

'You could try a little *minced* veal,' he was saying. '*Lean* veal, of course – not just scraps.'

Faustina was in her basket by the boiler, looking understandably complacent.

'Oh the best meat, of course,' said Sophia.

'Well, you know what they are,' said Edwin apologetically.

'Yes, and they can't let us know their wants,' said Sophia.

'Not in so many words perhaps,' said Mark, 'but they do manage somehow to make their wants known and perhaps even more persistently than we do.' He could smell fish cooking and wondered if it was Faustina's coley, then realised that in view of the conversation about the finest minced veal it was more likely to be something for themselves. All the same he rather hoped it wasn't coley, suitable Lenten fare though it might be.

'We were talking about the trip to Rome after Easter,' said Sophia, pouring out a cup of stewed tea for Mark. 'Edwin is hoping to be able to come, and of course Daisy will.'

'How many are going?' asked Edwin. 'Surely not the whole parish?'

'No – regular communicants only, if you see what I mean,' said Sophia. 'That is, our own friends and the people who really do come to church regularly. Of course that means Sister Dew, and Ianthe Broome.' Her face brightened as she saw herself walking down the Spanish Steps with Ianthe.

'How did the idea originate?' Edwin asked.

'Oh it was one of Mark's sermons, in a sense. He said something like "Those of you who are familiar with the church of Santa Maria Maggiore in Rome", and it turned out that hardly anybody was. So we thought we might make up a party from the parish and go to Rome.'

'Daisy has a friend living in Rome,' said Edwin, 'Nellie Musgrove – they were at school together. She teaches English and feeds the stray cats in the Forum.'

'Ah, what would these foreigners do without English ladies,' said Mark. 'And will you be able to leave somebody in charge of the animals?' he asked Edwin.

'Oh yes, Jim Mangold is shaping very well and I'm thinking of getting another assistant to do clerical work, keep the records and that sort of thing.'

'Yes, a girl would like that kind of work,' said Sophia, wishing that Penelope could take the job.

'I had thought of getting a young man,' said Edwin, 'though perhaps in a way it's hardly a job for a man. One feels that anything to do with card indexes is more in a woman's line.'

'You mean it's slightly degrading?' said Sophia.

'Oh no,' Edwin protested. 'A card index may be a noble thing, especially if it has to do with animals.'

Mark watched them arguing with a faint smile on his face.

'Yes, it could be noble work,' Sophia agreed. 'Think of Sir Edwin Landseer's portraits of animals,' she added, perhaps irrelevantly.

Edwin did not apparently need to think of them and rose to go.

'Was Faustina not well then?' Mark asked.

'A little off her food – nothing to worry about, Edwin said.'

'Is it coley for supper?'

'No, darling – that's Faustina's. We're having halibut.'

'I should have thought it would be the other way round.'

'I feel you need something nice tonight,' said Sophia. 'Ianthe wasn't in church last Sunday,' she added. 'I hope she isn't ill.'

'You could go round and see her,' said Mark, 'or telephone.'

'Yes, but the telephone is downstairs and if she's in

bed she would have to get out to answer it. I don't think Ianthe's the type of person to have a telephone by her bed,' Sophia mused. 'Not self-important enough, somehow. I think I'll go and call on her after supper.'

Sophia could see the light on in the hall as she came up to Ianthe's front door, but the front rooms were in darkness. She rang the bell and waited. There was silence, then the sound of footsteps coming downstairs. The door was opened and Rupert Stonebird stood before her, holding a hot water bottle in his hand.

'Oh . . .' they said together, staring at each other.

Sophia was the first to recover.

'I came to see Ianthe,' she said. 'I was worried because she wasn't in church on Sunday.'

'No, she's ill,' said Rupert almost eagerly. 'I called – quite unexpectedly – just before you came and found her in bed, so I'm filling her hot water bottle.'

'So I see,' said Sophia, unable to keep a note of indignation out of her tone, for it was most disquieting that the man she intended for her sister's husband should be discovered filling the hot water bottle of another woman. Besides, filling hot water bottles was not man's work – fetching coal, sawing wood, even opening a bottle of wine would have been suitable occupations for Rupert to be discovered in, but not this.

'You should have taken the cover off before you filled it,' she went on, taking the bottle, almost snatching it, out of Rupert's hand. 'Look, it's all wet.'

'Yes, the water spluttered up,' he said unhappily, uncomfortable with the new fierce Sophia. After all it hadn't been his fault that Ianthe was in bed with 'flu. He had called to ask her advice about the small dinner party he intended to give in the next week or so. He had been dismayed, almost horrified, when she had opened the front door a crack and displayed herself pale and ill and obviously in need of cherishing. He had not expected it of her and wished he could have gone away quickly without even asking if there was anything he could do for her.

Ianthe was also dismayed, for she had expected Sophia or some other female member of St Basil's congregation to be on the doorstep. And when she had seen a man's shape she had thought for one wild moment that Mervyn or even John had called with flowers. She did not know what to do with Rupert so had asked him to refill her hot water bottle. After all, there was something almost like a brother about him and he was a near neighbour.

'I'll take that up to her,' said Sophia, hugging the bottle to her.

'Oh, good – then I'll go,' said Rupert in a relieved tone. 'She won't want too many visitors at a time. Would you explain to her then?'

'Yes, certainly.' Sophia went up the stairs and heard Rupert leave the house. 'May I come in?' she asked, pausing outside Ianthe's door.

'Oh, it's you, Sophia – how nice.'

Sophia noticed with mingled pity and satisfaction that Ianthe was looking extremely plain in her sickness, with red nose and eyes, pale lips, and straggling hair.

'My dear, you look wretched,' she said.

'Yes, I feel awful anyone seeing me like this,' said Ianthe faintly. 'But as it was only Rupert Stonebird it didn't seem to matter.'

Sophia went over to the bed and started to tidy it.

'If you'll sit in that chair for a minute, I'll remake your bed – then you'll be more comfortable,' she said. 'And then I'll get you something to eat or drink – have you had supper?'

'Well, no – I had a cup of tea. I was just thinking of heating up some soup when Rupert came.'

'Now you get back into bed and I'll go and get you something – are there some eggs in your kitchen?'

'Yes, I think so.'

'How long have you been like this?' Sophia asked.

'Well, I didn't get up Sunday, then I thought I'd better go in to work on Monday, but I came home early and I've been in bed ever since.'

'And today's Wednesday. What a pity I didn't know – Sister Dew could have looked in on you.'

'Oh, I don't think that would be necessary,' said Ianthe quickly.

'Perhaps a trained nurse isn't quite what one wants at a time like this,' Sophia agreed.

Ianthe lay back on her pillows.

Down in the neat little kitchen Sophia made an omelette, cut thin bread and butter and arranged the quarters of a peeled orange on a crown Derby plate. 'Nice things' Ianthe had and it was a pleasure to use them. Sophia also reflected with some satisfaction on the way she had spoken about Rupert – 'only Rupert Stonebird', who 'didn't seem to matter'. Perhaps after all there was no need to fear that there might be anything between them. Rupert too had seemed glad to relinquish the hot water bottle and let her take over, though one never really knew what a man was feeling.

'We were talking about the trip to Rome just now,' said Sophia, going into Ianthe's room with the tray. 'It's only a few weeks away now. Just think of those lemon groves outside my aunt's villa in Ravello. You must see them!'

10

'No sooner do you get back than John chooses to go off,' said Mervyn peevishly on Ianthe's first day back after her illness. 'I suppose *he's* got flu now and I'm expected to manage as usual with only half of you here. Suppose I was to get ill, what would happen then?'

'I don't know,' said Ianthe meekly. 'We must hope it doesn't happen. But perhaps John's just late.'

'I suppose it could be that, though he isn't usually. Do you think he's satisfactory?' Mervyn lowered his voice, as if hoping that Ianthe might say something derogatory. 'His work, I mean.'

'Yes, I suppose he's all right,' said Ianthe reluctantly.

'I'm beginning to wonder if I wasn't a bit impetuous offering him the job just like that. But then that's what I'm like – you ask Mother. One day I bought six pomegranates on the way home – imagine it, *six*! We didn't know what to do with them. Of course Mother doesn't like anything with seeds, or anything foreign, come to that. She doesn't really like fruit at all.' He laughed. 'And another day I bought a hip bath in a junk shop – talk about Edwardian house parties...' Mervyn rambled on, but Ianthe was hardly conscious of what he was saying beyond feeling that he didn't seem to expect an answer.

At a quarter to eleven coffee was brought in, but there was still no sign of John.

'Perhaps he's too ill to get to a telephone,' said Mervyn in a satisfied tone – 'that's what it is.'

'But in that case somebody ought to go and see him,' said Ianthe, remembering her own recent illness and how forlorn she had felt.

'Yes, there ought to be somebody to bring him soup and toast and cooling drinks. And to shake the crumbs out of the bed,' said Mervyn. 'How dreadfully uncomfortable it is to be ill when one lives alone. I have to go to a cocktail party at the Library Association this evening,' he went on, 'so I'm afraid *I* shan't be able to be the ministering angel. Mother doesn't like me to be late for the evening meal. When is Mothering Sunday, by the way?'

'Next Sunday,' said Ianthe.

'Do remind me to get something for Mother before then – a potted plant or something growing. I suppose it's too late for cyclamen so it'll have to be tulips or daffs – which do you think?'

'I always like daffodils growing in a pot,' said Ianthe, 'then you can watch them coming out.'

'And then dying,' said Mervyn.

'Yes, but you don't think of that when you see them in bud,' Ianthe protested. 'What is John's address?' she asked, a flutter of nervousness starting up inside her.

'You mean *you'd* go? Oh, that is kind – much better than a visit from me. Women know what to do when you're ill.' Mervyn took out his diary and looked in the back. 'The address is 28 Montgomery Square, SW1. But don't let the SW1 deceive you. It's Pimlico, not Knightsbridge or Belgravia. Should you take some Beecham's powders along, do you think? Or will a cooling hand on the brow be enough?'

Ianthe, who had been thinking in terms of daffodils and lemon barley water, had not seen herself being so practical. And on the bus to Victoria she began to wish she had not been quite so rash in offering to visit John.

Supposing he were not ill at all? It was surely – the words came in the tone of voice her mother would have used – 'most unsuitable', and it seemed especially so when the bus passed the block of flats where she and her mother had lived. Ianthe was surprised not to feel the usual pang of nostalgia as she glanced down towards Westminister Cathedral. Instead she found herself remembering things she had disliked about the flat – the row of closed doors in the long dark passage, the kitchen looking out on to a brick wall, the occasional stiflingly hot summer evening when she had longed to be in the country. How much nicer her own house was. She realised that she was feeling almost excited, as if she were going on an adventurous journey into unknown country.

Montgomery Square turned out to be in that part of Pimlico which has not yet become fashionable again, though some of the houses at one end appeared to be newly painted. Ianthe remembered as she walked along looking for number 28 that her dressmaker had lived very near here, but somehow, after she had made one or two mourning dresses for her after her mother had died, Ianthe had lost touch with her. Today she happened to be wearing the dress of violet-coloured wool which was the last thing Miss Statham had made for her – drifts of its full skirt could be seen at the front of her grey squirrel coat.

'Oh, Miss Broome, that dress – I'd know that colour anywhere. And how are you, my dear?'

Ianthe was disconcerted to find the little dressmaker at her side, peering up into her face. If this rather delicate visit to John were to be carried out it must be done immediately, before her courage failed. She didn't feel she had the strength to face an interruption now.

'I'm quite well, thank you,' she said, 'but I'm on my way to visit a friend who is ill.'

'A friend who is ill....' Miss Statham took her

words and repeated them so that they sounded like a line from a Victorian poem. She looked down at Ianthe's basket with the bunch of daffodils and bottle of lemon barley water. 'Someone in bed?' she asked.

'Yes, someone in bed.' *That* sounded more like the title of a modern television play, Ianthe thought. And would he be in bed? She supposed it was quite likely that he would be.

Now she was at the door of number 28, which had not been repainted, but still Miss Statham lingered.

'This is a lodging house, Miss Broome,' she explained. 'Are you sure you've got the number right? I think it's mostly Indians and commercial travellers here.'

'Yes, my friend lives here,' said Ianthe firmly, feeling almost tempted to add that he *was* an Indian commercial traveller.

'Poor soul, she *will* be glad to see you,' said Miss Statham. 'You'll let me know if there's any work I can do for you, won't you, Miss Broome. Skirts have gone so much shorter — you'd hardly believe the hems I've taken up. Almost above the knees, some. Deaconness Blatt too.' She chuckled reminiscently. 'So nice to have run into you like this.'

Ianthe promised that she should make her a summer dress and with this managed to get rid of her. She mounted the steps to the front door of the house and stood looking for the right bell to ring. There were two windows on either side of the door with elaborately patterned lace curtains. Perhaps in one of these rooms John lay and tossed on a bed of fever. Ianthe rang what seemed to be the ground floor bell.

Let the door be opened by somebody ordinary and undemanding, she prayed, some comfortable woman who will ask no questions.

Perhaps the clergyman who eventually did open the

door might have been included in this category, surprised though she was to see him. Ordinary, undemanding, comfortable – though perhaps he should not be, a clergyman was sometimes all these.

'Good evening,' she said.

'Good evening,' he replied.

They stood then for a moment in mutual silence and surprise, rather as Sophia and Rupert had stood on Ianthe's doorstep, or like two strange cats meeting each other for the first time.

'I heard the bell ring,' he ventured at last. 'So I opened the door. I don't live here, but it seemed the obvious thing to do.'

'Thank you,' said Ianthe. 'I wanted to see Mr Challow. I hear he's ill.' Perhaps dead, she thought suddenly; that might explain the clergyman's presence. 'Perhaps you were visiting him?' she asked.

'Mr Challow? No – I was visiting Mrs Gammon who owns the house. I'm the vicar of St Mary's.'

'Is Mrs Gammon ill as well, then?' asked Ianthe helplessly.

'Not that I know of. She's not at home. It's her bingo night,' the vicar explained.

'*Bingo*?' Ianthe gave the word a horrified emphasis, for it sounded unsuitable coming from his pale lips. 'Tombola' would have seemed more dignified.

They were standing in a narrow hall, with a bicycle propped against one wall and stairs leading down to a basement. The floor was littered with papers – coupons offering '3d off' soap powder and frozen peas, and literature about television insurance and reconditioned sewing machines – which had evidently been thrust through the letter box. There was no sound in the house, apart from what might have been the twittering of a caged bird coming from one of the closed doors on the ground floor. Then a kind of muffled shouting could be

111

heard somewhere underneath them, as if somebody was having a fight or an argument. Ianthe felt tired and rather hopeless.

'I've come to see a young man from the place where I work,' she said, trying to sound firm and businesslike. 'He didn't come to work this morning and we're afraid he may be ill.'

'A non-appearance at work doesn't necessarily mean illness,' said the vicar, with what Ianthe considered unbecoming cynicism. 'He might have been at bingo.'

'Surely not in the morning?' Ianthe protested.

'I was speaking metaphorically – they do not as yet have morning sessions.'

'Well, I wonder where I can find him,' said Ianthe. She was getting tired of standing in the hall with this unhelpful clergyman.

'I expect Maureen – Mrs Gammon's daughter – will be able to tell you. She's in the basement watching "the telly"' – he picked out the words sarcastically – 'though she did glance away from the screen just long enough to tell me that it was her mother's bingo night. Perhaps she'll do the same for you. I hope you will not have had a fruitless journey, Mrs er—'

'Miss Broome,' said Ianthe firmly, putting down her shopping basket which was beginning to feel very heavy.

'Good night,' said the vicar, opening the front door.

'Good night,' said Ianthe, watching him go. She had not liked him very much but she judged him to be one of those unfortunate men who dislike their neighbours even more than they dislike themselves and as such he was to be pitied, plodding on from day to day among his bingo-playing telly-watching parishioners. How much nicer Mark Ainger was, assuming in his remote kindness that everybody knew about the things he was interested in himself and being much too charitable to

112

pass judgement on other people's amusements, however unlike his own though they might be.

The sounds of shouting and gunshots might have alarmed Ianthe had she not realised that they were coming from the television programme in the basement. As she stood uncertainly at the top of stairs leading down, she began to wonder how she was going to make herself heard above the noise. But fortunately at that moment there was a break in the programme. She heard a jolly male voice saying,

> Something something something means
> *Lots* and *lots* of chocolate beans.

What the 'something' was she didn't catch – perhaps Life itself?

'Excuse me,' she began, 'I wonder if you could tell me...'

A tall girl, her dark hair obviously just washed and half done up in rollers, came to the bottom of the stairs.

'...where I could find Mr John Challow,' Ianthe said.

'Number four – on the first floor,' said the girl, 'but I don't know if he's in yet.'

'He's all right then – not ill?'

'I don't know. I haven't seen him for a day or two,' said the girl, 'but he usually comes in about now.'

'Thank you – I'll go and see,' said Ianthe, hurrying away when she realised that the television programme was starting again. She felt disquieted at the lack of interest the girl had shown – anything might happen in this sort of house, she told herself indignantly. And supposing he were not ill at all – how embarrassing that would be.

As she mounted the stairs there was a sound of rushing water. An Indian wearing a turban came out of a door on the half landing and, with a slight bow, waited

113

for her to pass. Again her mother's face and voice came before her, and she hurried past the Indian, annoyed with herself for feeling embarrassed. It was with a considerable sense of agitation that she found herself opposite room number four.

She knocked – surely too timidly for anybody within to hear – and a faint voice said 'Come in.' Opening the door a crack she saw John lying in bed, unshaven and tousled, his pillows tumbled and the blue rayon eiderdown slipping on to the floor.

Although from her upbringing it might have been thought that 'visiting the sick' would be a part of her daily life she had hardly ever – thanks to the Welfare State – had to perform this duty, and then only with her mother or father. She had certainly never visited a sick young man alone.

'Ianthe – I knew you'd come,' he said simply.

She put down her basket and advanced towards the bed. The only chair she could see was being used as a bedside table and held a glass of water, a strip of Aspro tablets and a box of paper handkerchiefs. However romantically ill John might look, it seemed that he had nothing worse than an unromantic cold.

'We were worried about you,' Ianthe explained, sitting down on the edge of the narrow bed. 'So I told Mervyn I'd come and see if you were all right.'

'Were *you* worried about me?' he asked, his voice breaking into a croak.

'Well, of course,' she said in confusion, unable to meet the penetrating glance of his brown eyes. 'I've brought you a few things,' she said, glancing back to where her basket stood on the floor.

'Thank you,' he said. 'And you brought yourself – that's the most important thing.'

In a sense he was right. When one is ill it's the knowledge that somebody cared enough to come and see one

114

that matters more than the flowers and the lemon barley water. 'I must try and make you more comfortable,' she said. 'Hasn't anybody been looking after you or bringing you food?'

'I've only been ill since Saturday evening and of course yesterday was Sunday and most people stay in bed anyway then.'

Ianthe reflected for a moment on this depressing picture of the bed-sitting-room world, with no church-going to give meaning to the day, though presumably Mrs Gammon might go sometimes.

'You might have been seriously ill,' she said.

'Well, what happened when *you* were ill last week — did anybody come to see you?'

'Yes, the vicar's wife and...' Ianthe hesitated, unwilling to mention Rupert Stonebird.

'*I* nearly came,' said John, looking up at her, 'but then I thought you mightn't like it. I mean if you were in bed and not feeling and looking your best.'

Ianthe could think of no ready answer, so she looked round the room to see if there was anything practical she could do. In one corner there was a sink and a gas ring, partly hidden by a screen, a pile of unwashed crockery on a small table and a red plastic bucket filled with empty tins, tea leaves and broken egg shells.

Indignation surged up within her — that he should have to live like this.

'I'll wash up some of these things,' she said.

He tried to protest, but rather weakly. '*You* shouldn't be doing things like this for me,' he said.

'But one likes doing things for people,' said Ianthe firmly, for of course she had been brought up to think that one should, though perhaps this situation was a little different. As she worked she could not help contrasting this cheerless room with her own spare room where — had it not been impossible, she told herself

115

quickly – John might now be lying. The comfortable bed – she was sure this one was not – the restful pale green walls to look at instead of this busy pattern of soiled beige and brown abstract shapes – the soft cream Indian carpet instead of the one dirty patterned rug by the bed on the frayed chocolate brown linoleum. John loved beautiful things, she felt sure; it must be painful for him to live in such surroundings, perhaps humiliating too for him to have her realise that this was all he could afford to live in.

At last she had finished her work at the sink and looked doubtfully at his bed – surely it would be more comfortable if it were remade? The sheets were twisted and the blankets had slipped down to one side.

'You must get out of bed,' she said, 'and sit in this chair – then I can remake your bed.'

'Oh, I couldn't let you do that,' he said. 'They'll see to it for me.'

A disquieting picture of the girl in the basement came into Ianthe's mind and she was almost shocked to realise that she did not like to think of her looking after John. She stood in the middle of the room with a vase of daffodils in her hand, not quite knowing what to do.

'I'd rather see you like that than making my bed for me,' said John. 'I shall think of you every time I look at them.' He lay back on the pillows, smiling at her.

Somehow she wished he had not said that. It was too obvious, glib almost, and she did not know what answer to make.

'I suppose I ought to go now,' she said, picking up the eiderdown from the floor and making a vague attempt to straighten the blankets. 'I hope you'll soon be better.'

'It was sweet of you to come – it's done me so much good. I'm really ashamed of this awful place, but of course I'm not staying here long.' He raised his head and smiled to her again in a curious way, his eyes seeming to be laughing at her. 'I'm thinking of moving to a room on Campden Hill,' he added.

'Campden Hill? Oh, that's where my aunt's sister lives – my aunt by marriage, you see – in Aubrey Walk,' Ianthe said.

John was silent, perhaps because of this rather daunting information, the proximity of Ianthe's aunt's sister making his room on Campden Hill seem rather less likely.

Ianthe was trying to imagine what the room would be like and where exactly the house would be but somehow did not like to ask for further details. She gathered up her handbag, gloves, and empty basket and prepared to leave.

'Is there anything else you need?' she said.

'Well...' He hesitated. 'I hardly like to ask – it's so embarrassing.'

What could it be? Ianthe wondered. 'Something I can get for you?' she asked.

'No, not that exactly. It's only that I haven't been able to get to the bank, being ill and all that, and I haven't got any money for the rent. I suppose I could let it go for this week, though.'

'Oh no, you mustn't do that,' said Ianthe quickly. She found it most distasteful to think of him owing money to the bingo-playing woman in the basement. She took out her wallet and found that she had six pounds and ten shillings which she placed on the chair by his bed. 'Will that be enough to be going on with?' she asked.

'Oh, that's fine, but I feel so awful asking you. Are you sure you've left enough for yourself?'

'Yes, of course – I've got some silver and I can go to the bank tomorrow.'

'I couldn't ask just anyone.'

No, of course he couldn't ask just anyone, Ianthe thought, as she walked towards the bus stop, but she

117

was glad that he had felt able to ask her. She wanted to do things for him – it seemed to give some purpose to her life to have somebody depending even a little on her. That was what one was here for, she thought; doing things for people like Miss Grimes and John was, after all, one's Christian duty. The fact that it was much pleasanter doing things for John was really quite irrelevant. What a pity it was that he should have to live in that depressing room. If only conventions were not so rigid she could easily have had him for a lodger. But of course that wouldn't do at all.

As she passed the vicarage she was startled to see Faustina picking her way along the front wall with a palm cross in her mouth. How unsuitable, she thought censoriously, though of course the crosses had not yet been blessed. The cat had probably been in the vestry and undone the parcel they were in, though it was just as likely that Sophia had given her one to play with.

Ianthe entered her house, her thoughts now on John again. There was a folded note lying on the floor by the front door. It was an invitation from Rupert Stonebird to the dinner party he had mentioned some time ago. She put it down on the table in the hall and went upstairs smiling. She had been wondering if she would have gone to visit Rupert if *he* had been ill, or if she would have left it to Sophia.

11

The day comes in the life of every single man living alone when he must give a dinner party, however unpretentious, and that day had now arrived for Rupert Stonebird. 'My dining room faces north and is difficult to heat,' he had said to Ianthe, and now he stood in it looking out of the window at the cold March day, fully conscious of his words. Daffodils were coming up in the garden but it would be dark when his guests came to the house to eat their meal. He could not expect them to be warmed by the idea of daffodils coming up outside. Light the paraffin stove *now*, he thought, crouching uncertainly with a box of matches, wondering if it ought to be propitiated in some way. A libation of pink paraffin had already been poured into it – like a great can of pink gin – it ought to burn well on that. Mrs Purry, his daily woman, was due to arrive during the afternoon to polish and lay the table, hoover the carpet, dust the room, and – most important of all – cook the meal. Rupert was not one of those men with any sort of talent in the kitchen, but he could at least light the stove.

When the flame was burning blue and steady (as it said in the book of instructions) he left the room gladly, shutting the door firmly behind him. His study, with its big untidy desk strewn with folders of notes and the proofs of a book he was correcting, was to him the most congenial room in the house. He worked contentedly for some time and was deep in the intricacies of a genealogy when the telephone rang. It was a colleague, Everard Bone, who with his wife Mildred was to be one of the guests at the dinner party that evening.

'Such a nuisance, Mildred seems to have flu,' he said irritably. 'She thought it would be unwise to come out this evening, so I'm afraid that's that. She sends her apologies, of course.'

'I'm so sorry,' said Rupert, 'but I quite see that she shouldn't come out. I'd been looking forward to seeing you both, and I had wanted to discuss that Unesco thing with you.'

'Oh, *I* shall be coming,' said Everard. 'I only rang to say that Mildred can't.'

'But can you leave her? Will she be all right?' As a bachelor it seemed slightly shocking to Rupert that a colleague, even though an anthropologist, should think nothing of abandoning his wife when she was ill. It smacked a little too much of a primitive society.

'Oh yes, my mother is staying with us – so she'll look after Mildred.'

'That's all right, then – I'll see you this evening.' Rupert had never met Everard's mother, but remembering his own mother and how comforting she had been in his childhood illnesses he was immediately reassured. Now all that remained was to find a suitable woman to replace Mildred.

The other guests were to be two more anthropologists – Gervase Fairfax and his wife Robina – and of course Ianthe Broome. Rupert went over in his mind the unattached women he knew, beginning with Esther Clovis, the formidable secretary of the Foresight Research Centre, and ending with a pretty young typist who worked in the department of the University where he lectured. Then he suddenly remembered Sophia Ainger's sister, the rather odd young woman he had met in Bloomsbury that evening and taken out for a drink.

The Pre-Raphaelite beatnik, in other words. She would be suitable, but what was her name and where did she live? And was it likely that she would be free at such short notice? Dare he even ask her? The obvious thing to do was to ring Sophia at the vicarage.

'Penelope?' said Sophia. 'Well, she *might* be free. Though of course,' she added, good sister that she was, 'she does go out such a lot. And if it's *this* evening, I rather doubt.... Still, you could try. I'm sure she'd love to come if she could.'

So it was that about half an hour later the telephone rang again at the vicarage. It was Penelope, to tell Sophia that she had suddenly been asked to go to dinner at Rupert Stonebird's that evening, but that she wouldn't have time to go home and change first. She would come to the vicarage and borrow something of Sophia's.

Penelope arrived muffled up in a duffel coat and with her hair wild and untidy.

'And I'm in my old tartan skirt and black sweater,' she lamented. 'You'll have to lend me a dress.'

They went upstairs to Sophia's bedroom.

'There's my new green wool,' said Sophia a little reluctantly, 'but I haven't worn it yet.'

'Oh, not *wool*,' said Penelope in disgust. 'Besides, it's got long sleeves, hasn't it?'

'Well yes, but it's winter dress so it will be quite suitable. I dare say Ianthe Broome will be there and she'll probably be wearing a wool dress.'

'Yes, blue, I shouldn't wonder. Haven't you got anything else?'

'There's my old black one – you might do something with that.'

'But it would be down to my ankles! Besides, it's got Faustina's hairs all over it.'

'Yes, she particularly likes to lie on my lap when I'm wearing it,' said Sophia, examining the skirt of the dress. 'It's rather beautiful, really. The hairs are almost woven into the material, like a kind of mohair. I know,' she said suddenly, flinging down the black dress, 'Lady Selvedge's parcel. I told you she'd sent me some cast-offs and they're much too grand for me to wear. I'm sure we could find something for you.'

Half an hour later Penelope was encased – for it was a fraction too tight for her – in the lamé cocktail dress with the hem roughly tacked up, the sequin trimming torn away from the neck and a string of black beads hanging down below the waist. Sophia thought this looked rather odd and had offered to lend her a string of cultured pearls, but the beads seemed to go with the piled up hair style and the long pointed-toed shoes that Penelope was wearing.

'Good luck,' said Sophia, seeing her off on the doorstep. She felt somehow that her sister needed it, for it seemed only too probable that if Rupert was interested in any woman it was in Ianthe. Archdeacon's son and canon's daughter – what could be more suitable when one came to think of it. It was true that Penelope was a vicar's sister-in-law, but that was a poorer, meaner thing altogether. Sophia tried to see her sister as a spinster and it was not so very difficult – a rather eccentric spinster not even looking as if she might once have been ennobled by some tragic love affair. There was a precedent for it, too. Her father's eldest sister, the aunt who now had the villa near Ravello where Sophia hoped to spend a few days after the visit to Rome, was in some ways very much like an older version of Penelope.

'Ah, Penelope' – Rupert was pleased to have remembered her name – 'how nice to see you. It was good of you to come at such short notice and lucky for me that you had no date for this evening, as you so easily might have done.' He was talking rather too much, he knew, but her appearance in the dress of silver lamé – like some kind of armour remembered from childhood play-acting it looked to his inexperienced eyes – was quite startling and such a contrast to Ianthe's sober blue wool dress.

'No, I wasn't doing anything this evening,' said Penelope too brusquely, 'and one's always glad of a free meal.' Goodness, whatever had made her come out with that! she wondered in horror. It was so much the sort of remark one could only make to a girl friend, but Rupert took it very nicely and said with only slightly forced heartiness, 'Jolly good, and it's an excuse for me to have a better meal than usual, too. Mrs Purry generally turns up trumps,' he added, surprised at the rather strange effect Penelope seemed to be having on his conversation.

'Mrs Purry,' said Penelope, giggling a little. 'What a lovely name!'

'Yes, she's a good soul,' said Rupert, again uncharacteristically. 'Would you like to leave your coat in the spare bedroom? It's the door facing you at the top of the stairs. Ianthe's arranging some flowers on the table.'

So she's here already, thought Penelope, seeing that there was a fur jacket lying on the spare room bed. She fingered it. Moleskin! Did *anybody* have things made of moleskin nowadays? And Sophia said she had a grey squirrel fur coat too. Perhaps this one had belonged to her mother? It was an old lady's fur, somehow. And the silk scarf with it in a faded paisley design looked like something brought back by a missionary aunt from India about thirty years ago. But of course it was real silk, so tiresomely *good*, like all Ianthe's things. And what was *she* doing arranging flowers on the table – wasn't that Mrs Purry's job? No – she was presumably seeing to the food and Rupert didn't look the kind of man who would be good at arranging flowers.

Penelope went over to the long mirror to survey the general effect of her dress. It was certainly tight and the skirt was perhaps a little too short now, but none the worse for that, she told herself stoutly. Since she could not hope – and indeed did not wish – to be at all like Ianthe she could at least provide a complete contrast.

At the bottom of the stairs she met Ianthe coming out of the dining room with some leaves in her hands.

'Hullo, Penelope, I've been doing the flowers,' she said, as if an explanation of her emerging from the dining room with leaves seemed to be called for.

'Yes, so I heard.' Penelope glanced over Ianthe's shoulder through the open door of the dining room. Just a vase of red tulips on the table, she thought. Nothing very remarkable about *that*.

'The spring flowers are so lovely now,' Ianthe went on. 'In the shops, I mean.'

'And in the South of France and the Scilly Isles – or so one imagines,' said Penelope.

'Yes, of *course*,' said Ianthe with rather excessive enthusiasm. 'Rupert is with Dr Bone in the drawing room. I must go and dispose of these leaves, there were really too many.'

She's difficult to talk to, Penelope thought, moving towards a room where she could hear voices. Perhaps we shan't ever be jolly good friends. We've really nothing in common, except Rupert.

'Ah, Penelope.' Rupert repeated his earlier greeting and came towards her with a glass jug that looked as if it contained some kind of cocktail. 'I expect you're ready for a drink. Will you risk my dry Martini or would you rather stick to sherry?'

The idea of sticking to sherry sounded so very safe and dull that Penelope naturally chose the Martini. Rupert introduced Dr Everard Bone, who was tall and fair – rather good-looking in an austere way, she decided.

'Everard's wife has flu,' Rupert explained, 'so we owe the pleasure of *your* company this evening to that rather unfortunate occurrence,' he went on, feeling that in some obscure way he was being complimentary neither to Penelope nor to the absent Mildred Bone, but not quite seeing how else he could have put it.

At that moment Ianthe came into the room and accepted a glass of sherry. Then the front door bell rang and while Rupert went to answer it a somewhat uneasy conversation started up between the two women and Everard Bone about his wife's flu and the likelihood or not of his catching it from her.

'I particularly *don't* want to get it at the moment,' he said rather irritably. 'We've got this Unesco thing coming on – oh, here are the Fairfaxes,' he declared, as the door opened to admit a tall middle-aged man and an even taller woman, obviously husband and wife, who had grown to look like each other in a rather unfortunate way, their small heads and long stringy bodies seeming as if they must have combined the worst features of each.

'I'm sorry we're late, but these newly fashionable districts are so remote that we had difficulty in finding our way here,' said Gervase Fairfax. His voice had a sarcastic edge to it, once assumed for the benefit or otherwise of his students, and now its permanent tone.

'Gervase would not ask the way, and the street lamps were so few and far between that it was impossible to use our map.'

'And Robina would not take a taxi, even if we had seen one.'

'Well, here you are now, which is the main thing,' said Rupert a little awkwardly, yet determined not to apologise for the remoteness of his house when he remembered the hours he had spent waiting in the rush hour for a Green Line bus to their house at Warlingham or Woldingham or some such rustic name.

'Yes, here we are.' Robina Fairfax's mouth opened in a smile which revealed teeth that could only have been her own, so variously coloured and oddly shaped were they.

She gulped down the Martini offered to her and sat down on the sofa by Penelope, who edged away into her corner, recognising in Robina Fairfax's shapeless grey woollen dress and strings of painted wooden beads the kind of woman she sometimes met at her landlady's 'evenings'. It seemed almost as if she would have to side with Ianthe against the anthropologists, and this was not at all what she had intended.

But when they were sitting at the oval table in the diningroom, eating Mrs Purry's admirable steak and kidney pudding and drinking a full-bodied Burgundy, Penelope found herself next to Rupert, who talked very pleasantly about Italy, remembering that Penelope was shortly to visit Rome with the parish party, and told her of things she ought to see and restaurants where she might eat. He even dropped a hint that he had a conference in Perugia at about the same time and might very well find himself in Rome after it was over.

'Which could be fun,' he added, looking first at Penelope and then at Ianthe.

'We could have given you an introduction to Professor Vanchetti in Rome,' said Gervase Fairfax, who was Penelope's other neighbour, 'but unfortunately he dropped down dead the other day.'

'Oh dear,' Penelope murmured.

'Yes, near St Peter's, just by the obelisk, I believe. In the *Vatican City*' – the sarcastic edge of his voice seemed to sharpen – 'so *that* was all right.'

'He had borrowed a book of Gervase's,' said Robina. 'Now I suppose we shall never get it back.'

'It was an expensive book too, though fortunately I hadn't spent any money on it. It was sent to me as a review copy. Of course I haven't written the review – I doubt if I should have had time, my own work takes up too much.' He gave a short laugh.

'You are still working up your field material?' asked

Everard Bone politely.

'Certainly! And you too, I imagine?'

'But of course – my wife says that we anthropologists are like a housewife faced with the remains of yesterday's stew and wondering whether it can possibly be eked out to make another meal.'

'You can do that all right with a stew,' said Penelope. 'Add a few more vegetables, some carrots or a tin of peas, and a bouillon cube – or even just water – and serve rather a lot of potatoes with it.'

'But how does it work with an anthropologist's material?' asked Ianthe. 'Surely that's more difficult?'

'Surprisingly, it isn't,' said Everard.' Many have made only one short field trip and yet they go on using that material in articles and even books for the rest of their lives. Just a few more vegetables or a bouillon cube,' he turned to Penelope, smiling, 'and sometimes a *great* deal too many potatoes.'

'Lentils too,' said Robina, with her toothy laugh. 'I wonder what is the equivalent of lentils in anthropological writing?'

The laughter that greeted this remark was interrupted by her husband protesting that novelists were just as bad, writing the same book over and over again.

'But life can be interpreted in so many different ways,' said Ianthe in her quiet voice. 'Perhaps there the novelist has the advantage and he can let his imagination go where it will.' She saw herself again in John's room in Pimlico, washing up at the sink in the corner. 'Even the most apparently narrow and uneventful life,' she began thoughtfully, then stopped, uncertain of what she was going to say next. What did it mean for *her* – that little episode – what was its significance in the pattern?

'Haven't the novelist and the anthropologist more in common than some people think?' said Everard. 'After all, both study life in communities, though the novelist need not be so accurate or bother with statistics and kinship tables. How are you finding the church life here?' He turned to Rupert. 'Is it rewarding or amusing in any way?'

'Church life?' said Robina. 'What's that got to do with Rupert?'

'He has lately recovered his childhood faith,' Everard explained, 'as I also did some years ago.'

'Goodness – do people do *that*?' said Gervase incredulously.

'Oh, the church here is very pleasant,' said Rupert, seeming a little embarrassed, probably because of the presence of Ianthe and Penelope. 'Penelope is the vicar's sister-in-law,' he added quickly. 'And Ianthe is a canon's daughter.'

There was a short silence, as if in acknowledgement of or tribute to these facts.

'It's the hymns that are the great stumbling block,' Everard went on, 'but really the only thing is to abandon oneself to the words uncritically and let them flow over one.'

'The great translators of the Oxford Movement sitting in their gothic studies,' said Gervase. 'Hymns pouring off the assembly line.'

'Yes,' said Rupert. 'I think we must agree that Keble was not at his most inspired when he wrote the hymn – which we sang at Candlemas not so long ago – beginning, if I remember rightly,

> Ave Maria! Blessed maid,
> Lily of Eden's fragrant shade. . . .'

'But one must imagine the crowded churches in the East End of London,' said Everard, 'and the great processions – not just a few sophisticated Anglo-Catholic intellectuals pondering every word with critical detachment.'

'Personally I should find the endless cups of tea one of the more trying aspects of church life,' said Gervase. 'Women like them, I suppose – do they?' He turned to Ianthe. 'As far as I can gather from my limited field work they seem to be produced on every possible and impossible occasion. And I suppose they always were.'

'Yes, I can still see my mother at the urn.' Rupert smiled reminiscently.

'My Mother at the Urn – what's that? A newly discovered work by one of the minor Pre-Raphaelites?' said Robina. 'Well, I suppose at this point we retire and leave the gentlemen to their port. I know you all want to talk about that Unesco thing,' she added in a slightly threatening tone.

The three women went upstairs to the spare bedroom. Ianthe and Penelope waited while Robina tried various doors. Penelope sat down at the dressing table and tried to do something to her hair.

'Child, your dress has split at the back,' said Robina, coming back into the room.

'Oh, I wonder if there's a needle and cotton anywhere,' said Ianthe helpfully.

'The stuff has frayed and pulled away from the seam,' said Robina. 'I don't think sewing it together would be the slightest use.'

'The dress was rather tight to begin with and now I've eaten too much,' said Penelope despairingly. 'Steak and kidney pudding, baked apples and cream, and Stilton cheese – what can you expect! If only I had a stole or something to cover it up.'

'You could wear my fur jacket,' Ianthe suggested.

'But that would look rude – as if I thought the house wasn't warm enough, which it really is with all that paraffin burning away.'

'You could wear this Indian bedspread as a shawl,' suggested Robina, and even went so far as to pull it off the bed and advance towards Penelope with it.

'I couldn't wear *that*,'she said indignantly. 'He'd recognise it and it would look so odd.'

'I don't think men notice these things,' said Robina comfortingly, 'and that means they won't notice the split seam either.'

They went downstairs and into the drawing room. Penelope was careful to walk to her chair with a sort of sideways movement, so that nobody should see the back of her dress. Very shortly afterwards the men came in, Rupert carrying a decanter of port and a bottle of brandy. Mrs Purry, who looked suitably like a black Persian cat, then brought the coffee in.

'I thought you might like some brandy with your coffee,' said Rupert. 'Or there's port, of course.'

'Brandy for me, please,' said Robina.

'I don't think I will have either, thank you,' said Ianthe. 'I always feel port is really for men and brandy is rather associated with illness or disaster for me.'

Penelope hardly knew which to choose after this, but decided on brandy; she had a vague idea that for women port was a rather low-class drink, since they did not – perhaps could not – appreciate it in the rather ritualistic way that men did.

'You haven't allowed yourselves much time to thrash out the Unesco project,' said Robina vigorously.

'Well, it hardly seemed to need such drastic treatment as thrashing,' said Rupert.

'No,' said Gervase. 'Money has been offered and a very large amount, so it seems best to accept the assignment thankfully. We think we can produce what is wanted between us.'

The men talked on about the project, and the women feeling themselves to be excluded – as perhaps they were – started a conversation among themselves. But such conversations, unless they spring up spontaneously among friends, are usually poor and wretched things. I don't want to be talking to *you*, thought Penelope desperately, trying to appear interested in what Robina Fairfax was saying about a place in West London where she had bought a piece of statuary for her garden at a very reasonable price. Ianthe had gone into a kind of day dream and found herself wondering what John did in the evenings. It was a relief to all of them when at half-past ten Robina got up and declared firmly that they had a long journey and must now go. Everard Bone also remembered his sick wife, perhaps for the first time that evening, and offered to give the Fairfaxes a lift somewhere in his car.

Rupert, left alone with Ianthe and Penelope, found himself heaving a sigh of relief, flopping down into a chair, and suggesting a cup of tea.

'See how influenced by church life I've become,' he said.

Now that he was left alone with the two women, both of whom (he imagined) rather admired him, Rupert felt a sense of power, though there being two of them rather limited the scope of what he could do – cramped his style, he might almost have said. In the end, after the tea had been made and drunk, there seemed nothing for it but to escort them home, leaving Ianthe at her front door and walking the short distance to the vicarage with Penelope.

As he had helped her on with her coat, Rupert had noticed her dress had split at the back, which he found provocative and rather endearing. Had not Sophia been standing on the front steps of the vicarage calling Faustina in, he would have taken Penelope in his arms and kissed her. But she was not to know that he had had this desire, and went into the house with head bent, feeling that she had been a failure.

12

'Rome – you're welcome to it as far as I'm concerned,' said Mervyn spitefully, the day before Ianthe was due to leave with the party from St Basil's.

'But Rome in the spring, surely that will be lovely,' John protested.

'It's not like Paris, you know. I believe it can be uncomfortably hot. And I'm sure you won't like the food. All that canelloni – or all those canelloni, I should say – *very* much overrated.'

'Perhaps Ianthe will stick to spaghetti and ravioli,' said John, mentioning the better known varieties of pasta which English people would probably be familiar with in tinned form.

'Grated cheese on *everything*,' Mervyn went on, 'though it is Parmesan, I'll grant you that. Mother would find it much too rich, I know.'

'Well, it's a good thing she isn't going, then,' said John.

'They tell me you only get that very strong black espresso coffee – not even cappucino – and the cups are only half full,' Mervyn persisted, so that Ianthe had to protest that she wasn't going to Rome only to eat and drink.

'Of course he goes on like this because he's jealous,' said John, when he and Ianthe were alone. 'If only he could get away from his mother he'd love to go to Italy.'

'Yes, poor Mervyn, if only he could.' Ianthe spoke perfunctorily, for she was walking away from the library with John who had not left her as he usually did to go to his bus stop. He seemed to be about to ask her something.'

'I was wondering if you'd come and have a drink with me before you go home,' he said at last.

'That would be very nice, but surely it's too early for a drink?'

'No – it's half-past five. But perhaps a cup of tea would be better – cosier – if you know of anywhere round here?' He stopped in the middle of the pavement and took her arm.

'There's the Humming Bird,' said Ianthe, naming the café where she sometimes had lunch. It would be the first time she had ever been with John to a place that was part of her own particular world, unless one counted the Ash Wednesday lunchtime service at her uncle's church. But now that she came to think of it she had never been out to any sort of meal with John. There was to her something romantic about the idea of sitting with him in the place where she had so often sat alone, eating a poached egg or macaroni cheese at a shaky little oak table.

'No, we don't do evening meals,' Mrs Harper was saying to an obvious middle-aged civil servant as they entered. 'But I could knock you up a couple of poached eggs or a buck rarebit – how would that do?'

'Shall we have poached eggs?' John asked, as they sat down.

Ianthe hesitated. The eating of eggs together had not figured in the romantic picture, perhaps no actual food had suggested itself. Then she realised that he must be hungry and she felt a pang of that pity which is akin to love.

'Yes, let's have that,' she agreed.

'And cakes and China tea?'

'Yes, lovely.'

Mrs Harper gave Ianthe a piercing look through her pince-nez as she came to take the order. Ianthe felt that some kind of explanation for her presence at this unusual time and with a young man was expected, but did not feel herself capable of providing it.

'Do you want *milles feuilles*?' she asked in a tone of peculiar significance.

'Oh yes, please,' said John. When she had gone away he said to Ianthe, 'You won't forget to send me a post-card of that fountain, will you. The one where you throw the money and wish.'

'No, I won't forget.'

'Will *you* throw a coin in?'

'It depends.' Ianthe hesitated, seeing herself with the parish party. Perhaps it was easier to imagine Sister Dew doing it than Mark and Sophia.

'I wonder what you'll wish for,' John went on, looking at her intently.

Mrs Harper came up to the table with the tea so Ianthe's answer had to be delayed. In any case she did not know what it was to be and took refuge in the business of drawing the cups and the teapot towards her.

'I expect you'll wish *I* was with you – or at least I hope you will,' said John at last.

Poached eggs were placed before them.

'I thought your friend would probably be able to tackle two,' said Mrs Harper cheerfully to Ianthe.

'This is the first meal we've ever had together,' said John when she had gone.

'Yes, I suppose it is, really.'

'We'll have lots more together, won't we. We'll go to Italy together one day, don't you feel it?'

'I don't know,' said Ianthe, confused. 'Perhaps I'll go with Mervyn and his mother and we'll avoid canelloni and Parmesan cheese,' she added jokingly.

They ate their poached eggs, then John handed Ianthe the plate of cakes.

'I don't think I can eat any more,' said Ianthe.

'You must be in love or something,' said John. 'That's what loss of appetite usually means.'

'I'm not used to eating a meal at half-past five,' Ianthe protested. 'I suppose that's why I'm not hungry.'

'If you're not going to eat those *milles feuilles*,' said Mrs Harper, hovering reproachfully by the table, 'that gentleman over there would like them.'

'Of course it's lovely having tea,' said Ianthe, afraid that she had sounded ungracious. 'I have enjoyed it, John. But now I really must be going. I've still got most of my packing to do.

'I'll come to the station with you and get your ticket.'

'Oh, but I've got the return half, thank you.'

All the same John insisted on coming with her as far as the ticket barrier, and stood holding her hand while she attempted to say good-bye.

Suddenly he drew her towards him and kissed her.

'Good-bye, darling,' he said. 'I wish I was coming too. Take care of yourself.'

Ianthe hurried on to the escalator and began walking down. At the bottom the warm air blowing about her seemed to increase her agitation. A piece of newspaper was swirled against her legs and she collided surprisingly, almost nightmarishly, with a nun.

What was a nun doing, hurrying in the opposite direction in the rush hour, flashed into her mind as the nun spoke.

'Why, Ianthe Broome, of all people!' she exclaimed. 'Don't you remember me?'

She had an eager shining face and looked happy in a rather frightening way. She was grasping a large man's umbrella.

Ianthe hesitated for a moment, trying to remember.

'Agnes Dalby, isn't it,' she said. 'School, of course. You were in the Upper Fourth when I left.'

'And you were the Head Girl!'

'I didn't know about...' Ianthe looked at the black robes.

'My taking the veil?' said the nun, so that she appeared to be joking. Perhaps she had often had to put up this kind of defence Ianthe thought.

People surged forward, nearly knocking them over as a train came in.

'Mustn't keep you,' said the nun, 'and I'm dashing off to St Alban's, then supper at the Restful Tray with Mother Josephine.'

She seemed to vanish as quickly as she had appeared, leaving Ianthe to be pushed forward into the train, where she stood in a daze until she found herself sitting down in a seat offered to her by a small boy.

'You looked as if you could do with a sit-down,' said the boy's mother. 'I was watching that nun talking to you – it seems to have given you quite a turn.'

'I was surprised to see her,' Ianthe admitted.

The woman lowered her voice so that Ianthe could hardly hear it above the noise of the train. 'I don't think they ought to let them out, walking about like that in those black clothes. It gives me the creeps and I know it frightened the kiddies. I mean it's *not very nice*, is it.'

'Oh, I didn't mind,' said Ianthe. 'She's somebody I know.'

'How dreadful for you, somebody you know being like that.'

Ianthe was glad when the woman and her child got out at the next station, for not only did she find the conversation embarrassing but she also wanted to think about the moments before her unexpected meeting with Agnes Dalby – moments which she had so far had no chance of reliving or considering.

That John should have kissed her like that – in the way she had quite often seen boys kiss girls on their way home – and that she should not have minded, apart from the slight awkwardness of the people surging around them, would have seemed incredible to her a few months ago. One did not behave like that in a public place with a young man, suitable or otherwise, and John was so very much otherwise. It was not surprising that at this moment the image of her mother – the canon's widow in the dark flat near Westminster Cathedral – should rise up before her.

But there was obviously nothing she could do about it *now*, she decided, and the holiday in Rome would no doubt put him out of her mind. Resolutely, and determined to think no more than she could help about it, she opened her new copy of the *Church Times* which normally she would have looked forward to reading on her journey home. Yet she reached the station where she got out without having progressed any further than the first page.

Walking past the vicarage, she wondered whether to call in to see Mark and Sophia, but judged that they were probably busy doing their packing. When she got into her house she poured herself a glass of sherry and stood looking into the garden, not wanting any supper.

'You must be in love or something,' she heard John saying, then she remembered the unaccustomed poached egg and was glad to have found a sensible reason for her lack of appetite.

'Two men and five women – er – ladies,' said Mark rather despondently, as he and Sophia were doing their packing. 'Still, I suppose I can always creep off somewhere by myself.'

'Aren't most parties made up like that?' said Sophia

consolingly. 'And the odd thing is that of all the people who complained to you after that sermon that they'd never been to Rome only Sister Dew has taken advantage of this opportunity to go there.'

'The others prefer to go to Broadstairs and Ilfracombe as usual. Where they'll have the usual bad weather so that they can go on complaining.'

'Yes, of course,' said Sophia,' and I suppose we didn't really ask them to come with us, did we. As it is, I don't know how Sister Dew is likely to fit in. And I can't help feeling a *tiny* bit worried about leaving Faustina with both Edwin and Daisy away. Though Daisy's tightened up the rules at the Cattery – did I show you her new brochure?'

Mark took from Sophia the cyclostyled leaflet – hardly a 'brochure' he felt – and read through the rules starting with 'Sex (undoctored ... and Siamese cats *cannot* be accepted)', going on to invite owners to bring bedding but 'no bowls, please', and ending with the injunction 'This year we must ask you to leave your cat at the house and *not* go down to the Cattery. We find that the cats already in the Cattery become unsettled with the noise that is made when settling new cats.'

'I suppose *you* could go down,' he said soothingly. 'After all you are such an old friend.'

'Yes, but one doesn't want to unsettle the other cats, and Faustina herself might become upset.'

'I'm sure Jim Mangold will look after her splendidly. You've often said yourself how good he is with her, and he has such a reassuring name.'

'Oh, certainly – Jim loves Faustina. I shan't worry really, but she's all I've got.'

For a moment Sophia was afraid that Mark was going to speak sternly to her, for his eyes had their rather distant look and his mouth was in a firm line. But when he spoke again it was only to express some anxiety about the conduct of the services while he was away. Father Anstruther, the former vicar who lived rather too near, was to do duty for the time of Mark's absence – not an entirely satisfactory arrangement but the best that could be made.

'Now indeed the dog will return to his vomit, as he so happily put it,' said Sophia.

'I only hope he won't upset anybody,' said Mark anxiously.

13

A party of people sets out on a journey with all its different components like the jumbled up pieces of a jigsaw puzzle, Sophia thought, waiting for something – some event or just the passing of time – to fit them together into a whole. In the bus going to the airport she looked around her to see what sort of people went to Rome in April. She was not surprised to see two or three elderly ladies and nondescript middle-aged couples, but where were all the priests and nuns she had expected, the real glory of a flight to Rome?

The answer to this question was that they had other means of transport. As the bus arrived at the airport a shooting brake drew up and a party of nuns got out of it. Sophia commented on this to Ianthe who was sitting in front of her.

Ianthe was reminded of her meeting with the nun in the Underground the day before and Sophia remarked that nowadays some of them seemed hardly to be cloistered at all.

'But it doesn't seem right for them to drive about like that,' said Sister Dew. 'It always gives me a bit of a turn to see a nun driving a car.'

Now priests and even a couple of bishops appeared and Sophia felt a sense of relief, as if their presence were some sort of guarantee of a safe flight.

'Don't you feel a slight envy of the Roman Catholics

when it comes to making a trip like this?' said Edwin Pettigrew to Mark.

'Ah yes,' Mark sighed. 'The English College, the Irish College – there's a sort of cosiness about it all. It must be like a homecoming to them. An Anglican feels almost an intruder.'

'Darling, you mustn't say such things,' said Sophia indignantly. 'You who so often preach about the catholicity of the Anglican Church, and believe it too.'

'Oh yes, Father,' said Sister Dew unctuously, 'we always say that's one of your little hobby horses.'

'We', the stupid, ignorant, umbrage-taking members of Mark's congregation, thought Sophia, moving closer to her husband as if to protect him from them. Now she took care to change the subject and what could be more natural than to talk to the vet and his sister about Faustina and to speculate on what she might be doing at this moment. But Faustina's remoteness, now of distance also, made it difficult to guess. Mark, too, after the slightly disquieting observations about Roman Catholic priests, seemed to have removed himself from her. Looking for Ianthe and Penelope, Sophia saw that they were deep in conversation, which she welcomed as a good sign.

The two unattached women seemed to have been drawn together perhaps by their very unattachedness but more certainly by Rupert Stonebird's dinner party and the idea that they might meet him in Rome.

'Perugia,' Sophia heard Penelope murmur. 'Is that far from Rome?'

'It isn't really very far,' said Ianthe. 'I looked it up on the map as a matter of interest.'

'But distance is only relative,' said Sophia. Love will find out the way, she thought, though it was a little difficult to picture Rupert like the lover in the poem, galloping over the earth and swimming the seas to reach the

141

loved one, especially as he had not as yet shown much sign of loving either of the two women.

The presence of the two bishops, not to mention the priests and nuns, gave confidence to everybody as the plane rose into the air.

Sister Dew, who had not flown before, let out a cry at seeing fields and houses beneath her.

'Jim Mangold will be feeding them now,' said Daisy Pettigrew comfortingly, 'and I expect Faustina will be getting her share. I can almost hear them crying out for their dinner. Look, dear,' she opened her capacious shopping bag and invited Sophia to peer into its depths.

Sophia saw some tins of a well-known brand of cat food, neatly packed into the bottom of the bag.

'For those poor deprived ones in Rome,' Daisy murmured.

'I hope you remembered to bring a tin-opener,' said Sophia, in confusion, for the idea of taking food to the deprived Roman cats had set up in her head a muddled train of thought, which had something to do with Anglo- and Roman Catholicism, as if the latter had need of nourishment from the former.

When the stewardess came round with cigarettes and miniature bottles of spirits and liqueurs, the St Basil's party bought them eagerly. Cigarettes, so cheap and in such large numbers, were snapped up even by non-smokers, who regarded them as some new kind of currency; and the little bottles, so exquisitely miniature, 'twee', as Sister Dew put it, could have nothing wicked about them even for teetotallers.

'Of course *I'm* thinking of the bottle stall for the Christmas bazaar,' said Sister Dew virtuously, tucking the little bottles into her bag.

Sophia noticed that the tall handsome priest sitting over the other side from her also bought a great many of the little bottles.

In what seemed a very short time the plane began to come down and bits of northern Italy could be seen below. Sophia, who had not made this flight before, was disappointed that it did not look more like the Italian landscape she remembered from the ground. This green-ish greyish land with patches of dark trees might have been anywhere.

The Italians, and indeed all foreigners, are known to be cruel to animals, thought Daisy, looking down to see if she could catch some peasant beating a horse or kicking a dog.

Now there is a whole ocean between John and me, Ianthe thought, but soon she was caught up in the bustle of landing. Groups of priests and nuns, the latter waving handkerchiefs and carrying bunches of flowers, came into view. It was almost as if they had been hired to give the tourist a suitable first impression of the Eternal City.

'Look,' said Edwin Pettigrew to Mark, 'our Roman Catholic friends are being whisked through all the for-malities, and Mark saw that the priests had been gathered into a little group under the leadership of a jolly-looking, curly-haired Irishman with a strong brogue. 'Did ye get the little bottles?' Mark heard him ask.

Leonardo da Vinci, thought Penelope, seeing the curious angular statue from the bus. Presumably this identified the place as being Italy, but it might have been anywhere. Depression had descended on her, hemmed in by all these people, driving along a straight dreary road. Where were all the handsome Italians of good family? The only Italian she might have got an introduc-tion to – and though elderly he might have had a son – had dropped down dead in the Vatican Square. And Rupert Stonebird was in Perugia, which was *miles* away. He had not said definitely that he would be coming to Rome, only that he *might*. . . .

Italy, thought Sister Dew, well it doesn't seem very romantic so far. She was beginning to wish she had gone to the toilet again on the plane – it had been so nice and clean, and who knew when she would get another chance? Tea, too – that was what she wanted now, a good cup, and where was she going to get *that*? Yet she was not downhearted. With a vicar's wife and a canon's daughter in the party she had faith that somehow all her wants would be taken care of.

Ruins, thought Mark, as the bus wound up the road by the Colosseum, the glory that was Rome. 'Have we not all,' he heard himself saying from the pulpit, 'as we have gazed on the ruins of the mighty Colosseum. . . .' Well, a few more of his congregation would have done that by then. They should have a sermon about Rome when he got back. Perhaps another 'Why I am not a Roman Catholic' would be salutary from him as well as for them. Again he heard the strong Irish voice ring out – 'Did ye get the little bottles?' – and knew that however cosy it might seem in imagination he would never be one of the party hurried through the customs to the English or Irish or Scottish College. He was too old now and the whole thing was altogether too complicated. There was Sophia too, his beloved wife, and even Faustina who was, he felt sure, fiercely Protestant.

Turning to Sophia he touched her hand. She was looking tired and a little sad. The journey had been too much for her, he thought apprehensively, but when she spoke it was in a cheerful raised voice.

'I think we'll go first to the pensione and leave our luggage and then *straight* to Babbington's', she said. 'I'm sure we could all do with a good cup of tea.'

14

When they got to the pensione Sophia prayed quickly to whatever saint arranged such things – one of the less well known women saints, she felt – that it was going to be all right about the rooms. She and Mark would of course be sharing a room; Ianthe and Penelope had also expressed their willingness to share. Edwin Pettigrew would have a single room, but it had not been possble to get more than one, which meant that Daisy would have to share with Sister Dew. Fortunately neither had raised any objection to this arrangement, but Sophia could not help fearing that there might be difficulties.

The pensione was of the reassuringly old-fashioned type which was used to catering mainly for parties of middle-aged English, American, German or Scandinavian women, though a few men in the shape of clergymen and husbands were also accommodated. But women always seemed to be in the majority and the proprietor and his wife, both of whom spoke excellent English and German, could be seen at every hour of the day advising parties of determined-looking women in sensible shoes how to get to St Peter's or the Piazza Venezia or the English church, or which were the best shops to buy presents and souvenirs to take home.

Sophia had stayed here several times before, which was one reason why it had been chosen as suitable for the St Basil's party. She greeted the proprietor in her careful

Italian and was welcomed by him in his careful English.

Penelope, standing behind her sister, wished that a more exciting hotel would have been chosen. This was the wrong way to come to Rome, in such uninspiring company. One should visit Italy for the first time either alone or with a lover, she decided. When she and Ianthe were shown into their room she sat down on what looked to be the best bed and lit a cigarette. Ianthe went over to the window and flung open the shutters and it occurred to Penelope that she was probably one of those people who didn't approve of smoking in bedrooms. If that was so, she would just have to put up with it.

But Ianthe had not even noticed Penelope's cigarette. She was conscious only that she was now in Rome for the first time in her life. She wanted to stand on the balcony and look out over the roofs, listen to the strange sounds and watch the cars and scooters rushing by in the street below. She was too tired to be aware of much except the slight headache which a long journey always gave her, yet she felt curiously light-headed and carefree.

'There seems to be quite a lot of room for our clothes,' said Penelope. 'Two chests of drawers and this big wardrobe – which side will you have?'

'Oh, I don't mind,' said Ianthe, watching an old woman watering plants on a nearby roof. 'How I long for a cup of tea!' she went on, coming back into the room.

'Well, we're just going out to have one,' said Penelope, thinking how typical it was that Ianthe should long for such a dull and essentially English thing as a cup of tea. She hardly liked to admit that she wanted one herself.

'Shall we go out now and meet the others then?' Ianthe suggested.

The party was already waiting, and with Sophia leading the way they walked rather briskly to Babbington's tea room at the foot of the Spanish Steps. All the women exclaimed at the sight of the red, pink and white azaleas massed on the steps, but each thought privately that only she could appreciate the true beauty and significance of the flowers – Sophia feeling that here was the essence of the Italy she knew and loved, Penelope experiencing a lift of the heart as if the flowers held a promise of future romantic adventures, Ianthe knowing as she looked at the flower what she had only suspected before – that she was in love with John. The emotions of Daisy and Sister Dew were of a different type. Daisy thought, a people that loves flowers yet is cruel to animals; Sister Dew said to herself, I must get a coloured postcard of that to send to my friend. The men's feelings were not so well defined and they were not to be diverted from their search for tea.

In the tea room their spirits were at once raised and depressed by the English-looking cakes, pots of jam and packets of tea in the showcases on the counter, but the dim interior, with its Kardomah-like décor, reassured and encouraged them. The whole place suggested tea, and a good cup at that.

They found two adjacent tables and settled down, the men a little aloof from the women. A waitress came and took their order in broken English though Sophia had started to speak Italian to her. There were a few obvious English tourists, but even more elderly Italians, and even a few young couples, as if it were the fashionable thing to do.

'Or perhaps they just like tea,' said Ianthe, grateful for the cup that Sophia had poured out for her. Oh, the benison of it, she thought, for she seemed to need comfort now, not only because she was tired after the journey and far away from John, but because she had admitted to herself that she loved him, had let her love sweep over her like a kind of illness, 'giving in' to flu, conscious only of the present moment. She tried to imagine what John would be doing; it would be past the time for office tea but not yet time to go home. Was he thinking of her as she was of him? She gazed ahead of her, seeing neither the pots of Chivers jam in the glass showcase nor the dark handsome young man in the opposite corner, who was staring at her fixedly.

Penelope had noticed him, staring at Ianthe like that, and wondered who he was. It almost seemed for a moment as if he would come over to the table and speak, but then he turned away, looking rather puzzled and began to order his tea. At that moment, too, there was another diversion – a large black and white cat appeared from some kitchen region and stalked down the passage between the tables. Their first Italian cat and it was disappointingly sleek and well fed looking.

'Come here, pussy,' said Sister Dew. 'Oh, I suppose he doesn't understand English – and isn't he *fat*,' she added, with a reproachful glance at Daisy.

'That's because it's in the English tea room,' said Daisy. 'One would naturally expect him to be well fed.'

'Pettigrew and I are going for a stroll,' said Mark, who had been finding the atmosphere of the tea room rather oppressive and not really what he had come to Rome for.

'I expect they want to see a bit of night life,' said Sister Dew.

'Hardly at half-past five in the afternoon,' said Penelope coldly. She was finding the presence of Sister Dew intolerable and couldn't think why Mark and Sophia had invited her. Surely she wasn't going to go everywhere with them.

'Well, I expect it starts earlier on the Continent,' said Sister Dew happily.

Now that the women were by themselves, the man whom Penelope had noticed staring at Ianthe seemed to pluck up courage to come over to their table. Could it be that Ianthe *knew* this good-looking young Italian? she wondered enviously.

'It *is* Ianthe Broome?' he asked tentatively and with no trace of foreign accent.

'Why, yes.' Ianthe looked puzzled for a moment. 'And you're...?'

'Basil Branche.'

'Basil Branche, of course! Father Branche was one of my father's curates,' she explained to the rest of the party, and began making introductions.

So he was a clergyman, thought Penelope, a little disappointed. Still, he was very good-looking and not being dressed as a clergyman might be quite an asset to their party. She began to wonder if he was unattached.

'Are you staying long in Rome?' asked Sophia politely.

'I've already been here a fornight and shall probably stay a week or two longer before moving south,' said Father Branche vaguely.

'My word, you *are* having a nice long holiday! Won a football pool or something on Ernie?' asked Sister Dew.

He smiled faintly. 'No, my health broke down and I was ordered to take a long holiday in the South of France or Italy.'

Goodness, were people 'ordered' to do such things in these days Sophia wondered, seeing the crowded waiting-room at the doctor's surgery. But perhaps he had been to a Harley Street specialist – it was easier to imagine the long holiday being recommended behind thick net curtains in one of those tall houses with several brass plates on the door.

'How lucky that you were able to arrange it,' said Ianthe, not in the least sarcastically.

'Yes, a most extraordinary thing happened. I was glancing through the personal column of the *Church Times* when I saw an advertisement for "a curate in poor

149

health" – those were the very words – to accompany two elderly ladies on an Italian tour, all expenses paid.' He smiled. 'So naturally I applied.'

'They must have had a lot of replies,' said Penelope. 'How lucky that you were chosen.'

'No, the strange thing is that I was the only applicant. I suppose no other curate happened to be in poor health at that time.' Father Branche looked puzzled for a moment, as if he might have said something amusing. 'Or perhaps others didn't feel they could give in to it as I did.'

'No, they felt it their duty to *struggle on*,' said Daisy, half to herself.

'I suppose it was a nervous breakdown, that sort of thing,' said Sister Dew knowingly.

'What do you do – act as chaplain to these ladies?' Sophia asked quickly, feeling that Sister Dew might go too far.

'Not really, they just like to have an escort sometimes.'

'They are able to get about, then?'

'Goodness, yes – they're in their seventies and very active, especially the younger sister. She was left some property in Italy by an elderly Count who had always admired her, even wanted to marry her, I believe.'

'How romantic,' said Sophia. 'It seems to be not quite of this age, a story like that.' Neither was Father Branche, she thought, a kind of 'tame curate' of the old-fashioned type beloved by elderly ladies. One did not seem to meet many of them now. 'I expect we shall run into you again, as English people do in Rome,' she added, as they were leaving the tea room. 'We are staying at the Pensione Laura.'

'And we are at the Albergo di Risorgimento,' said Father Branche, his voice seeming to rise in triumph at the noble word.

'Perhaps we could all stroll back together,' said

Ianthe. 'I expect we shall just be spending the evening quietly – dinner at the pensione and then an early night.'

Penelope looked appealingly at her sister, but Sophia was no help.

'Yes, we're all rather tired,' she agreed. 'We only arrived this afternoon – I think that's the best plan.'

'I want to visit my old school friend Nellie Musgrove, who lives in the Via Botteghe Oscure,' said Daisy firmly, 'so I may get Edwin to take me along there. I have some tins of cat food for her.'

If Father Branche was surprised he did not show it, but no doubt he was well used to English women in Rome and the kind of things they were likely to do. Before they parted it seemed to Sophia that he was trying to draw Ianthe aside, as if to make an assignation with her, but she gave him so little encouragement, indeed seemed almost to avoid him, that he had to be content with looking forward to the doubtful pleasure of meeting the whole party the next evening after dinner at the Trevi fountain. If it was fine, of course.

Dinner seemed to be hardly Italian at all, except that there was spaghetti, so English and German was the company. But the Roman evening was not to be disposed of in quite the way they had imagined, with an early night because they were tired after the journey. Everyone felt a desire to go out, even if only for a moment, to feel the pleasure of walking in a foreign city at night. Edwin and Daisy marched off with a map and the numbers of suitable trams to find the Via Botteghe Oscure; Sister Dew, Ianthe, and a rather unwilling Penelope went to buy postcards; Mark and Sophia, the cares of the parish temporarily forgotten, strolled up to the Trinità dei Monti and down the Spanish Steps.

At this moment she is all mine and without Faustina, Mark thought, then added quickly, 'I wonder what Faustina is doing now,' for he could afford to be generous among the azaleas, with Sophia's hand in his.

'I don't know, she's so unpredictable. Perhaps she's even giving to somebody else the love and devotion she's never given to me.'

Mark pressed her hand.

Sophia, looking up at him, saw that his usual remote look had gone and that he was smiling.

'What amuses you?' she asked.

'I was thinking that an obviously romantic setting has something to be said for it. I suppose I don't love you any more here than when we're walking together in Ladbroke Grove – how romantic *that* might sound to a foreigner, by the way – and yet it seems as if I do.'

'But *do* we walk in Ladbroke Grove?' Sophia murmured.

One of many photographers who had been lurking among the azaleas seemed to take hope at the sight of such an obviously affectionate couple and presented himself before them.

'Why not?' said Mark. 'We could print it in the parish magazine.'

'Or at least look at it in the winter,' said Sophia. 'If only Penelope could find love here. What did you think of Father Branche? Oh – I forget – you and Edwin had gone for a walk. He's a sort of curate we met in Babbington's. Apparently he used to know Ianthe and now he's here with two old ladies, for his health.'

'He sounds an improbable sort of curate,' Mark commented.

'Yes, but very good-looking. There *might* be something. . . . Oh, Mark, she does need to love and be loved.'

'It isn't given to everyone to have that good fortune,' he said rather stiffly, for he often found it difficult to know what to say about Penelope.

'Oh don't talk like that – it's inhuman. What is there

for women but love?'

'Now, darling, you know there are many things,' said Mark, the usual stern note coming back into his voice.

'I've been taught to believe that there are – perhaps I've even seen it, but I don't *know*,' Sophia protested. 'And mustn't all these things be a second best? Oh, not to God – I know what you're going to say.'

They had now reached the house where Keats died and Sophia was diverted – fortunately, Mark felt.

'And there *is* poor Penny with Ianthe and Sister Dew,' Sophia went on. 'They've been buying postcards. What a way to spend one's first evening in Rome. Still, I have hopes for tomorrow and the Trevi fountain.'

'Oh, Mrs Ainger, such lovely cards,' said Sister Dew. 'I'm going to send this one to my friend' – she lowered her voice – 'the one who's had that big operation. It'll cheer her up. We've had ever such a nice walk.'

Ianthe and Penelope seemed less enthusiastic. When they were in their room together they agreed that Sister Dew was 'a bit of a trial' and that seemed to draw them together. And then there was the other bond between them.

'I suppose Rupert Stonebird will be at that conference in Perugia now,' said Penelope casually.

'Yes, with a lot of odd anthropologists,' said Ianthe, who was unpacking her suitcase and arranging her various possessions. Penelope noticed a leather photograph frame and wondered whose photograph Ianthe carried about with her. When the frame was unfolded and set up she saw that it contained two photographs – one of a good-looking white-haired clergyman wearing a biretta, and the other of a 'sweet-faced' woman, her slender hand fondling the large cameo brooch at the throat of her dark dress. Her parents, of course, and like so much that was connected with Ianthe, almost too good to be true.

The conversation about Rupert petered out; perhaps the thought of a crowd of anthropologists was somehow unfruitful and put a stop to the wanderings of the imagination. It seemed easier to discuss the encounter in Babbington's.

'Do you think we'll be seeing much of Father Branche?' Penelope asked.

'Basil Branche,' Ianthe murmured, a smile playing about her lips. 'I can *hardly* remember him, really. He stayed such a short time.'

'*Did* his health break down?'

'Yes, I believe it did. He was said not to be very strong. Of course the work in my father's parish wasn't particularly exhausting.'

Ianthe moved over to the balcony and stood looking out into the noisy Roman night. She could not concentrate on Basil Branche when John was so much in her mind. For one whose thoughts were normally disciplined it was disconcerting and humiliating to find how much he was creeping into them. Perhaps 'creep' was hardly the word, though there was something appropriate about its insidiousness. Still, she had promised to send him a postcard and the wording of that would need careful consideration.

'Look,' she called to Penelope, 'such a strange illuminated sign – BANCO DI SANTO SPIRITO,' she spelled out.

'Bank of the Holy Spirit?' said Penelope. 'Is it a real bank or something to do with the Vatican? It reminds one of those great red signs you sometimes see in London – TAKE COURAGE – have you ever noticed them?'

'Yes,' said Ianthe, 'I believe it's a kind of beer – but how many people must have been strengthened and comforted by seeing that message shining out into the night.'

15

Both Daisy and Sister Dew woke early the next morning. My hospital training, Sister Dew said to herself complacently, confident that she would be the first up. She felt cheated when she saw that Daisy was already standing on the balcony in a shapeless white winceyette nightdress, looking as if she were performing some kind of ritual sun or nature worship.

Sister Dew lay in bed, uncertain whether to get up or to pretend that she was not yet awake. She turned over to look at her watch on the table between the two beds. Twenty past seven. Daisy was taking up more than her share of the table with a guide-book, a Bible, two novels, and a large bottle of Kitzymes, which Sister Dew happened to know were yeast tablets for cats. Surely she didn't take them herself? Perhaps she had forgotten to take them to the lady she'd been to see last night. Quite late coming in she'd been, so that Sister Dew was already in bed and there had been no embarrassment about washing or getting undressed. Oh well, no doubt they'd come to some arrangement to suit them both. Live and let live sort of thing, thought Sister Dew, a little confused.

'Good morning, Miss Pettigrew,' she said. 'I see you're one for early rising like I am. Best part of the day, I always think.'

'Yes, lovely morning,' said Daisy rather gruffly.

'Mind if I wash first?'

'No – you do. I won't look,' said Sister Dew coyly.

'Oh, I don't mind. After all we're all made alike.'

'Well, not *quite*, Miss Pettigrew.'

'No – male and female created He them, more or less, or as near as makes no matter,' said Daisy. 'But you and I are both too old to have any false modesty.' And with this she stripped off her nightdress, and flung it on the bed and advanced to the wash basin.

Sister Dew was so surprised that she forgot to look the other way.

'I ordered breakfast for a quarter to eight,' said Daisy, putting on various garments. 'Of course we have it in our rooms here.'

'Oh, a continental breakfast, I suppose.' Sister Dew paused, as if considering the implications of her statement. The continental breakfast, like the continental Sunday, was something she had heard about and when some time later there was a violent knocking on the door, it seemed suitable that the tray should be born in shoulder-high by a very good looking young waiter.

'*Well*,' she said, turning to Daisy half shocked and half delighted, 'fancy *that*.'

'I should have it in bed if I were you,' Daisy suggested, seeing that Sister Dew was not yet dressed.

'Breakfast in bed! Well I never – if people could see me now,' she said, removing an old-fashioned metal curler from her front hair. 'I'd better smarten myself up in case anyone comes in, hadn't I. You never know!'

It had been decided that the morning should be spent visiting St Peter's and the Vatican, for whatever one did *not* see one must see that. Ruins were more easily glossed over, one church or one fountain could be confused with another, but St Peter's was not to be so easily disposed of.

Sophia had visited the basilica several times before and, as one might say, thought nothing of it, but Mark was always impressed and overawed. It did not give him the same comfortable feeling as seeing the hurrying priests at the airport had done. He tried to think of Canterbury Cathedral, as being perhaps the nearest Anglican equivalent, but all that came into his mind was the irrelevant picture – vignette almost – of a tall thin English lady he and Sophia had once seen arranging long-stalked thornless red roses on the high altar one Saturday morning. He experienced a sudden wave of homesickness, yet no sermon suggested itself to him. He slipped away to a side altar to say his prayers.

Edwin Pettigrew looked around him perfunctorily, yet impressed by the sheer size of everything. He was not a believer, though he sometimes went to church out of politeness to Mark and Sophia. He had to keep reminding himself that this was a holiday which his sister had persuaded him to take because he needed it. Therefore he should be deriving benefit from it and the sight of so much gilt and marble must be doing him good. Yet his thoughts kept returning to the Aberdeen terrier he and Daisy had seen the evening before in the Via Botteghe Oscure. Such an unexpected sight, an Aberdeen terrier in Rome, and with an interesting condition of the tail glands which he had spotted immediately, though professional etiquette prevented him from drawing the owner's attention to it.

Those confessionals, Daisy thought. Confessions in all languages. And there was somebody actually making use of one, with all those crowds of sightseers shuffling past. Not a black-shawled Italian peasant woman or a Spanish donna with a lace mantilla thrown over her head, but an Irish lady in tweeds and a felt hat. Or so she looked to be. What must it feel like to confess one's sins? Mark was always urging them to do so and Daisy had listened, tight-lipped and disapproving, to many such sermons. This will give him an opening, she thought – yet who could blame him for wasting such a golden opportunity.

Penelope hadn't really wanted to come to St Peter's, though she felt she 'ought' to see it. She kept thinking of Rupert Stonebird's dinner party and the Fairfaxes who would have given her an introduction to the man who had so inconsiderately dropped down dead by the obelisk in the square. When they saw St Peter's foot, worn away by the devotion of countless pilgrims, she had a superstitious desire to kiss it, as if doing so could bring her good luck, but when the moment came she couldn't do it. She became fiercely hygienic and Protestant and held back.

'How *can* they,' she whispered to Ianthe, then realised that a young Italian was pressing too close to her and sprang away in horror, both at this episode and the whole idea of kissing the foot.

Ianthe's feelings were as mixed as those of the rest of the party. She had dutifully 'read up' something about St Peter's, but a guide book springs to life in unexpected ways and now she found herself wondering what John's comments would have been. Would it be possible to go round sightseeing with him and expect him to say the sort of things appropriate to the occasion? But perhaps if they were to have any kind of life together, none of it – or very little – would be spent in looking at churches and picture galleries, so it wouldn't matter. Plenty of people did without that sort of thing and were perfectly happy.... Ianthe stopped short at the boldness of her thoughts, wondering what she could have meant, and then she felt Penelope clutch her arm, as if in need of her protection.

'*Really*,' she whispered fiercely, 'that man – even in *church*. You'd think, wouldn't you, that even an

Italian . . .'

Ianthe kept hold of Penelope's arm, for she felt in need of protection too, or perhaps not protection so much as the comfort and advice of a woman friend. Perhaps she could tell Penelope about John – for she longed to tell somebody – though Sophia would really be a more suitable confidant.

'I suppose you'd say that the Pope was the vicar of St Peter's in a manner of speaking,' declared Sister Dew, bringing everybody's thoughts back to the matter in hand. 'I wonder what the lady workers here use to keep all that marble clean?'

'One doesn't somehow think of ladies working here,' said Sophia, daunted by the idea. 'Our little brass-cleaning party would be quite lost in all this. Shall we go and have something to eat? I know a restaurant here where we can get a good cheap osso buco.'

They walked for some time until they came to a modest-looking restaurant. Just as they were about to go in Daisy saw a chicken's head lying on the dusty pavement.

'A severed head,' said Penelope facetiously. 'It seems appropriate to find one here.'

'I don't think I shall want to patronise this restaurant,' said Daisy firmly. 'It looks as if there has been something not quite as it should be in the way that chicken was killed.'

'Oh come now, Daisy,' said her brother. 'You needn't eat chicken – you can have spaghetti or something like that.'

'Of course you wouldn't see that sort of thing in France,' Daisy went on. 'They waste nothing there.'

'No, I suppose the head would have gone into the stock-pot,' Sophia agreed, feeling that Daisy was being somewhat illogical. 'Well, are we going in? I think we're all hungry.'

159

Spaghetti was ordered for Daisy and osso buco for the others.

'A sort of savoury rice with a bone in the middle,' said Sister Dew, when she was served. 'Osso means a bone, doesn't it.'

'And wine?' said Mark. 'What do you think?' he turned to Edwin for his opinion.

'Oh, something of the country,' said Edwin easily, for he hardly noticed what he ate or drank.

'The wines that do not travel,' said Sophia, her eyes filling with tears.

'You mean Frascati,' said Mark doubtfully. 'I should have thought perhaps with osso buco ... what would you like?' he asked, turning to Ianthe.

'I don't know,' she said in confusion. 'I don't know anything about wine.' She was a little shocked that Sophia appeared to, unless it had been just a sentimental fancy that had prompted her remark.

'Let's have some red and some white,' said Penelope sensibly.

'I don't usually take wine in the middle of the day,' said Daisy.

'My dear, you hardly ever take it at any time,' said her brother.

'Not in England, but it seems ungrateful not to in a foreign and wine-producing country,' said Daisy surprisingly. 'The fruits of the earth are given to us so that in due time we may enjoy them.'

Mark looked a little self-conscious, as if Daisy's remark was one he ought to have made himself, but then he applied himself to his Chianti, feeling that – with all due respect – her reason for drinking was dutiful rather than joyous.

Sister Dew also drank Chianti, saying that she 'quite' liked it and found it 'something similar to Wincarnis'.

Sophia and Ianthe had Frascati – Sophia thinking of

160

the little hill town in the autumn, Ianthe of the old Frascati's restaurant in Holborn where she had once been
taken to lunch as a schoolgirl by her uncle and aunt.

Afterwards they all felt tired and went back to the pensione to rest. It was not really hot enough to have a
siesta, but as they were on holiday and abroad, no excuse
was needed for an afternoon sleep.

'I think I shall write a few postcards,' said Ianthe. 'It
seems a good opportunity to send them now.' She ran
over in her mind the people to whom she would send
them. The Spanish Steps and the flowers to poor Miss
Grimes – as Ianthe still though of her – in her room off
the Finchley Road; the Colosseum to her uncle and aunt;
St Peter's to Mervyn Cantrell; and the Trevi fountain to
John. It was all quite simple, really; one need not write
very much – remarks about the weather and what they
had seen and done would be enough. It was only when
she came to John's card that she hesitated for a moment.
Sitting at the little table in the window, she looked out
over the roof tops, her hand on her brow and her pen
pressed to her right temple.

Penelope, watching her from her bed where she lay
pretending to be asleep, thought, now perhaps she is
wondering what to say to Rupert Stonebird, sending
him a card to Perugia. Of course he would have given
her his address. Penelope remembered her that evening
coming out of his dining room with tulip leaves in her
hands, and there was that other occasion – more difficult
to visualise – when she had brought him a portion of ox
tail in a basin.

At last Ianthe wrote something on the postcard, but it
seemed to be very little as far as Penelope could judge.

'Hope to see this fountain tonight and make a wish,'
was what she had written to John – the kind of message
that might seem disastrous when remembered after
posting. Emotion, or the too careful lack of emotion,

recollected in tranquillity. A woman is apt to worry, perhaps unnecessarily, about such things, for a man will interpret what she writes in his own way and it is almost certain to be not the way she intended. John might think that she meant to wish that he was in Rome with her, when she hardly knew whether she wished it or not, but it was certain that by choosing that particular card and having to think so carefully what to write she was in some way irrevocably committing herself to him.

When she had written it she put her pen away, took off her shoes, and lay down on her bed. But it was a self-conscious kind of resting, sleepless and unrelaxed, and she was glad when Penelope, who also seemed not to have slept, suggested that they should go out by themselves for a cup of tea or coffee. As they threaded their way along the narrow pavements Ianthe felt again the desire to confide in Penelope, but it was difficult, impossible really, to know how to bring up the subject. Her experience as a canon's daughter of having to make conversation in sticky social situations had not included anything like this, and the occasion passed off with small talk that was unsatisfying to both of them.

It was dark by the time the party arrived at the Trevi fountain after dinner. The evening sky was a bright electric blue and against it the fountain reared itself monumentally like scenery in an opera. Yet nothing dramatic was to be expected of this cast, Sophia thought, and there was no sign of Father Branche.

'Perhaps we shouldn't wait for him to throw in our coins,' said Mark, rather as if he were organising the children on a parish outing. 'It's rather cold standing about.'

'I know what I'm going to wish for,' said Sister Dew, advancing dangerously near to the water, as if about to fling herself in among the straining, rearing horses.

Mark explained that strictly speaking the legend was that if you threw a coin into the fountain you would ensure your return to Rome.

'I feel that should be enough without any other wish,' said Sophia; but privately she added a kind of prayer that Faustina might be safe and happy.

Mark also threw a coin because he did not want to seem superior by refusing to make a fool of himself, and Edwin did the same, to humour the women. Daisy frowned as she threw hers, as if she hardly wished to return to a country where animals were not treated as they should be.

'Now you mustn't tell anyone what you wish,' said Sister Dew to Ianthe and Penelope, for obviously the two younger unmarried women would have the most interesting and secret wishes. She herself wanted nothing in the romantic line, just that one of her numbers should come up on Ernie – Premium Bonds, that is, she added in case the spirit of the fountain didn't know what she meant.

'You go next,' said Penelope to Ianthe, for she had a childish feeling that it would be lucky to be last.

'Oh, all right.' Ianthe laughed but inwardly she felt quite serious. That I may return to Rome with the man I love, she said to herself, and quickly threw her coin into the water.

Penelope barely had time to frame her wish when there was a commotion among the rest of the party and she realised that Father Branche had arrived.

'Perhaps we might go to a café,' he suggested, 'if you've all thrown your coins in. Would you find that agreeable?'

'*Agreeable*,' Sister Dew giggled. 'It would be nice to sit down.'

'What a typically English reaction,' said Penelope scornfully. 'And does he really mean *everybody* to tag along?' She had decided that if possible she would go off by herself with him. It was a rather desperate plan and she did not know what was likely to come of it, or indeed what she wished to come of it, but anything would be better than the parish party.

'I don't know really,' said Sophia vaguely. 'Some of us walk rather slowly, you know, and it's quite easy to get lost in Rome.' Her sister would be quite safe with a clergyman, she thought.

They were walking rather a long way, it seemed, and in a direction Sophia did not know. At one point they had to cross the road by a subway. As they walked down the steps eyes glowed at them in the dark and grey shapes slunk past them, so that Sister Dew let out a cry and clung on to Sophia.

'Look, so many of them,' said Daisy, 'and I've brought nothing with me. Still, we can find this place again. I shall come back in the morning.'

'Somebody seems to be feeding them,' said Ianthe.

A kind-hearted Italian lady with a basket was crouching down by the cats, encouraging them with gentle murmurings, and setting out food in little dishes.

'Left-overs, I suppose,' said Sister Dew thoughtfully, for what would *Roman* left-overs be? A bit of that osso buco, perhaps, or spaghetti – fancy a cat eating spaghetti. 'I shouldn't think *your* pussy would fancy that,' she said to Mark.

'Would Faustina like spaghetti, do you think?' he asked Sophia.

'I don't know, we must try her with some when we get back. She might like the sauce.' Basil, she thought, that was what gave it the Italian flavour.

'We seem to have lost Basil and Penelope,' said Ianthe, linking their names cosily together. 'Did anyone see which way they went?'

Apparently nobody had, but as there was a convenient

164

café where they had stopped it seemed sensible not to go on any further.

'I'm sure Basil will look after Penelope,' Ianthe reassured Sophia. 'After all he *is* a clergyman.'

'Yes, of course,' said Sophia, for had she not been thinking that herself?

'We seem to have lost the others,' said Basil, 'but this was the café I meant. If we sit near the window they'll see us when they arrive.'

'Yes, they will,' said Penelope. She was beginning to realise that she had meant to throw Ianthe and Basil together so that when Rupert came – as he surely would – Ianthe might seem to be involved with him.

'What would you like?' asked Basil. 'Coffee and brandy?'

'Thank you.'

When the waiter had brought their drinks they sat in a rather awkward silence.

'Do you know Ianthe well?' Penelope asked.

'Not really – I was a curate in her father's parish for a short time.'

'Before he was a canon?'

'Yes, before that.'

'She's a charming person,' said Penelope, feeling that this was expected of her.

'Yes, charming, I suppose, but a little inhuman, don't you think? Just a little too good to be true?'

Penelope looked at him suspiciously. It did not seem quite natural that he should feel as she did about Ianthe.

He fitted a cigarette into a rather too long holder.

'I suppose I ought not to say this, but she was a bit keen on me at one time.'

Penelope smiled to herself at the old-fashioned phrase 'a bit keen on me'. It seemed to make him rather 'caddish' in a way that men weren't nowadays. She took a sip of brandy, wondering what he expected her to say.

Then she realised that he was smiling at her indulgently and it suddenly occurred to her that he was one of those men who imagine that all women are running after them. So she had got herself into another of her ludicrous situations. What she would have said or done was still uncertain, when there was a commotion in the doorway of the café, and a stout handsome elderly woman, in a tight silk dress printed with tiger lilies, rushed past the waiters to the table where Penelope and Basil were sitting.

'*There* you are!' she called out in a ringing tone. 'I've been looking for you *everywhere*. You went out without your scarf and you know how treacherous these Italian nights are.' She was brandishing in her hand what looked like a hand-knitted muffler in two shades of ecclesiastical purple.

She sat down heavily in a vacant chair at the table and summoned the waiter with a gesture.

'Coffee is *not* good,' she said, 'it will keep you awake. You know you must have your nine hours sleep. My sister is a great believer in a little brandy – not more than a teaspoonful – in cases of biliousness,' she added to Penelope.

'Milk,' she said to the waiter, '*latte* – hot,' she hesitated for the Italian word, '*bolente*,' she brought out at last.

'But I don't want boiling milk,' protested Father Branche unhappily. 'One never knows what milk will be like abroad. It might be goat's milk, or even sheep's milk – imagine that!'

'It would probably be very nourishing,' said Penelope.

'Oh, Miss Bede, let me introduce...' Basil began, then realised that he had forgotten Penelope's name, if he had ever known it.

'How do you do,' murmured Penelope. 'I'm Penelope

Grandison.'

'She is a vicar's wife's sister,' Basil went on.

'A vicar – *what* vicar?' asked Miss Bede suspiciously.

'The vicar of a north London parish.'

'Oh, I see.' Miss Bede nodded, obviously not quite satisfied.

'My brother-in-law is the Reverend Mark Ainger,' said Penelope.

'Ainger,' Miss Bede repeated. 'Is he in *Crockford's Clerical Directory*?'

'Yes, I'm sure he is,' said Penelope, rather taken aback. 'I haven't actually looked, but he must be.'

'I always believe in checking up,' said Miss Bede firmly. 'There are so many impostors nowadays. Not, I'm sure,' she said, smiling graciously at Penelope, 'that your brother-in-law is an impostor.'

'No, he isn't, I assure you. . . .'

'Still, it will be interesting to look him up.'

'Well, you can hardly do that here,' said Basil smugly.

'There must be a *Crockford* somewhere in Rome – in the Vatican Library, no doubt. *They* like to check up, of course. Do you know,' Miss Bede turned to Penelope, 'the Jesuits have a list of every Church of England clergyman who is visiting Italy and know exactly what he is doing at every minute of the day *or night*?'

'Goodness, I didn't know that,' said Penelope weakly. Surely they couldn't know about every *minute*, she thought, but decided not to pursue the subject. She wondered if Mark knew about it.

Fortunately, perhaps because of some confusion in the order, the hot milk did not appear and soon Miss Bede seemed to want to lead Basil away. As they were staying quite near to each other the three of them walked back together, rather slowly, for Miss Bede was wearing very high-heeled shoes – most unsuitable for an elderly lady, Penelope thought.

'The night air is so treacherous – in more ways than one!' Miss Bede said, suddenly roguish. 'My sister will wonder where I've been. She decided to have an early night with *Adonaïs* – a poem by Shelley, you know. If one must read in Rome that seems very suitable, don't you think.'

'Oh yes,' said Penelope, rather confused.

'Here we are then,' said Miss Bede. 'Good-night, Miss Grandison. Basil, say good-night to Miss Grandison.'

Basil did as he was ordered and followed Miss Bede into the Albergo di Risorgimento. He was like some tame animal being led away, thought Penelope scornfully. She didn't see how anyone could take him seriously, not even a clergyman's daughter, who might be thought to have to make do with her father's curates.

She supposed she would have to explain how she and Basil had gone ahead of the others and lost them, but to her surprise there was nobody to explain to. The others were not yet in, so she got undressed quickly and was lying in bed reading when she heard Ianthe at the door.

'Oh, that's a relief,' said Ianthe. 'I'll just go and tell Sophia you're here.'

'Surely you weren't worried about me?' said Penelope.

'Not *worried* exactly, and of course we both knew you would be all right with Basil. Did you have a jolly time?'

Penelope could not help smiling at Ianthe's choice of adjective, but perhaps 'jolly' was what the 'time' had been. Yet 'ludicrous' would be more accurate, she felt.

'A lady came and fetched him away,' she said. 'A Miss Bede.'

'One of the ladies he is in Rome with, I suppose.'

'Well yes, one does suppose so.'

Ianthe smiled. 'Something of the kind happened when I knew him,' she said. 'The lady was a rich widow and wanted to marry him.'

Penelope remembered what Basil had said about Ianthe being 'a bit keen' on him and wondered if she had been jealous of his attentions to the widow. It was difficult to imagine Ianthe feeling such a strong emotion.

'Did you ever feel anything for him?' she asked boldly.

'*I* – feel anything for Basil Branche?' Ianthe's astonishment seemed genuine. 'Well, I suppose I quite liked him, as one usually did like the curates, but there was no other feeling.'

'I thought you might have been passionately in love with him at one time,' said Penelope, wondering if she was going too far.

But Ianthe laughed good-humouredly.

'Actually,' Penelope went on, 'it's difficult to imagine you falling in love with anybody – if you see what I mean,' she added hastily. 'You're so cool and collected and I'm sure a man would have to be almost perfect to come up to your standards.'

'What a strange idea you must have of me,' said Ianthe. 'I'm just like anybody else in that way. I could fall in love,' she began and then broke off in embarrassment, for now that the opportunity had presented itself she found it was not so easy to tell Penelope about John. There was not much to tell and a girl like Penelope would think very little of a bunch of violets, tea in a café, and a kiss in public.

'You sound as if you *are* in love with somebody,' said Penelope, 'but I suppose I mustn't ask who it is.'

Ianthe's silence confirmed her worst fears. Obviously she must be in love with Rupert Stonebird, but as they both knew him it was awkward to discuss the subject further. If only he would come to Rome and put them out of their misery!

16

The next few days passed happily and profitably in a whirl of sightseeing. Churches were reverently admired, views exclaimed over, ruins gave rise to solemn or facetious comments. Feet and backs ached in a good cause and Sister Dew's ankles swelled in the unaccustomed heat. Basil Branche was seen frequently in the distance, but always with the ladies he was escorting. Penelope's scorn for him increased.

'A tame donkey – that's what he's like, letting himself be led about like that,' she said to Ianthe, who was contemplating a slab of marble fallen in the grass. They were spending the afternoon at Ostia, and Ianthe and the two sisters had drawn away from the rest of the party for some feminine small talk.

'Some young men seem to be fated to that kind of life,' said Ianthe. 'I suppose it isn't always as easy as it sounds and we know that it has its disadvantages.' She smiled, remembering that Penelope had told her about Miss Bede ordering hot milk for him in the café.

'I think men should be more – well – *manly*,' said Penelope in disgust.

'Oh darling, we know they can't always be that, and why should we expect them to be,' said Sophia. 'I'm sure Father Branche *is* rather delicate, you know. He doesn't look at all strong and it would be a great strain trying to be manly all the time.'

'Miss Bede won't let him out of her sight,' said Penelope. 'I suppose he's like a son to her.'

'We must suppose so,' said Sophia, 'though it's often difficult to guess what a man may be to a woman – age doesn't seem to enter into it.'

'But Miss Bede must be more than twice as old as Basil Branche,' said Ianthe, almost protesting, for she had seen Penelope's disgusted expression when Sophia was speaking and could not forget that John was five years younger than she was.

'I *couldn't* be in love with a man younger than myself,' Penelope declared.

'But then you're so very much younger than the rest of us,' said Ianthe. 'A man younger than you would be just a boy. When you're older you may feel differently.'

'Yes, Penny, you don't really know what you're talking about,' said Sophia sensibly. 'I don't think it matters at all a man being a few years younger than a woman – provided he's suitable in other ways, of course.'

She smiled as she watched her sister run ahead to where the guide was pointing out a particularly interesting mosaic pavement. In her pocket Sophia had a postcard from Rupert Stonebird saying that he was arriving in Rome from Perugia that evening; she was keeping the news as a surprise for Penelope.

'But when he isn't particularly suitable,' Ianthe continued, her tone almost agitated, when Penelope was out of earshot. 'I mean, doesn't *appear* to be suitable . . . what then?'

'Well . . .' Sophia felt embarrassed and confused, as if she had heard something not meant to be spoken aloud. 'Perhaps then it doesn't concern anybody but the woman herself – obviously it doesn't. *She* is the one who must know in her heart whether he's suitable or not, whatever other people may think.' She was remembering that her mother had not considered Mark a suitable match for her, Sophia, the older daughter, though nobody could exactly *disapprove* of a clergyman. So if Ianthe really fancied Basil Branche – and it suddenly occurred to Sophia that this could be the reason for her unexpected outburst – it was difficult to see why a few years difference in age should be holding her back. And she had no parents to disapprove of her choice or to find him 'unsuitable' in any other way. Sophia was just about to say something that might draw Ianthe out still further, while being at the same time sympathetic and comforting, when Edwin Pettigrew, guide book in hand, came up to them and began talking about the amphitheatre which they were now approaching.

'Remarkable carrying power sound has in such a structure,' he said. 'We must put it to the test. Perhaps your husband will oblige us, being the one most accustomed to public speaking.'

'It will be a new beginning for one of his sermons,' said Daisy. 'Let's run up to the top and see if we can hear him.'

'My friends,' Mark began, 'many of you have no doubt stood in the amphitheatre at Ostia Antica, marvelling...' then suddenly he broke off, for Sister Dew in her scramble up the steps to the top had stumbled and fallen and appeared to be unable to get up.

'Sister Dew, are you hurt?' called out Sophia anxiously.

'It's my ankle – something seems to have gone. I can't move.'

'Quick, Edwin, go to her,' said Daisy, 'and see what you can do.'

Edwin hurried to where Sister Dew lay in a tumbled heap. In his veterinary practice he specialised in the treatment of small animals, and the sheer bulkiness of Sister Dew reminded him that his work had been with cats and pet dogs rather than with horses and cows, but he examined her ankle as best he could.

'We must get her to hospital for an x-ray,' he said. 'Something may be broken.'

'But we don't know where the hospital is,' moaned Sister Dew, forgetting to be splendid for a moment. 'I never did like these old places. There should be a notice up saying these steps are dangerous – you wouldn't have this kind of accident in England.'

'Well, there aren't any amphitheatres in England,' murmured Penelope. She could not help wanting to laugh, for Sister Dew looked so comic lying there, and it was even funnier when two burly-looking middle-aged Italians offered to take her to hospital in their car and attempted to carry her shoulder high to the place where it was parked.

'Ought I to go with her?' Sophia asked.

'No, my dear,' said Daisy firmly. 'Edwin and I will go. I should like to see inside one of those hospitals.'

'Well, we can't all go,' said Sophia, sounding relieved. 'And one of those Italians does seem to speak English.'

'She couldn't be in better hands,' said Mark. 'I suppose they will take her to the English hospital? And of course I shall visit her there – if she is detained.'

'Yes, darling – but don't forget that this evening we're going to have dinner in Trastevere,' said Sophia. And without Sister Dew it would really be a more suitable party, if, as she very much hoped, Rupert Stonebird could be persuaded to join them. 'Of course you must visit her,' said Sophia, 'but there's an English chaplain and you must leave him something to do.'

'I expect he has plenty to do,' said Penelope. 'I'm sure English tourists, especially women, are always falling about in ruins and getting taken to hospital. And getting upset by the food and wine, too.'

'And English people are dying everywhere,' said Sophia. 'Rome is full of their bones.' Here lies one whose name was writ in water – she felt she could not bear to visit the English cemetery with Sister Dew.

Back at the pensione there seemed to be some agitation at the reception desk. Rupert Stonebird was trying to explain to the little man in the striped jacket that he wanted a room for a few nights.

'It isn't enough to have read Colucci when it comes to ordinary conversation,' he said, turning to Sophia thankfully. 'Somehow the things one wants to say aren't to be found in that excellent work.'

Behind Sophia he could see Ianthe and Penelope standing side by side. He was struck immediately by Ianthe's absolute rightness here – the Englishwoman in Rome – in her cool green linen suit and straw hat. Penelope looked slightly grotesque by contrast, in dusty black cotton, with red sandals on her stumpy little bare feet. She reminded him of some of the women who had been at the conference in Perugia. And yet Penelope was more appealing than these and seemed genuinely pleased to see him. Her dusty little toes amused him, for they were such a contrast to Ianthe's smooth beige linen shoes. When Sophia, tentatively yet somehow firmly, put forward her plan for the evening he found himself thinking that it would be fun and was delighted to accept. There had not been much time for romance or even flirtation at the conference. A handsome Italian girl to whom he had been attracted had turned out to be disappointingly serious-minded, wanting from him only a secondhand copy of a long out of print anthropological book which he had promised to look for in Kegan Paul's and other suitable shops. Somehow it had not seemed a promising start to an affair, though it might well have provided a solid basis for marriage. But perhaps it was something lacking in himself that made an attractive woman see him rather as a procurer of secondhand books than as a lover. With this thought in mind he set out for the evening in a rather subdued mood – dark-suited, with his spectacles in his hand. Nor was he encouraged to find that a possible rival – a good-looking dark man some years younger than himself – had been invited to join the party. Sophia addressed him as 'Father Branche', which made Rupert think that he must be a celibate Roman Catholic priest – so perhaps he was not a rival in the true sense of the word after all. Apparently they were fortunate in having his company that evening, since the two ladies he was with had another engagement.

'The Misses Bede are dining with Cardinal Pirelli this evening,' he said, or seemed to have said, for the name 'Cardinal Pirelli' seemed to Rupert at once familiar and unlikely. Yet English ladies in Rome no doubt did dine with Cardinals – it seemed right for both parties for they would have much to learn from each other.

Edwin and Daisy, after reassuring Sophia about Sister Dew's ankle, which was only a severe sprain, decided not to join the others for dinner but to go in search of more Roman cats to feed. Edwin even hoped to get another sight of the Aberdeen terrier he had seen a few evenings ago in the Via Botteghe Oscure. Their absence left a rather suitable party of six to dine at the restaurant in Trastevere. Nicely paired off, Sophia thought happily, dividing the party between two taxis.

'You come with us, Ianthe,' she said, 'and Penny can go with Rupert and Father Branche.'

Two taxis, thought Rupert, what extravagance! The anthropologists in Perugia had gone everywhere by tram or on foot. Indeed, the dusty-looking group, most of them carrying briefcases and raincoats, had been quite a familiar sight in the town. Still, he could hardly question Sophia's arrangements, though he did wish that Ianthe could have been in his taxi. All the same Penelope looked attractive in an outlandish sort of way, in a black skirt and orange velvet top. She wore no jewellery and her lips were pale, though her eyes seemed to be heavily made up. The heavy scent she wore tantalised him because it was one he knew though he could not remember its name – whether it was an evocative French phrase or a downright English word like 'Carpet' or 'Swamp'. He wondered if Basil Branche knew, then decided that a celibate priest – or at least not an English one – would probably not know such things.

Mark sat back complacently in his taxi with Sophia and Ianthe. Sophia wore a black dress and an antique silver necklace set with turquoises; Ianthe was in flowered silk with pearls. She smelt rather faintly of lily of the valley and was in a mood to match the sweetness of that flower, smiling and finding everything delightful. What an asset to our congregation, Mark found himself thinking, without realising what an odd thought it was to have in a taxi in Rome.

'How interesting and mysterious all this looks,' said Ianthe, as the taxi nosed its way through the narrow alleys and little squares of Trastevere and finally came to a stop in what seemed to be a dead end, a blank wall on which mysterious scrawls – perhaps even a ghostly DUCE – could be discerned. A few gesticulations and shouted phrases between Sophia and the driver had them turning round and threading their way down another dark alley, until suddenly the headlights picked out Rupert, Penelope and Basil Branche standing in front of a doorway, like characters in an opera. Perhaps here will be enacted the drama which was lacking at the Trevi fountain, Sophia thought hopefully.

'We've been here ages,' said Penelope, running up to the taxi. 'Did you get lost?' She had quite enjoyed her ride, though she kept remembering Miss Bede and the hot milk whenever she looked at Basil. He, however, seemed not at all embarrassed and had rather irritatingly told Rupert of all the things he had apparently missed seeing in Perugia.

Now they entered a narrow doorway with a lantern hanging from it, from which a grey cat scuttled away into the shadows, and found themselves in a kind of ante-room leading to the restaurant proper. One wall was taken up with an elaborate gilt-framed mirror under which stood a marble-topped table laden with a still life of food. There was a joint of meat, raw steak, a large fish and a lobster, flanked by a pile of artichokes, apples, and oranges, with rough-looking skins and withered leaves still clinging to them.

'I wonder if pussy was at that fish,' said Penelope, in Sister Dew's manner. 'I shouldn't fancy it after that.'

They were shown to a table in an inner room by a wall covered with signed photographs of celebrities of some kind, with an occasional face almost recognisable among so many flashing sets of teeth and gleaming waves of hair.

'It reminds me of Edwin Pettigrew's waiting room,' said Sophia 'except that his are animal celebrities.'

'All this smiling humanity is a bit overwhelming,' said Basil in an affected way. 'I feel I should enjoy my meal more if I couldn't see them.'

'It's hardly the still sad music of humanity, is it,' said Rupert.

'Nor harsh nor grating, though of ample power to chasten and subdue,' said Mark, smiling. 'Wordsworth, isn't it?'

'How tiresome the men are being,' said Sophia, who was studying the menu. 'Showing off their knowledge when they should be advising us what we ought to eat. We really don't want to be thinking of Wordsworth at a time like this.'

'We must all have *carciofi*,' sighed Basil extravagantly.

'That's artichokes,' Sophia explained briskly, 'and they certainly are very good here. And then perhaps...' she suggested various dishes which sounded perhaps even more delicious than they could possibly be, so musical were their names. Mark and Basil consulted together about the wine, while Rupert sat quietly, feeling that he was showing himself to be not quite a man by allowing them to do this. He wondered if Penelope had noticed and would hold it against him; he was sure Ianthe would not.

The least he could do was to suggest a toast, when their glasses were filled – it was only Chianti, after all the fuss – but here again Mark forestalled him.

'I think we should all like to drink to poor Enid Dew's speedy recovery,' he suggested dutifully.

They sipped their wine in a slightly awkward silence.

'*Enid*,' said Sophia, 'so *that's* her Christian name – I never knew what it was.'

'One seems unable to get away from the poets,' said Rupert. 'Tennyson is so very much...' he began and then realised that he had been about to betray something private – the volume of Tennyson discovered in Ianthe's sitting room that January evening. He glanced to where she sat, on his right, dealing neatly and carefully with her artichoke. It should be possible for him to escort her home alone after dinner, he thought. It would surely be natural, even with two clergymen present – for the party to separate in three couples.

Ianthe herself, having no interest in any of the men present, was thinking how delicious the canelloni looked and wondering how Mervyn could possibly have disliked them. If only John could have been with them instead of Rupert or Basil, how much nicer the evening would have been! Not that it wasn't very pleasant and she was thoroughly enjoying it, but Rupert with his

178

rather stiff conversation and Basil with his tiresome affectation seemed to add nothing to it. Of course Mark was a dear and it was lovely to see him and Sophia so happy – she had not once mentioned Faustina the whole evening.

Penelope was eating and drinking with a kind of stolid fatalism, feeling that she was destined to spend yet another evening with Basil. There was nothing she could do to make Rupert take any particular notice of her. He was talking almost entirely to Sophia and Ianthe, telling them about the conference in Perugia, which seemed to interest them.

Rupert called for more wine, feeling that the evening was going well, and comparing it very favourably with those he had spent with the anthropologists. He was looking forward to being alone with Ianthe, who seemed to him to have gained in attractiveness since he last saw her, so that she now seemed to be rather more than just 'suitable'.

But plans do not always materialise in the anticipated way and somehow – perhaps by some subtle action of Sophia's (he would never know) – Rupert found himself alone with Penelope, the others having somehow got away before them.

Penelope sensed that he was surprised at the way things had turned out, and this feeling, together with the kind of desolation that much wine can sometimes bring, made her sulky and on the verge of tears. She had wanted to be alone with him but now that she was she knew that he would have preferred to be with Ianthe.

'I suppose we should get a taxi,' he said, feeling that he was being ineffectual and that no taxi would come. Had he been with Ianthe it would not have mattered and probably a taxi would have appeared immediately. A walk in the balmy Roman evening would be pleasant, he thought hopefully, but it was miles back to where they were staying and he had no idea where he was.

'Here's a taxi,' said Penelope. 'Should we take it?'

'Oh, yes – by all means.'

'What happened to the others?' Penelope asked. 'Did they go off together?'

'I don't know – I suppose they did.'

'And you were left only with me.'

'Yes.' He could think of nothing to soften or adorn the bare affirmative.

'You must have been disappointed,' said Penelope, turning her head away from him.

'On the contrary – I couldn't imagine a pleasanter ending to a delightful evening.'

Rupert's gallantry sounded forced and mocking even to himself. He really must try harder, but her rather curious behaviour didn't make things easy for him. He longed for the sensible maturity of Ianthe.

'But I've never brought you an oxtail like Ianthe did,' Penelope suddenly burst out in a defiant tone.

'Ianthe ... an *oxtail*?' he repeated incredulously. He felt as Penelope had when he first told her of the incident – that it was impossible to imagine Ianthe doing anything with an oxtail. When, indeed, had *anyone* brought him such an unlikely thing? he asked himself. Then he remembered and began to laugh. 'Oh, *that* ...' he said.

'Had you forgotten?'

'Yes, for the moment. But it wasn't Ianthe who brought it. It was Sister Dew – Enid, as we should perhaps now call her.'

'Sister Dew?' Shame and relief sounded in her voice. She ought to have known, for obviously it was Sister Dew one would imagine coming up to the door with a covered basin.

'Yes, Enid Dew.' He smiled at the remembrance of her Tennysonian Christian name.

'Oh, I see.'

Penelope sat apart from him saying nothing until after some minutes she looked out of the window and said, 'Aren't we nearly there? This looks like that Church at the top of the Spanish Steps.'

'Yes, so it is,' he said, realising that he had forgotten what the Italian word for 'stop' was.

But Penelope seemed to have told the driver where they wanted to go, and all Rupert had to do was to fumble with notes and coins while she stood a little distance away with her back to him.

'There,' he said, 'that's done. Shall we stand here for a bit and look at the view?'

'If you like,' said Penelope unhelpfully.

They leaned on the stone balustrade, surrounded by American tourists, and looked down into the azaleas. Still Penelope seemed quiet and sulky, so Rupert, after commenting on the beauty of the flowers, lapsed into silence too. After a while he stole a sideways glance at her and saw to his dismay that tears were running down her cheeks.

What have I done – or *not* done – he asked himself, but he knew that the question was unanswerable. Women were so hopelessly irrational, though Ianthe would not have behaved like this, he thought complacently. All the same, the sight of Penelope's distress on what should have been – indeed, what *had* been – a very enjoyable evening was upsetting. Rather tentatively he put his arm round her shoulders and drew her closer to him.

'What is it?' he asked. 'I can't bear to see you cry – is it my fault in some way?' Could it have been something to do with the oxtail? he wondered wildly.

She uttered some strangled sound that might have been 'no', but her crying did not stop.

The American lady on her other side was beginning to take a sympathetic interest. Her eyes behind their odd shaped spectacles gave Rupert an appraising and rather steely stare. It was really most unjust and not a little unnerving.

'Please, Penny, don't cry,' he said more urgently. 'I can't bear to see you unhappy. You're always such a jolly little thing.'

She stopped crying in astonishment – 'a jolly little thing'! So that was how he thought of her – what could be worse. *Jolly* and a *thing* . . . she began to cry again.

'Poor little Pre-Raphaelite beatnik,' he murmured, stroking her hair. Gently he started to lead her down the steps with the idea of finding some more secluded spot where he might kiss her.

As they walked she managed to regain control of herself and began to apologise, wondering what on earth he must think of her and begging him to forget all about it if he could.

Rupert hardly knew what to say. If only he could take her to bed with him, he thought as they approached the pensione, so much might be smoothed out there. But perhaps it was just as well that circumstances made it impossible at this moment, for that might bring about even deeper complications.

'It must have been the Chianti,' said Penelope, smiling and sniffing. 'Some wines are said to have a depressing effect.'

'Well, as long as it's nothing I've done,' said Rupert, relieved but not altogether convinced.

She wondered how she was going to be able to face him again after this dreadful evening, but perhaps they need never meet again. The bitterness of being described as a jolly little thing would remain with her for a long time, she felt.

As for Rupert, he could not help reflecting on the irony of a situation that now made him want to take Penelope to bed when he had intended to have a decorous flirtation with Ianthe. Was he in some way irrevocably committed to her? Perhaps it was a good thing that he had already decided to spend a few days working in the Vatican Library – that convenient hiding place and haven of scholars, to name only the least obvious of its uses. He was too modest to believe that Penelope could have fallen in love with him, yet the memory of her tears disquieted him and he realised that he could hardly at this stage start paying attention to Ianthe. That would have to wait until they were back in England.

17

It was a grey morning when Sophia and Ianthe left Rome, the kind of morning one might just as easily have had in England. From the train the country looked uninteresting except when a small town came into view on a distant hill top.

'I feel rather guilty coming away with you like this,' said Ianthe, after they had exclaimed together over one such pretty little town.

'It's only a few days,' said Sophia, 'and it's such a waste for you not to see a bit of the south while you're here.' She hoped Ianthe wasn't going to spoil this part of the holiday by having dreary scruples about her work.

'Yes, it does, after coming all this way,' said Ianthe. 'I've written to Mervyn Cantrell at the library and he should get the letter today or tomorrow. Of course these few days will come off my summer holiday so it isn't as if I'm taking any *extra* time off.'

'Mark and the Pettigrews *had* to get home and Sister Dew was well enough to travel with them, and Penelope...' Sophia hesitated, not quite knowing what to say about her sister. She had appeared to be upset about something to do with Rupert Stonebird, but Sophia had not been able to gather exactly what had taken place between them on that evening in Trastevere. Some little scene – wine and kisses – tears and the beauty of the Roman evening – it was not difficult to imagine. Could it have been a lovers' 'tiff'? Sophia wondered hopefully. Whatever it had been, Penelope had seemed anxious to go back to London and Rupert had hidden himself away in the Vatican Library to work – a natural but perhaps slightly cowardly thing for a man to do. It was obviously better to remove Ianthe from Rome in case he should emerge, as he was bound to eventually, and find her there. Not that Ianthe had wanted to stay on by herself; she had seemed eager to go with Sophia to her aunt's villa for a few days. The idea of Basil Branche being still in Rome evidently had no attraction for her. Unless she was purposely fleeing from him in the hope that ... here Sophia realised that she was tired and closed her eyes, as if by so doing she could shut out further tortuous imaginings. She decided to meditate on Faustina, to try to picture what she would be doing at this moment. Various little scenes came into her mind – Faustina at her dish, her head on one side, vigorously chewing a piece of meat; sitting upright and thumping her tail, demanding for the door to be opened; reposing on a bed, curled up in a circle; sharpening her claws on the leg of an armchair – so many of these pictures brought the cat before her, so that she could almost smell her fresh furry smell and her warm sweet breath.

Ianthe meditated on the landscape and the other people in the train, who were as unremarkable – though in an Italian way – as a similar collection of people in an English train might have been. The only differences were that the priest looked somehow dirty, and the young couple were gazing at each other in a way not found in England. Yet here Ianthe became doubtful – did a Church of England clergyman never look dirty? – did young English couples never gaze at each other so devouringly? After all, John had kissed her at the station, she thought, lowering her eyes as she felt Sophia looking at her.

185

'You can tell we're getting to the south,' she said enthusiastically. 'The sun's shining and the houses look different.'

'Yes – the flat roofs are rather ugly, aren't they.'

'But look at the oranges,' said Sophia reproachfully.

'Are we nearly at Naples, then?'

'Yes – we have to change there. In fact here, at Mergellina. Isn't the air wonderfully different?' said Sophia as they stepped out of the high train.

'There's a sort of peculiar smell,' said Ianthe uncertainly.

'Yes – the Bay – it's a kind of emanation. You sometimes get it in London at unexpected times.'

Ianthe was glad that Sophia was with her and knew what to do and where to find the train to Salerno. It was not until they were in the bus winding along the coast road towards Amalfi that she began to feel her spirits rising again. A journey, especially a foreign one, is always tiring, with the added fear or excitement of not knowing exactly what one is going to find at the end of it. Ianthe thought sympathetically of English governesses going out to strange families. Then the bus turned up the road to Ravello and she forgot her strangeness in the more immediate excitement of the twisting road and the view revealed at each bend of it.

When they reached the square an old woman in a black dress and a young boy were there to meet them. Sophia embraced the old woman and said something to her in Italian which made her cackle with laughter.

Surely this couldn't be Sophia's aunt? Ianthe wondered. The boy had seized their suitcases and was hurrying on ahead up a rough path.

'This is Anna,' Sophia explained. 'I'm afraid she doesn't speak English, but she'll get you anything you want – she's very quick at understanding one's needs. And here is the Villa Faustina!'

186

So the cat had been named after the villa, thought Ianthe in confusion, not quite knowing what the significance of this might be. 'It's lovely,' she said. 'It reminds me of *The Enchanted April* – the wistaria and the roses. . . .'

Sophia had forgotten exactly what happened in that book, but remembered enough to realise that there was a sort of bringing together of husbands and wives and that in the end everybody was satisfactorily and happily paired off. She imagined Rupert Stonebird coming up the steep path to the villa, wearing a dark suit and carrying a briefcase. And Ianthe running, tumbling, falling into his arms. *That* was not the sort of thing she wanted to happen and must be prevented at all costs, but somehow she did not see Basil Branche coming up the path and Ianthe falling into *his* arms.

'This is my aunt,' she said firmly, as a tall thin elderly woman came out on to the terrace to greet them.

'How do you do,' said Ianthe, taking the hand extended to her. Sophia's aunt had rather mad-looking dark eyes and was dressed in black. There was a family likeness between her and Sophia. After so many years in Italy she spoke English with a trace of foreign accent.

Ianthe was relieved to be shown to her room and left to unpack. She stepped out onto the little balcony rather nervously, for it did not seem to be very safe, and looked down over acres of lemon groves. The trees were covered with matting so that the fruit was almost hidden, but Ianthe could feel that there were hundreds, perhaps thousands, of lemons hanging there among the leaves. All those lemons, she thought, Sister Dew would say that they almost gave one the creeps. Beyond the lemon groves she could see the sea which she found more reassuring because beyond it lay England, her little house, the library, and John.

She began to unpack, taking out the photographs of

her father and mother and placing them almost defiantly on the dressing table. Again she was reminded of the governesses of a hundred or even fifty years ago, coming to a strange country to live and work, and felt grateful that she would never have to experience the loneliness of that kind of life. A canon's daughter, left alone in the world but with enough money to live comfortably in her own house – it seemed a contradiction in terms.

She sat down on the bed and looked around her. The room had a blue and white tiled floor and was sparsely, almost meanly, furnished. 'Spotlessly clean' was how one usually described such rooms, particularly if they were 'abroad', but this did not seem to be all that clean. Ianthe began to wonder why she had come here and her strangeness and homesickness returned in full force. Rome had seemed almost like England in a curious way, but here even Sophia seemed different – not the vicar's wife but a stranger who appeared to be quite at home, and could speak and understand the harsh unmusical Italian of the south. 'You *must* see the lemon groves,' she had said and Ianthe had been glad of an excuse to prolong her holiday, perhaps not to have to return to London just yet to face Mervyn's curiosity and questions.

There was a knock on the door. Ianthe started up guiltily, unable to remember what one said in Italian.

'It's only me,' said Sophia's voice. 'We're having drinks on the terrace when you're ready to come down. My aunt has a guest – an old friend of hers.'

On the terrace chairs were set out and a dilapidated little white table, on which stood a bottle of vermouth, four glasses and a plate of sliced lemon. It looked like a picture in a glossy magazine, but there was something subtly wrong with it, for the terrace was shabby, the little statue too much broken, and the oleander not quite out. The people were not right, either – Sophia's aunt, black and sinister – almost raffish, with hair that was surely dyed; Sophia herself, thin and awkward, holding a capacious brown plastic handbag; Ianthe, neat and timid and too English-looking, in a blue-flowered cotton dress and a white orlon cardigan. A fourth person now joined them, and there were introductions and kissing of hands. Signor – Professore – Dottore – Ianthe could not quite make out which he was – perhaps all three – was a good-looking solid sort of man of about sixty, tall for an Italian, wearing a suit of a particularly foreign-looking tweed, striped in such a way that it looked like the distinctively marked skin of some wild animal.

'The Dottore has been much in Ethiopia,' declared Sophia's aunt, 'where he has made a study of Konso funeral statues.'

Ianthe was used to meeting strangers and trying to put them at their ease. She had often herself introduced somebody at a parish function with a descriptive phrase, so that conversation might be encouraged. 'Mrs Noakes lives in Haslemere and does Jacobean embroidery' was perhaps only a little less daunting an introduction than the mention of Ethiopia and funeral statues. Ethiopia surely conjured up a good deal; there ought to be something for conversation there.

She had no idea what Konso funeral statues were, but she could at least ask intelligent questions about them.

'Miss Broome is an English lady from north-west London,' went on Miss Grandison precisely. 'She attends the church where my niece's husband is vicar.'

So they confronted each other – Ianthe and the Dottore – north-west London and Ethiopia, 'the church where my niece's husband is vicar' and Konso funeral statues.

'North-*west* London,' said the Dottore. 'Highgate?

189

No? Kensal Green, perhaps – a fine cemetery, I have heard, but alas I have never been there.'

'Yes,' said Ianthe eagerly, relieved that a link had been established so easily. She had forgotten about Kensal Green, and had never dreamed – for who indeed would – that it could be useful to her socially in Italy.

'You go there often, perhaps?' he asked.

'Well, I have been,' Ianthe hesitated, 'but I don't go there *very* often.'

'No,' said Sophia, breaking into the conversation. 'One could go – oh, every day – and yet one doesn't. *Why* doesn't one?' she asked extravagantly.

'Well, we have our work to do,' said Ianthe a little reproachfully.

'Yes, I suppose that's why. We have to spend our days doing dull unnecessary things rather than wandering about cemeteries – but that's what life is,' said Sophia.

Ianthe looked at her in surprise and perhaps disapproval. Life surely was and ought to be 'doing dull necessary things rather than wandering about cemetries' and Sophia, as a vicar's wife, should not speak as if she regretted it. Disconcerted, Ianthe sipped her vermouth, savouring the slight bitterness under the aromatic taste as if it were a medicine.

'You like our weak Italian drinks?' asked the Dottore politely.

'Oh, I do – this is delicious,' said Ianthe. 'It makes one feel really in Italy, somehow.'

'More so than drinking "Scotch" in a bar in the Via Veneto,' said the Dottore scornfully.

'But *we* didn't spend our time in Rome doing that,' said Sophia indignantly. 'We hardly saw the Via Veneto. Our Rome was *very* different, wasn't it, Ianthe.'

Ianthe agreed it had been. Rome for her was a confused mixture of St Peters and other churches, fountains, flower stalls and cafés, cats slinking in dark underground places and priests dashing along on scooters – perhaps no more the ideal picture of Rome than what one saw from the bar in the Via Veneto, where the Dottore imagined all the English tourists drinking whisky.

After taking another glass of vermouth he left them. Ianthe wondered if he had patients to see to, though it seemed unlikely.

'Has your aunt known him a long time?' she asked Sophia.

'Oh, *years* – they were – perhaps still are . . .' she hesitated, thinking that Ianthe would not need her to go further.

'Great friends, I suppose,' said Ianthe uncertainly.

'The most, as Penny would say.' Sophia smiled and drained her glass.

'And they have never thought of getting married?' Ianthe asked.

'Who knows what their *thoughts* may have been,' said Sophia. 'Come along – I think we're going to eat now and I believe Anna has done us a *fritto misto.*'

The next day Sophia took Ianthe for a walk. There was a villa she wanted her to see which had wonderful gardens and had once been the setting for an illicit love affair between well-known persons, now long dead. As they strolled among the cypresses Ianthe found herself remembering Sophia's aunt and the Dottore – surely Sophia could not really have meant that anything like *that* was going on between them. Yet why, otherwise, should the aunt have dyed her hair? In her confusion it was a relief to think of John, so far away in the library, perhaps even at this moment compiling a bibliography or assisting a reader with a sociological query.

'Of course this magical setting is almost *too* obvious,' Sophia was saying. 'One can imagine the lovers stroll-

191

ing here only too well, but it amuses me to think of totally unsuitable and incongruous people here – parties of English schoolgirls or priests from a seminary, or even Basil Branche and his two elderly ladies. Of course in the season people like that *do* come here, but this morning we seem to have it to ourselves. Perhaps the flowers are really at their best now – all the roses and these apricot pansies.'

'Yes, they are most unusual,' said Ianthe a little stiffly.

'Shall we sit down here?' asked Sophia. 'I always love this marble lion licking its cub – don't you find it charming and touching, somehow?'

Ianthe was unequal to the marble lion and its cub, but she was glad to sit down and look down at the sea.

'The "panorama" is almost too much at times, isn't it,' said Sophia in a slightly mocking tone.

'Yes, it's overwhelming,' Ianthe admitted. 'In England we're starved of this kind of scenery – at least in our everyday lives – and I suppose not many Italians see this view, when you come to think of it.'

'No – or they don't notice it,' Sophia agreed. 'Life everywhere is lived on a lower more humdrum plane. It's only when one comes to Italy that one imagines – oh such things!' She flung out her arms in an exaggerated gesture as if she would gather the sea and the lemon groves to her bosom. Then she laughed. 'I did hope that you and Penelope might find romance in Rome – perhaps in a sense you have.'

'It's such a beautiful city – one couldn't help finding it romantic,' said Ianthe evasively.

'Now you know *that* wasn't what I meant,' said Sophia, 'though I was surprised that you didn't want to stay longer in Rome, for quite another reason.'

'Well, of course one could spend months in Rome and still find plenty to do and see.'

'I expect Basil is missing you,' said Sophia.

'Basil, missing *me*?' said Ianthe in surprise. 'I don't think he'll miss me in particular, though I think he enjoyed meeting our party.'

'But you do like him, don't you?' Sophia persisted.

'How funny you should ask that,' said Ianthe, 'because Penelope asked me almost the same question.'

'Oh?' Penny never told me, Sophia thought. 'You must think we're a couple of matchmakers, like...' she paused, thinking she might bring in some respectable literary allusion to make the whole thing somehow 'better'. But Ianthe did not give her time for this because she said quickly, 'You surely couldn't imagine that I should want to marry Basil Branche?'

'No?' said Sophia doubtfully. 'But then how can another person ever tell – you *might* have been in love with him or wanted to marry him.'

'Well, as it happens you've guessed the wrong person,' said Ianthe.

Sophia realised that she had been snubbed, but remembering her duty to her sister she was determined to persevere.

'Then there could be a *right* person?' she went on. 'I mean, there *is* someone you love?'

They were leaning on a stone balustrade, looking out towards the sea. Why shouldn't she tell Sophia, Ianthe thought, the beauty of the view and its unreality overwhelming her.

'Yes, there is someone,' she said. 'Somebody at the library.'

'But how *suitable* – that librarian, I suppose, the one who came to the Christmas Bazaar?' Sophia sounded almost jubilant with relief that it was not Rupert Stonebird Ianthe loved.

'Mervyn Cantrell? Oh no – not him!'

'That's a blessing, in a way,' said Sophia. 'I didn't think it could be him. Librarians aren't really very lovable sort of people, are they.'

'Oh, I don't know – I suppose some of them are, *must* be, when one comes to think about it,' said Ianthe, feeling that Sophia's generalisation was difficult to comment on. 'And this – er person is a *sort* of librarian.' Ianthe's lips curved into a smile.

'A *sort* of librarian,' repeated Sophia dubiously, for that sounded somewhat disturbing, almost sinister.

'Yes, he was at the Bazaar too – it's John Challow.' Ianthe experienced the relief and pleasure of having spoken his name which is familiar to women in love.

'Oh, the *other* one – the good-looking dark young man? But surely . . .' Sophia broke off.

'Surely what?'

'He isn't the sort of person one would *marry*?'

'I don't know . . .' stammered Ianthe, 'I haven't . . . it hasn't . . . I mean, got to that stage yet, and I don't suppose it ever will.'

'Oh, I see,' said Sophia. 'You just *love* him.' Of course, she thought, Ianthe might well love somebody in a sort of general Christian way. She remembered some lines from a hymn

> For the love of human kind
> Brother, sister, parent, child. . . .

There was no mention of unrelated handsome young men there, indeed it had always seemed hard to Sophia that one's love was to be limited in this way. Yet for Ianthe it seemed ideal.

'I rather feel that you're one of those women who shouldn't marry,' Sophia said.

'I don't suppose I shall now,' said Ianthe. 'But of course one never knows – people *do* marry quite late in life.'

'I always think that's such a mistake,' said Sophia. 'You seem to me to be somehow *destined* not to marry,' she went on, perhaps too enthusiastically. 'I think you'll grow into one of those splendid spinsters – oh, don't think I mean it nastily or cattily – who are pillars of the Church and whom the Church certainly couldn't do without.'

Ianthe was silent, as well she might be before this daunting description. Yet until lately she too had seen herself like this.

'What about your sister,' she said at last, 'will she marry?'

'Oh, Penny will marry,' said Sophia confidently, 'she's made for it. In fact,' she added, with a laugh, 'I've arranged that she shall marry Rupert Stonebird.'

Ianthe looked surprised. 'But she may not want to – or he may not. I don't think one can – or should – arrange people's lives for them like that.'

'No, you're right – one shouldn't. Do you know, I often ask myself, did I do wrong to deprive Faustina of the opportunity of motherhood? You knew that she'd had the operation?'

'The operation?' repeated Ianthe stupidly. 'Oh, you mean your cat can't have kittens.' Somehow the mention of Faustina had turned her against Sophia; she remembered another time when the cat had been brought into a serious discussion. On occasions like this she found herself disliking Sophia; such lack of proportion, frivolity almost, were highly unsuitable in a vicar's wife.

They turned away from the view as if by mutual consent and began to walk out of the gardens. Ianthe suddenly realised the full significance of having told Sophia of her love for John. Perhaps it had been a mistake to confide in her.

'Of course you won't say anything about...' she began.

'What you've told me? Oh, my dear' – Sophia took

195

her arm impulsively – '*of course* I won't.'

Nevertheless her thoughts returned to Ianthe later that day when, at the end of their evening meal, she untied one of the little bundles of lemon leaves and began to remove leaf after leaf until the fragrant raisins were revealed at the centre. This process surely had something in common with uncovering the secrets of the heart, as Ianthe, aided by Sophia's probings, had uncovered hers. This would not have happened in north-west London over a cup of tea, Sophia felt. Perhaps it had taken Italy to show Ianthe that she loved this young man, though – since she was destined not to marry – it was a love that could hardly find fulfilment.

Having settled Ianthe, Sophia turned her thoughts to the others. What had the visit to Italy done for them? she wondered. Sister Dew has tasted osso buco and Chianti and found them as good as savoury rice and Wincarnis; she had also been carried shoulder-high by Italians. Edwin and Daisy Pettigrew had studied the life and conditions of Roman domestic animals and brought sustenance to some of them. Penelope had 'seen more' of Rupert – had even had some kind of a quarrel with him, which was surely better than going on in a neutral humdrum way. As for Mark and herself, she supposed people might say that they had had a 'second honeymoon', away from the cares of the parish. And now here she was alone, unwrapping another little bundle of lemon leaves to reach the deliciously flavoured raisins at the heart, and feeling that this trivial delight was almost enough to have brought away from a visit to Italy.

18

This Library is for the use of bona fide Scholars and may only be used at the discretion of the Librarian.

Ianthe stared at the repressive new notice which confronted her on her first morning back at work. It was written in red ink in Mervyn's italic hand and made her realise as nothing else could have done that she was now back in the closed world of the library after the open promise of life in Italy. And yet, when she was feeling homesick, this was the world she had thought of so longingly.

Mervyn was in one of his bad moods and his first words to her could hardly have been less welcoming.

'Nobody need think they're indispensable,' he declared, 'especially in a library. The work just has to go on and it does go on. Books are written and published; they find their way into libraries and are catalogued,' he continued, as if he were reciting a psalm.

'Then they're put on the shelves and forgotten,' said John sarcastically.

'Well, some books are destined never to be read,' said Mervyn. 'It's the natural order of things.'

Like the women who are destined never to marry, thought Ianthe, remembering Sophia's words to her in the gardens at Ravello.

There had been something almost cruel in the way she had spoken and Ianthe felt that she had left Italy liking

Sophia a little less than before. Yet a kind of defiance had risen up in her as if she might yet prove her wrong.

'I'm sure you and John and Shirley managed perfectly well without me,' she said quietly. 'And after all I haven't been away very long.'

'You've put on a bit of weight, haven't you,' said Mervyn cattily. 'It must be the pasta you've eaten – all that canelloni.'

'It suits her to be fatter,' said John. 'She was a little too thin before.'

His tone sounded almost fond which gave Ianthe a glow of pleasure and made up for the rather off-hand way he had greeted her when they had first met that morning. Not that she should have expected anything else, for if there had been any change it had been in her own feelings towards him and he was not to know how much she had looked forward to seeing him. Yet that first sight of him had been a shock to her, for she had forgotten not only how good-looking he was but how different from the men she had been seeing on her holiday and indeed all her life – different from Mark Ainger and Basil Branche, from Edwin Pettigrew and Rupert Stonebird, and from all the ranks of clergymen and schoolmasters stretching back into the past like pale imitations of men, it now seemed.

When lunchtime came she hoped that he might ask her to go out with him, but he made no move and hurried off at half-past five saying that he was going to see a man about a second hand car – the kind of thing that sounded almost as if it might not be true. So, feeling rather cast down, she began to pack up her work and prepare to go home. Just as she was ready to leave Mervyn came into the room and asked if she had any plans for the evening.

'I was just going home,' she said flatly.

'But have you planned your evening meal?' Mervyn

asked.

'Not really – there's a tin of pork luncheon meat I opened yesterday,' she said. 'I thought I'd finish that up with salad.'

'Pork luncheon meat and salad – ugh....' Mervyn shuddered. 'In that case I think it's my duty as well as my pleasure to take you out for a meal tonight.'

Ianthe was so taken aback – for Mervyn had never before asked her out for a meal – that it was a few seconds before she could answer him.

'That would be nice,' she said, 'but aren't you going home this evening as usual?'

'No – Mother is spending a few days with a friend at Sittingbourne, so I'm on my own and making the most of it.'

Ianthe supposed that she ought to feel flattered that he had thought of asking her out to dinner, but just as some women rate themselves too highly so she undervalued herself and thought only that it seemed pathetic that 'making the most of it' could mean something as dull as taking a woman colleague out to dinner. But of course his pleasure would be in the food rather than in her company, she thought.

'I suppose these clothes will be all right?' she said. 'I hadn't expected to be going out.'

'Oh, a woman always looks suitably dressed in a grey costume,' he said, in a way which did not add to her feeling of gaiety. 'Anyway, we're not going to the Caprice or the Savoy. I'm afraid I can't quite rise to that, but a friend of mine has opened a new restaurant in South Ken. and I think the food should be worth eating there.'

They took the Underground and arrived at the restaurant at about half-past six.

'Of course it's unfashionably early to eat, I know,' said Mervyn, 'but they start serving dinners from six o'clock onwards, life being what it is. Shall we go to this table in the corner?'

They sat down and Ianthe took off her gloves and looked around her a little apprehensively. The room was papered in a design of fishing boats and nets which did not seem altogether appropriate for the early diners scattered at the tables round the walls. The tablecloths were dark green and the china white. Ianthe commented on this rather striking arrangement.

'Oh, a friend of Eric's did the décor,' said Mervyn. 'At least he *was* a friend but they've split up now.'

'How sad,' she said, then felt she had expressed herself too strongly.

'Well, these things happen, don't they,' said Mervyn, studying the menu. 'Now I can recommend the pâté because Eric makes it all himself from pig's liver and fat bacon.'

Ianthe felt sickened by this description and chose soup instead. Afterwards they were to have some special lobster dish.

'Fish is one of his things,' Mervyn explained. 'Of course he's a Catholic – a convert – very devout, so that may have something to do with it.'

'Oh, surely not,' said Ianthe, rather shocked.

'As a matter of fact it was he who got that bouillabaisse flown over from Marseilles on Ash Wednesday for that clergyman I was telling you about.'

'An Anglican clergyman?' asked Ianthe. 'It sounds rather unlikely.'

'Well, I can't remember now,' said Mervyn impatiently. 'I expect Eric'll come and have a word with us later on, so you can ask him if you like.'

The food was certainly very good and Ianthe was surprised to find herself enjoying the meal, for she had not imagined herself being able to eat anything at all. Conversation was not difficult because Mervyn kept up a continuous commentary on the food itself and recalled dishes he had eaten on other occasions. While Ianthe listened to him it occurred to her that Mervyn was one of the few people to whom she could talk about John and she was just planning how she could introduce his name into the conversation when a man in a white coat and chef's hat came up to their table and Mervyn introduced him as his friend Eric. He was about Mervyn's age, rather fat and wearing a gold bracelet on one wrist, which struck Ianthe as unusual for a man. He had a slight Cockney accent and was not quite Mervyn's 'class', she felt. He did not look at all like her idea of a devout Catholic convert. After he had received their compliments on the dinner he leaned over towards Mervyn and said in a confidential tone, 'I *was* sorry to hear that about your mum.'

'My mum?' Mervyn repeated the word – unsuitable, surely, when applied to a man of his age.

'Yes – I heard she's passed on. I *am* sorry, knowing how devoted you were to her.'

'But *my* mum hasn't passed on,' said Mervyn, with a rather inappropriate little laugh, 'she's very much with us – staying with some spiritualist friends at Sittingbourne at the moment.'

'Sittingbourne? Well, I never! Then it must have been somebody else's mum that passed on. Now whose mum could it have been?'

They were all three silent before the ridiculous question.

'Oh well,' said Eric at last, 'it'll come to me whose mum it was – probably in the middle of the night. Does that ever happen to you?' he asked suddenly, turning to Ianthe.

'Yes, one does sometimes remember things then,' she said. 'Forgotten names or quotations do seem to come back.'

When Eric had left them to talk to friends at another table Mervyn said, 'Funny him saying that about my mother, wasn't it. I hope it isn't a portent or anything.'

'Oh, don't be silly,' said Ianthe briskly, for she had had the same feeling. 'Things like that don't happen. Besides, your mother is at Sittingbourne.'

'Yes, of course she is.' Mervyn took up the bottle of hock they had been drinking and refilled their glasses.

'I like this wine,' said Ianthe politely.

'Yes, I thought you might. I hoped you would – that's why I chose it.'

He was talking almost like John, she thought. Yet it was only natural that a good meal with a pleasant wine should soften his usual sharpness. Had he really chosen it to please her, though? Ianthe sat with her head bent, fingering the stem of her glass, uncertain how to take this implied compliment.

'Of course,' Mervyn went on, 'my mother won't live for ever. I shall have to face up to that.'

'Yes, of course,' said Ianthe, 'but she's in good health, isn't she.'

'Oh yes, Mother's as right as a trivet,' he said awkwardly, 'but after all death comes to everyone.'

'Of course. . . .'

'I mean, *your* mother died – passed on,' he added, as if the expression needed to be softened for a woman.

'Yes, but she wasn't very strong and older than your mother, I think.'

'I expect you were very lonely at first, until you got your lovely little house and all your nice things around you.'

Ianthe hardly knew what to say to this. 'I suppose we're all alone, in a sense,' she brought out at last.

'If *my* mother died, we should *both* be alone,' Mervyn declared.

'Yes, I suppose we would be,' said Ianthe in a puzzled

202

tone. 'But people's parents are dying all the time – people of our age, I mean – there must be quite a lot of us living alone.'

'Supposing we were to join forces,' said Mervyn almost eagerly. 'It would be silly keeping on two houses.'

'Do you mean we should live together?' she asked, thinking that she must have misunderstood him.

'Well, not in sin – I wasn't suggesting that.' He giggled. 'Get married – that's what I meant, of course.'

Ianthe felt herself go hot and cold with surprise and horror. That Mervyn of all people should make such a suggestion!

'But I couldn't marry *you!*' she burst out.

'And why not, might I ask?' he said petulantly, almost nastily.

'We don't love each other.'

'Perhaps not, but there's marriage and marriage, if you see what I mean.'

Ianthe thought she did see but there was no comment she could make.

'We get on well together,' Mervyn continued, 'and we've many interests in common, after all. The library. . . .' He paused, for that indeed was something to contemplate in solemn silence. 'And we both like nice furniture.'

'Whose house would we live in?' asked Ianthe.

'Oh, yours!' he answered without hesitation. 'Ours isn't at all nice and besides it's only leasehold.'

Ianthe sat in a dismayed silence. Then she remembered that the whole idea was a fantasy, for his mother was still comfortably alive in Sittingbourne. There was no cause for alarm or the slightest agitation.

The waiter came to the table with more coffee.

'I like this restaurant,' said Ianthe in a relieved tone, grateful to be able to change the subject.

But Mervyn was not to be diverted yet. 'You said you couldn't marry *me*,' he persisted, 'as if you had somebody else in mind.'

'Oh, I didn't mean anything like that – you misunderstood me,' she said quickly. 'I don't suppose I shall ever get married.'

She nerved herself to look at him sitting opposite to her – fair-haired with distinguished-looking features, light-coloured horn-rimmed glasses, neat clothes. . . . She supposed she must regard him differently now; her feelings towards him could never be quite the same again. Had he always loved her? she wondered. No – she was honest enough not to flatter herself in that way. It was after seeing her house and furniture – the Heppelwhite chairs and the Pembroke table – that his feelings had changed. She only hoped this evening wasn't going to make any difference to their relationship at the library, which had always been quite a pleasant one.

'That's not what John thinks,' said Mervyn, much to her surprise for she had not expected any further comment on her statement. 'He's determined that if anyone marries you it shall be him,' Mervyn went on, in a way that might have been serious or joking. 'I suppose he sees himself in your house too.'

Was it only for her house and furniture that she was to be loved? Ianthe wondered, hardly knowing how to feel about Mervyn's revelation of John's intentions. She had not imagined *him* coveting the Hepplewhite chairs.

'Seriously though, you want to be careful of John,' he said.

'I shall behave just as I always do,' she said stiffly to hide her feelings of disquiet. 'Oh, hullo, Penelope,' she said, seeing Penelope Grandison and another girl sitting at a table near the door. 'I didn't realise you were here.'

'No, I didn't see you either,' said Penelope gruffly, for she felt deeply the shame of being caught dining out with a woman friend when Ianthe was with a man. To make matters worse, the restaurant had turned out to be rather more expensive than she had bargained for. Her friend Jocasta had suggested it as she had thought it would be 'fun'. It was disconcerting to meet Ianthe of all people under such circumstances.

'I expect we'll be meeting at St Basil's some time,' said Ianthe in a perfunctory social way, for she did not want to stay and make conversation with Penelope and her friend. She wanted to go home and brood over what Mervyn had said about John. Could it be that he really did want to marry her, and what did Mervyn mean by saying that she should be careful of him.

It was not until the small hours of the morning when she was lying awake that she remembered something. Perhaps at this moment Eric was also remembering whose mum it was who had passed on. Ianthe remembered that she had lent John some money when he was ill and that he had never paid her back.

19

Rupert Stonebird stood in the hall looking at the invitation which had just come by post. It was to a garden party, to be held in the grounds of the anthropological research centre of which his friend – if such she could be called – Esther Clovis was the secretary. 'Dr R. Stonebird and guest', it said. 'Dress optional'. This last would be one of Esther's touches, he decided, with its implication that anything from nakedness upwards would be acceptable.

And guest, he pondered, going into his study. Little Penelope Grandison, perhaps; here would be a chance to atone for whatever he had done to make her cry on the Spanish Steps that evening some weeks ago. The stupid thing was, though, that he hadn't been in touch with her since the visit to Italy. Several times he had thought of asking her out to dinner but something had always happened to prevent it. He had not seen Ianthe either, except to say good-morning in the road. She, of course, would be another person he might ask to the garden party, an easier and more suitable choice than Penelope. And yet, need he ask either of them? Couldn't he go alone or break away from St Basil's and ask somebody unconnected with the parish? He toyed with the idea for a moment, but the uncomfortable conscience he seemed to have developed lately would keep returning to Penelope, and in the end he found himself calling in at the vicarage to ask Sophia for her sister's telephone number.

He found Sophia in the garden with Faustina. The cat was lying stretched out in the sun, her creamy underside exposed for stroking. Sophia was beside her in a deck-chair, a piece of petit-point on her lap though her hands were idle.

'Was she glad to see you back?' Rupert asked, wishing he could remember the cat's name.

'I like to think so,' said Sophia, 'but one can't assume anything with Faustina. And have you recovered from Italy?'

'Recovered? I suppose so. I managed to do some useful reading in the Vatican Library,' said Rupert, more primly than he had intended.

'That's very good then,' said Sophia. 'I was just think-ing the other day that we must all have brought some-thing away – impossible to go to Italy and *not* do that – but your benefit does seem to have been rather more tan-gible – to have been in the Vatican Library and read all those books.'

Was she making fun of him? he wondered, glancing at her quickly. But Sophia, lying back in her chair, her eyes closed against the evening sun, looked perfectly serious, even a little sad.

'I came to ask for Penelope's telephone number,' he went on. 'So stupid – I don't seem to have it. I wondered if she'd come to an anthropological garden party with me.'

'I'm sure she'd love to,' said Sophia. 'The only thing is though that she probably wouldn't be able to get away from work if it's a weekday.'

'Oh, I hadn't thought of that. Still, I can try – if she can't manage the garden party perhaps she'd have dinner with me one evening,' he said quickly, feeling Sophia's eyes on him. Did she know about the tears on the

207

Spanish Steps? he wondered. He could not meet her glance but looked instead at Faustina, who glared at him disconcertingly.

Sophia gave him the telephone number and he hurried away, not wishing to reveal his alternative plan to her, for it seemed now as if he would have to ask Ianthe. Yet she also worked, and it was just as likely that she too would be unable to get the afternoon off. The whole scheme was turning out to be more complicated than he had bargained for, perhaps too difficult to be carried out. All the same later that evening he went to the telephone and dialled Penelope's number, not sure what he was going to say.

She did not recognise his voice and when he announced himself there was a perceptible stiffening in her manner, almost a chilling of the air that he could sense coming at him over the wires all the way from South Kensington to north-west London.

'I can't get an afternoon off in the middle of the week,' she said brusquely.

'Oh, I'm sorry – I'd hoped perhaps you might be able to. . . .'

'No, I can't, and I've just had this holiday in Rome.'

'Yes, of course.'

The conversation flagged. Ask her out to dinner, he told himself, but somehow he could not get the words out and then the line started to crackle as if it were a long distance call over oceans and continents.

'We must have a talk some time,' he said, trying to be cosy, but she did not hear properly and put the receiver down thinking he had said 'walk'. She saw herself tramping over Hampstead Heath or Richmond Park in unsuitable shoes – for one just didn't have shoes for *that* kind of thing. He was like an old-fashioned undergraduate, she thought in disgust, offering her that kind of entertainment. He might at least have asked her out to a meal. In her disappointment and misery Penelope flung herself down on the divan among the rose-coloured velvet cushions and lay sulkily eating a Mars bar she had happened to find conveniently to hand among the jumble of things on her bedside table. She was too depressed to reflect that his having asked her to the garden party was better than nothing.

Ianthe, rather to Rupert's surprise, was able to come to the garden party with him. She was glad to be taken out of herself, to get away from the library and her own thoughts which were a miserable confusion of Mervyn's proposal, John's possible feelings for her and the remembrance of the money he had borrowed and not paid back. It was a fortunate coincidence that she should have been entitled to take an afternoon off because she was due to work the next Saturday morning.

Rupert called for her at her house. It was a fine afternoon, and Ianthe's blue and white silk dress and jacket and large-brimmed blue straw hat brought back to him memories of his mother at parish garden parties of his childhood. But was this quite as it should be? he asked himself anxiously – that Ianthe should remind him of his mother? It was a comforting rather than a promising beginning to the afternoon.

'I'll ring for a taxi,' he said.

'Oh, do we need a taxi?' said Ianthe. 'It's such a fine afternoon and a bus will take us all the way, surely?'

'Yes, of course – but I thought...' he began, then realised that, on the whole, women should be encouraged not to take taxis.

'I always like riding on the top of a bus in the middle of the afternoon,' said Ianthe. 'It seems like a holiday when one's usually working.'

'Yes, I suppose it does. I don't have any set hours, except for lectures and seminars.'

'Seminars,' Ianthe echoed in a wondering tone and

was then silent.

Strange and perhaps rather sad, Rupert thought, the way any mention of his work seemed to inhibit her.

They passed along a street of peeling stuccoed houses. Ianthe was reminded of the house where she had been to visit John, except that these were even more decayed. Oh, what was he doing now, she wondered unhappily.

'This is all part of St Basil's parish,' she said quickly, to take her mind off John. 'I suppose Mark has to come visiting along here – it must be a thankless task in many ways.'

'Yes – I expect he meets with as little response as the anthropologist in the field sometimes does,' said Rupert.

'Oh, but that's hardly the same,' said Ianthe, sounding shocked at the comparison.

'Why not?'

'Well, the anthropologist is asking prying, personal questions that people might not want to answer, whereas a parish priest is bringing them something,' she said.

'Something they don't always want.'

'Yes, in a way, but. . . .'

'All right then – we won't go any further,' he said lightly. 'Perhaps it isn't a valid comparison after all. Look, we get off here, then it's just a short walk.'

'It's here, then?' said Ianthe, as they came up to a square of large houses.

'Yes, we go through the library and there's a garden at the back,' Rupert explained. 'Oh,' he exclaimed, as they passed through the hall into the library, 'it seems not to be quite as usual today.'

'No, I suppose today is different,' said Ianthe, for at a table, among the piles of learned journals that seemed appropriate to such a library, sat two elderly women hulling strawberries and arranging them in small dishes, counting aloud so that the portions were scrupulously equal. Cut loaves and pats of butter balanced on top of the journals, while African sculptures had been pushed aside to make room for plates of cakes. Bottles of milk stood on shelves half full of books and an urn appeared to be boiling furiously and spurting steam on some valuable-looking old bindings.

'Oh dear,' said Rupert, leading Ianthe quickly through.

'Have we come too early?' she asked.

'I think we shouldn't have come through the library – perhaps we weren't meant to see quite so much. It's a side of things one would rather *not* see, don't you think?'

'Well, one knows that tea must be got ready,' said Ianthe, 'and that people have to do it – like a parish function – only it does seem odd in a library. Perhaps it would have been easier to have left it to a catering firm?'

'Ah, but that would have added to the expense and the place has little money to spare at the moment. Besides, life isn't meant to be easy,' said Rupert. 'Not for *ever* in green pastures, as the hymn reminds us.'

'What a beautiful lawn,' said Ianthe, as they stepped out on to the grass.

'Yes, it is nourished by the bones of former presidents,' said Rupert.

'You mean they are buried here?' asked Ianthe, startled.

'Not exactly buried, but it has been fashionable – perhaps I should say customary – to have one's ashes scattered here. The old rationalist likes to feel that others of similar beliefs will be treading on his earthly remains . . . but let me get you a cup of tea, there does seem to be some now, and strawberries too.'

Ianthe accepted the tea gratefully. She did not feel quite at ease with Rupert's talk of rationalists and their ashes, and the sight of the elderly ladies preparing tea in the library had made her feel slightly uncomfortable, as if she ought to be there helping them. In some ways the garden party was like a parish function for there is a certain sameness about all these occasions. This realisation comforted her and she was about to say so to Rupert when he was approached by a short bald man, who began talking about an article Rupert had evidently just written for a journal of which he was editor.

Rupert introduced him to Ianthe as Dr Apfelbaum, but as is often the way in the academic world he made no further effort to include her in the conversation. And indeed, how would it have been possible, she wondered, listening to the snatches of their talk that came over to her – something about a controversy on the introduction of maize into West Africa which had been going on in one of the learned journals for five years – 'Digby and Mrs What's-it going at each other hammer and tongs – oh, you mean Digby *Fox*? But I thought he was one of the ethnohistory boys?'

'What's ethnohistory?' she asked, feeling she should make an effort.

To her surprise they both smiled, as if she had said something funny.

'A word we're not supposed to use,' said Rupert kindly.

'You will be glad to know that Rupert doesn't dabble in such dangerous waters,' said Dr Apfelbaum unhelpfully. 'Now what is the length?'

'Sixteen thousand?'

'My dear boy...' Dr Apfelbaum flung out his hands in a gesture of despair.

'All right, then – two parts of eight thousand each.'

'We'll see – I'll tell you when I get back from – where is it we're going first? – Prague, Leipzig, Brazzaville....'

'Conferences,' Rupert explained. 'We have them

every summer.'

'How nice,' said Ianthe.

'Sorry about all that,' said Rupert when they were alone again, 'but as you've probably gathered Apfelbaum is going to publish an article of mine in his journal.'

'Oh, that's good, isn't it,' she said. 'What's the title of your article?'

He hesitated, then thought, why not – no point in mincing matters, it would only be like teaching somebody to swim by throwing them in at the deep end. 'The implication of jural processes among the Ngumu: a structural dichotomy,' he declared.

'Oh . . .' she turned her head away as if she were in pain or distress.

At least she had not been facetious or made some cheaply witty rejoinder, he thought. 'It's quite simple, really,' he began, but he knew that it was not. It was the kind of thing that could be, and so often was, the stumbling block between men and women, or, if a relationship had progressed through several stages, the last straw. 'Let's have some more tea,' he said.

'Oh, there's Mrs Fairfax, isn't it – she was at your dinner party!' Ianthe cried out. 'And Professor Fairfax too.' It was a relief to see them, odd though they looked.

'Wild animals in their natural setting,' said Robina Fairfax, approaching them, 'that's what I always say when I come here.'

'Oh, I think we're pretty mild and harmless, aren't we,' said Rupert.

'Tamed and shabby tigers, perhaps,' said Gervase Fairfax, on his usual sarcastic note.

Ianthe did not know what answer to make. People at church garden parties did not make such remarks and she could not imagine that she would ever feel at ease with Rupert's colleagues. Now a short rough-haired woman in a grey suit joined them and was introduced as Esther Clovis, the secretary of the research centre. She began asking Ianthe searching questions about herself, almost as if she were Rupert's fiancée and needed to be 'vetted'.

'Are you a statistician?' she asked gruffly.

'No I'm not,' said Ianthe, puzzled.

'A pity – it's useful when the woman is, but perhaps you're an economist or a social worker?'

This last seemed almost the kind of thing one might be, Ianthe felt, and she ventured to say that she was 'interested' in social work, feeling that she must do her best if only out of politeness to Rupert.

'A vague interest in social work won't get us very far,' said Esther sharply. 'Have you a degree in it?'

'Oh come now, Esther,' said Rupert, detaching himself from Gervase Fairfax with whom he had been discussing the Unesco project, 'Ianthe is a librarian.'

'Good heavens!' Esther exclaimed. 'It seems as if I've been barking up the wrong tree.' And with that she turned on her heel and left them.

Ianthe felt a little shaken by the encounter and was glad when Rupert suggested that they should leave.

'I'm sorry about that,' he said. 'Esther evidently thought you were going into the field – she's so keen you know.'

'Has she been often herself?'

'Oh, never – but she likes to direct others, and to see that the right people get together.' He hurried over these last words, afraid that Ianthe might take fright and leave him, and suggested that as it was now the rush hour they should take a taxi home. Perhaps she would come and have a glass of sherry at his house?

Leaning back in the taxi Ianthe realised that she was tired and one of her shoes was hurting. Her unhappiness, pushed away for a couple of hours, also came back

214

to her.

'Tired?' said Rupert, in a sympathetic tone, laying his hand on her arm.

'No, not really,' she said politely. 'I enjoyed it very much, though I suppose one's feet get a bit tired standing about in one's best shoes,' she added, trying to make a joke of it.

'Take them off then,' he said.

'Oh, I couldn't!' she said, sounding genuinely shocked.

'Well, you can when we get home.'

Rupert had a pleasant little terrace at the back of his house, something rather better than a yard, where he had put a seat under an old vine which grew against the south wall of the house.

'What would you like?' he asked. 'Sherry, gin and something – or Cinzano, perhaps, to remind you of Italy?'

'No, not that,' she said. 'Sherry would be nicer.'

'Did you enjoy Italy?' he asked. 'I haven't really heard much about it from you.'

He came and sat beside her, stretching his arm along the back of the seat so that it almost touched her shoulders.

'Yes, it was lovely.' Imperceptibly she drew herself a little away from him.

'You were lucky to see Ravello and Amalfi – I believe it's very lovely there and Sophia's company must have been delightful.'

'Yes, delightful,' Ianthe said mechanically. There was a silence and then she went on, 'Sophia's rather – well, I don't quite know how to put it.'

'Strange, were you going to say?'

'Yes – one thinks one knows her and then suddenly one seems not to at all.'

'But isn't everybody like that to some extent?'

215

'I suppose so, in a way,' said Ianthe uneasily, thinking of John. 'It's that cat, too.'

'Ah, yes, Faustina – isn't that her name? I was trying to remember it when I was at the vicarage the other day.'

'Sophia brings it into everything, the cat. *She*, I suppose I should say, not *it*.'

'I feel Sophia knows about life,' Rupert went on.

'You mean living in this poor parish and being married to a clergyman – yes, I suppose she would know about life.'

'Yes, that would be the conventional view of course – that a woman in those circumstances would know about life, but I meant something a little different.' Rupert frowned with the effort of trying to explain himself. 'Something that the pessimistic Victorians had, not the women, the men. Perhaps I was thinking of Matthew Arnold.'

'Oh?' Ianthe looked puzzled and uncomprehending, but he did not see her face and went on, 'I think she sometimes feels that there really is neither joy nor love nor light. . . .'

'But she is devoted to Mark,' said Ianthe almost sharply, 'anyone can see that.' And how did Rupert know all this about Sophia? Ianthe wondered. Was it because he was an anthropologist and used to studying people? Yet anthropologists did not seem to do exactly that; it would be difficult to imagine, say, Gervase Fairfax, talking in this way. Had Rupert talked to Sophia about such things, then? It seemed unlikely that he had ever had the opportunity.

'I think the feeling would go beyond a happy marriage,' said Rupert. 'I suppose we all experience it sometimes.'

'I don't think one should feel like that about life,' said Ianthe, a little shocked. 'A clergyman's wife certainly shouldn't anyway.'

Poor Sophia, Rupert thought, breaking the silence by refilling Ianthe's glass, to be classified in this way. Ianthe seemed to be very much the canon's daughter this afternoon.

'Well, don't let's talk any more about it,' he said, 'when it's so pleasant being here. I think Esther Clovis has decided to bring us together. I rather like the idea, don't you?'

'I couldn't be a statistician,' said Ianthe unhappily.

'I should hope not – I should hate you to be that. I like you too much as you are,' he said affectionately, moving his arm so that it tightened around her shoulders and drew her closer to him. There was now no doubt that he was about to kiss her.

'Oh, no! Please, no,' she cried out in agitation.

'I was only going to kiss you, Ianthe; surely. . . .'

'But I'd rather you didn't, please.'

'Don't you like me at all, then?' he asked, feeling very foolish.

'Yes, of course I do. But I'm in love with somebody else,' she said simply. The effect of this flat statement was devastating, for it was the last thing Rupert had expected. Then he saw that her eyes were full of tears which were beginning to course slowly down her cheeks. So for the second time within not much more than a month he – the meekest and kindest of men – had made a woman cry.

'But who can you be in love with,' he said stupidly, as if that could make any difference.

'Nobody you know.'

'Oh. And does he love you?'

'I don't know,' she said miserably.

'My dear, I'm sorry – of course I never guessed. I'll take you home.'

'It's only across the road,' she said, trying to smile. 'I've behaved so stupidly and you've been so kind – I did

217

enjoy the afternoon. It's all hopeless anyway,' she sobbed.

Rupert took her arm in a brotherly way and they walked in silence the few yards to her front door. Some married man, he thought, probably a clergyman with a wife in a mental home, or was that being too melodramatic and old-fashioned?

Such a nice couple they made, Sister Dew thought, seeing him return alone to his own house. She wondered if she should take him one of the steak and kidney pies she had baked that morning, but then – with unusual delicacy – judged it to be not quite the moment. And of course there was no question of taking one to Miss Broome – one did not take cooked food to lone women in the same way as to lone men.

Yet, had she but known it, Rupert would have welcomed a gesture of such solid kindness at that moment, for he felt depressed and at a loose end with the whole of the evening before him. He went to his study automatically and settled himself down with a new journal of linguistic articles, thinking that it would 'take him out of himself', which in a sense it did. The examples cited in one article – 'I eat meat, I beat the child, I do not eat toad' – conjured up a drab picture of life in a primitive tribe in all its brutal simplicity. Only in a word-list from a more sophisticated area did a more civilized, and therefore more depressing, picture emerge – 'pyorrhea, beard, maternal aunt' he read gloomily. Perhaps it would be best if he let Esther Clovis find him a suitable wife after all.

In her house Ianthe made a determined effort to pull herself together, as her upbringing and training told her that she should. She bathed her eyes and face in cold water, changed into a cotton dress and comfortable sandals, and went into the garden. She did not fling herself down on the grass as Penelope might have done, but lay in a deckchair with her eyes closed. If only she could have loved Rupert Stonebird! Could she not even now, by some effort of the will, turn her thoughts towards him and make herself care for him? It would be much easier to love Rupert than to love Mervyn, she thought.

Being in the garden she did not hear the front-door bell ring the first time and had John not been persistent enough to ring several times she might have lain in her deckchair wondering if she could love Rupert while John crept unnoticed away from the house. But he had come all this way to see her and to pay back the money which – to his horror – he had suddenly remembered that she had lent him when he was ill. All that time ago – whatever must she think! And when the money had been handed over and refused and handed over again, there were other things to be talked about, misunderstandings to be cleared up, and – at last – mutual love to be declared and brought out into the open.

'But when I came back after my holiday,' Ianthe said at last, 'I thought. . . .'

'Oh, that was all Mervyn's fault,' John interrupted her quickly, 'something he said – almost as if he wanted to marry you himself and as if you'd given him to understand that you wouldn't be unwilling. And then he went on about our different backgrounds – you know how catty he can be.'

What did it matter now! thought Ianthe in her happiness.

20

'Take an apostle spoon,' Edwin Pettigrew had said, in that calm way that inspired so much confidence, making it all sound so easy. And certainly one would have thought that a vicarage was the one place where one could be sure of finding plenty of apostle spoons. Trying to hold Faustina firmly under one arm, Sophia rummaged in the silver drawer but could not find one. Then she remembered the coffee spoons that had been a wedding present and were kept in a satin-lined case. Surely those were apostle spoons? They looked something like them, but then she realised that they were miniature replicas of the coronation anointing spoon – not so unsuitable, really, for with a jerk of her head Faustina sent the spoonful of liquid paraffin running down her face and brindled front so that she had, in a sense, anointed herself with oil.

Sophia let out a cry of exasperation as the cat jumped to the ground and stalked away. Who would ever have thought that a miniature anointing spoon could have contained so much, she asked herself, for her hands and the front of her skirt seemed to be covered with liquid paraffin. It was not the best moment for the front-door bell to ring, but those who live in vicarages are used to people calling at awkward times. Sophia rubbed her skirt and hands with a towel and composed her face into the patient sympathetic mask she wore when confronted with one of her husband's black parishioners wanting to know about getting married or having a child baptised.

But her expression changed when she saw an elderly clergyman and a woman – both total strangers to her – standing on the doorstep. Ah, people to see Mark, she thought with relief; they did not look as if they would be troublesome in any way.

'I'm afraid my husband's out at the moment,' she said, 'but I'm expecting him back any time now. Perhaps you'd like to wait for him?'

'Mrs Ainger, it is really you we want to see,' said the woman. 'I think you know my niece, Ianthe Broome.'

'Ianthe? Yes, of course – do come in,' said Sophia, for now she was beginning to realise who they were. The memory of the Lenten addresses on those cold Wednesday evenings came back to her. Even today, when the weather was warm, the woman was wearing a light fur coat, summer ermine, Sophia believed it was. Could it be that Ianthe's uncle and aunt had come to 'call' in a rather splendid Edwardian way? And had there been nobody at home, would Mrs Burdon have left one of her own cards and two of her husband's? One of them might even have been turned down at the corner for some mysterious reason which Sophia had now forgotten.

'I was just going to make tea,' she said, showing them into the drawing room.

'Well, thank you – a cup of tea will certainly make things easier,' said Bertha Burdon, rather to Sophia's surprise, for surely that was the kind of thing one thought rather than said?

'What my wife means is that it will make it easier to discuss this rather worrying business,' said Randolph Burdon hastily.

'Of course I meant that,' said Bertha sharply. 'Mrs Ainger would think me very discourteous if I had meant anything else.'

Fortunately Sophia had made a cake that morning and it looked almost as good as one of Sister Dew's. She made the tea, deciding that Earl Grey would be appropriate just as wines are on various occasions, and cut some thin brown bread and butter. It was only when she was wondering whether they would prefer strawberry jam or quince jelly that it occurred to her to wonder what 'this rather worrying business' could be. Had something happened to Ianthe that she didn't know about? Sophia went back into the drawing room with the tea-tray feeling rather apprehensive.

'I hope Ianthe is all right?' she said.

'Then you haven't heard?' Bertha asked.

'No.' What could it be? Sophia wondered. Something to do with a man, perhaps, though that seemed unlike Ianthe. But what was it she had said at Ravello about being in love with somebody? Sophia had hardly taken it seriously at the time.

'She has announced her intention of marrying,' said Randolph. 'Ah, is that *quince* jelly, I see? How delicious!'

'A most unfortunate choice,' Bertha continued, obviously irritated by her husband's allowing himself to be diverted by the quince jelly. 'The man is several years younger than she is and inferior to her socially.'

'Then it must be the young man from the library?' Sophia asked. Her feelings on hearing the news were mixed; surprise and disappointment that Ianthe should be acting out of character – disregarding the advice she had been given at Ravello – and relief that she had not chosen to marry Rupert Stonebird.

'You know him, then?' asked Bertha sharply.

'Not really – he came to our Christmas bazaar but I can't remember much about him.'

'From what Ianthe tells us he doesn't sound at all what one would have wished for her.'

Sophia refilled the tea cups. 'I don't quite see what *I*

can do,' she said at last. 'Ianthe is old enough to know what she's doing.'

'You could tell her what a mistake she is making – she would respect your opinion,' said Bertha.

'But do people respect each other's opinions in cases like this, unless they happen to agree with their own?' Sophia protested. People have been doing this from time immemorial, she thought, advising each other to marry or not to marry and how often does it do any good. Indeed, she began to wonder uneasily if it had been her advice to Ianthe not to marry that had decided her to take this step. 'I had a conversation with Ianthe when we were in Italy,' she said, 'and we certainly did talk about marriage and that sort of thing.'

'And did she reveal anything?' asked Bertha eagerly.

'She told me she loved this young man – John, isn't it – but I never realised that she wanted to *marry* him,' said Sophia.

'At least he works in a library,' Bertha murmured, 'one does feel that is *something*.'

'He is not, I understand, a *qualified* librarian?' asked Randolph in a brisker tone, as if he had decided to make the best of a bad job.

'No, I don't think so,' said Sophia.

'Perhaps if they love each other...' Bertha seemed to bring out the words with difficulty, perhaps because she had heard rather than experienced what love was and what it could drive people to. In her case there had been no love and no driving, only a good and suitable match that her parents had encouraged, but it was only at this moment, contemplating Ianthe's foolishness, that she realised almost with regret that she herself had never loved.

'But there is the rest of their lives,' said Sophia, 'and marriage is for a long time. What will they talk about in the evenings when the novelty has worn off?'

'In the *evenings*?' asked Bertha in a puzzled tone which made Sophia think that perhaps her life with Randolph Burdon did not have evenings in the way that of other married couples did.

'The man can go to his club while the woman does needlework or watches the television,' said Randolph, 'so conversation in the evenings need not be a problem. She could always make quince jelly of course,' he added, with a distressing lack of seriousness. 'This is so delicious, Mrs Ainger, that I am going to take the last spoonful. A pity my wife has not the strength to do these things.'

'And quinces do not grow in Mayfair, anyway,' said Bertha complacently.

'My mother sends them up from the country,' said Sophia. 'I'll give you a pot to take away with you.'

'So kind of you,' said Randolph. 'You have really been most helpful.'

At least he would be taking away a pot of his favourite jelly, Sophia thought, which was a great deal more than one usually got out of trying to interfere in other people's business.

'I suppose Ianthe didn't give you any idea when she was going to get married? I imagine she'd want you to marry them?' Sophia asked, as she saw her visitors out of the gate.

'That's another thing,' said Randolph. 'She suggested August, if you please.'

'August? Yes, that does seem rather soon,' said Sophia.

'It is quite out of the question as far as we are concerned,' said Randolph. 'She must know that my church is always closed in August – none of my parishioners would *dream* of being in London in August and Bertha and I always go either to the Riviera or the Italian lakes at that time. This year, we have arranged to go to Estoril where I believe the climate is delightful. By the way, do you think your husband could be persuaded to preach at our dedication festival in October? We need a man with experience of a parish like this to shake my good people up a bit.'

'I'm sure they don't need shaking up any more than people do here,' said Sophia, 'and I'm sure Mark would like to preach very much.' What a splendid opportunity it would be for him to use one of his famous 'openings'. 'A few months ago, as I was sitting in Doney's on the Via Veneto, where many of you....' She would suggest it to him.

'But as I keep telling Randolph,' Bertha was saying rather plaintively, '*somebody* must minister to the rich.'

'I expected Mark would be in before now,' said Sophia. 'He'll be so sorry to have missed you.'

They continued a little longer chatting by the Burdon's car, the main purpose of their visit temporarily forgotten.

'Perhaps we shouldn't have come,' said Bertha, arranging her fur coat so that she should not squash the fur by sitting on it, 'but we were worried about Ianthe. I never really cared for my sister-in-law,' she said to Sophia in a low voice, 'but I know how upset she would be at the idea of Ianthe making this mistake. Of course Ianthe was too much with her mother after my brother died – otherwise she might have got this sort of foolishness over when she was younger. But there they were living on top of each other in that flat, *much* too near Westminster Cathedral – I always felt it most oppressive when I went to see them, the cathedral towering over them like that. And one could even see the canons going in and out – *Roman* canons, of course...' her voice trailed off uncertainly and she began to fuss with the pot of quince jelly which was balanced rather unsafely in the glove compartment.

'I dare say nothing will come of this business,' said Randolph, getting into the car. 'Ianthe may come to her senses.'

They drove off, waving to Sophia. She strolled back into the house, wondering why Ianthe had not told *her* that she was going to marry John and feeling a little hurt by her lack of friendliness. Then it occurred to her suddenly that perhaps Ianthe didn't really like her. We assume that nice women – clergymen's wives and canons' daughters – who go to the same church will get on well together and be friends, that they must of necessity be friends, but why should they be? All this time Sophia had thought that she knew Ianthe and could predict how she would behave, and now she had done this. I must have left out 'the human element', she thought, the phrase coming into her mind as a convenient tag to explain unexpected behaviour. She was still brooding over her failure when Mark came in.

'I've got some news for you,' she said, when a decent interval had elapsed. 'Guess what it is?'

'Something to do with Faustina?' he suggested indulgently.

'No, though I was just trying to give her some liquid paraffin when they came.'

'Who came?'

'Ianthe's aunt and uncle – the Burdons – and he wants you to preach at their dedication festival.'

'I should like to very much – when is it?'

'In October, I think. He'll be writing to you. And you're to give them a sermon suitable for rich people.'

'How do they differ spiritually from others?' Mark asked.

'That's what I wondered,' said Sophia. 'But at least you'll be justified in giving them one of your best beginnings.'

'Yes, they will surely have stood in St Peter's or at

Delphi and even further afield than that.'

'There was other news too,' said Sophia, unable to contain herself any longer. 'Rather surprising, almost dreadful, news. Apparently Ianthe has told them that she intends to marry that young man from the library where she works – you remember, he came to the Christmas bazaar.'

'Really?' said Mark absently.

'But she wants to *marry* him,' Sophia persisted, 'and that surely can't be a good thing.'

'No, better not to marry,' he agreed, but he was thinking not of Ianthe and the young man from the library, but rather of the clergy in general and perhaps at that moment of himself in particular. How could Faustina's hairs have got *here*, he had asked himself at the early Mass that morning, seeing them on the fair linen cloth on the altar.

'And apparently he isn't a qualified librarian.'

'Oh, I don't see why librarians as such shouldn't marry, whether qualified or not,' said Mark, still not quite appreciating the point Sophia was trying to make.

'Darling, the celibacy or not of librarians is neither here nor there,' she said a little impatiently, 'but this young man is quite unsuitable for Ianthe.'

'Ianthe?' he said suddenly realising who Sophia was talking about. 'What does she want to get married for? Isn't she quite happy as she is in her charming little house?'

'No, that doesn't seem to be enough,' said Sophia. 'We've both had this picture of her which was so pleasing and comfortable and all the time she's been wanting something more.'

'Well, yes...' said Mark feeling rather at a loss. 'It's difficult to see what one can do to dissuade a woman of Ianthe's age from making what seems to us an unsuitable marriage.'

'Penny will be interested to hear about this,' Sophia went on. 'I suppose there's no harm in telling her tonight.'

'Tonight?'

'Yes – had you forgotten? We've been invited to supper with her.'

'But can she cook anything on that gas ring?' asked Mark apprehensively, for he was hungry and had been looking forward to one of Sophia's spaghettis which she had been cooking enthusiastically since the visit to Italy.

'At least I can provide you with a reasonable spaghetti,' said Penelope, welcoming them at the front door. 'And I've got a bottle of Chianti.'

'I didn't know you could cook,' said Mark.

'Well, I'm learning. It seems the best thing to do now and it gives me an interest.' Penelope sounded subdued and looked somehow different. Her hair was smoother and neater and she wore an ostentatiously simple dark blue dress.

'But this is excellent!' exclaimed Mark, in the rather unflatteringly surprised way people sometimes talk when provided with unexpectedly good food.

'And you've put basil in it, like I told you,' said Sophia.

'Yes, and I used a *tin* of tomatoes, and cooked it all very slowly for hours and hours.'

Mark felt rather out of place in the bed-sitting room, too big for the small space which seemed only just big enough for the two women so obviously wanting to have a sisterly talk.

After they had all drunk an indefinite toast in the Chianti Sophia came out with the news about Ianthe.

'The *dark* man?' asked Penelope. 'And I saw her with the other – the *fair* one – having dinner in a restaurant that's just opened near here. And now she's going to

228

marry the dark one. Oh, well. . . .'

'I should have thought Rupert Stonebird would be the one for her,' said Mark, feeling able to make this rather intelligent comment.

'Oh no,' said Sophia firmly. 'I made that *quite* clear when we were in Ravello. I said that I'd arranged for Rupert to marry Penny.'

'Sophia, you *didn't*!' Penelope burst out in horror.

'And why not?' Sophia protested.

'No, what difference can it make,' said Penelope more calmly. 'It doesn't really matter – I shall never marry now.'

Mark sat silent, not unduly surprised by her statement, for he was used to people, especially women, not marrying. But Ianthe had been the one he had seen as the splendid unmarried woman, so dependable and such a pillar of the church. He felt slightly apprehensive at the idea of Penelope attempting to fill this role. Drinking his coffee he watched the sisters warily as they, now forgetting his presence, began talking about why Penelope would never marry. It seemed to be something that had happened in Rome, some sort of disaster ending in tears, and then somebody – perhaps the same person? – had actually suggested they might go for a *walk* some time. . . . Mark couldn't make out what it was all about.

His attention strayed to Penelope's bookshelves to see if he could find something there to while away the time. He saw a volume of Donne's poetry and prose and turning to the sermons he began to consider what he could preach about at Ianthe's uncle's dedication festival. 'A sermon suitable for rich people,' Sophia had said, and he came upon the words 'Our critical day is not the very day of our death: but the whole course of our life', which might well do as a text for rich and poor alike. He remembered with irritation that somebody had approached him that afternoon with a complaint about Father Anstruther, who had taken the services when he had been away after Easter. After all this time some 'uncalled-for' remark had been brought up – Mark couldn't even remember now exactly what it had been – and he had found himself having to make excuses for Father Anstruther and protest that he couldn't really have meant what he had seemed to. . . .

'And then,' said Penelope, 'it wasn't so much that as what he called me – a jolly little thing – wasn't it *terrible?* . . .'

Mark turned away from the sermons to the love poems at which the book seemed to open more easily. A pressed flower fell out on to the floor and lay on the carpet, dark and dry. The things women did, he thought with resignation. Stooping down he picked up the flower and replaced it, wondering if he had put it in at the right poem and if it really mattered if he hadn't.

21

Ianthe was surprised how much courage it took to break the news of her engagement to Mervyn. She and John had decided that it would be better if she did it, not only because of her senior status in the library, but also because of the unusual and in some way privileged relationship she had with Mervyn, who could now be seen as a rejected suitor.

Obviously it would have been better to have broken the news first thing in the morning, without thinking of repercussions, but after Mervyn had come into the room and nothing had been said then it seemed that the opportunity had gone. Besides, Mervyn was in a bad temper because of a letter he had received.

'I will not have books taken away from the library,' he declared.

Ianthe did not improve matters by protesting mildly that books were meant to be read and that she saw no harm in people taking them away if they were known to be bona fide scholars.

'And how is one to know that?' Mervyn asked. 'This letter from somebody called R. J. Stonebird claims that this young man is one of his students – how am I to know that it's genuine?'

'Rupert Stonebird?' said Ianthe, feeling rather uncomfortable. 'He's a lecturer in Anthropology at London University.'

'So he says, but it doesn't impress me,' said Mervyn. 'These red brick universities don't impress me at all.'

'Well, you can hardly call London "red brick",' said Ianthe. 'Just think of the Senate House, all grey. And University College in Gower Street is really quite classical. As a matter of fact, you've met Rupert Stonebird – he's one of my neighbours.'

'Oh, then I suppose *you* put him up to writing this letter?'

'No, of course I didn't – but don't you remember after the Christmas bazaar, you and John and I and the vicar's sister-in-law and Rupert Stonebird. . . .'

'And Uncle Tom Cobley too, I suppose,' interrupted Mervyn sarcastically.

'You came and had a glass of sherry at my house,' said Ianthe.

'Of course, dear – your charming little house,' he said, softening a little at the idea of the house. 'But I don't remember this Stonebird.'

How much easier it would have been had Rupert been the man! Ianthe thought, for this would have been a good opportunity to break the news. It was ridiculous that she hadn't managed to tell Mervyn yet. John was going to buy her an engagement ring at lunchtime and it was nearly that now. If only the subject could be brought round to something connected with marriage.

'What are the books this man wants to take away?' she asked at last.

'That's the annoying thing – books that nobody ever asks for,' said Mervyn, perhaps illogically. 'Some old-fashioned monographs on African marriage and that sort of thing.'

Ianthe nerved herself. 'Talking of marriage,' she began, for really they almost had been, 'I want you to know that John and I are going to be married – quite soon.' Her voice died away on a kind of gasp. There was a silence. 'Perhaps you guessed,' she went on nervously.

'Oh come now, dear,' Mervyn exclaimed, 'you can't expect me to have guessed anything as fantastic and un-likely as *that*! Whatever next!'

'But it's true – one doesn't usually joke about such things.'

'Doesn't one? I should have thought it was one of the most popular subjects for joking.'

Ianthe was disconcerted by the unexpected way Mervyn was taking her news. She wished that John would come in, but she knew that he was in the library helping a reader with a query.

'John and I are going to be married,' she repeated, beginning to wonder if it could be true.

'Well, even if you are you're certainly cradle-snatching, aren't you?' said Mervyn spitefully. 'John must be a good ten years younger than you are.'

'Only five years,' said Ianthe, wishing she could have maintained a dignified silence. 'That's not much of a dif-ference.'

'You wait till you're over forty, my dear, and he's still in his thirties.'

Ianthe was silent, for she too had thought of this.

'So *that* was why you didn't fancy the idea of marry-ing me,' Mervyn went on.

'I didn't know then that John and I. . . .'

'You mean he hadn't popped the question?'

'No, he hadn't asked me, but I . . .' the door opened before Ianthe could finish her sentence and she was re-lieved to see John coming into the room.

'What's this I hear about you and Ianthe getting married?' said Mervyn truculently. 'It isn't true, is it?'

'Of course it is,' said John, going over to Ianthe and taking her arm. 'Aren't you going to congratulate me?'

'I might congratulate *you* but I certainly won't con-gratulate *her*.'

'Well, I don't have to get your permission to marry her,' said John.

'No, but you'll need a job if you're going to support a wife, won't you,' said Mervyn in a threatening tone. 'And I'm not at all sure that I'm going to have you working here.'

'Then I'll work somewhere else,' shouted John, approaching Mervyn as if he were about to strike him. 'I suppose you wanted to marry her yourself – that's what it is!'

None of the actors of the little scene realised that the door between the reading room and the library office had been left open when John came in, so that the raised voices were plainly audible to the three readers who sat at the long table working. One, a moon-faced sociologist, went on reading as if he had heard nothing, nor was a bearded Dutchman in the least disturbed, for his understanding of the English language did not go beyond a knowledge of written sociological jargon. Only the third reader, a youngish woman of about thirty-five who had come in to shelter from a heavy shower of rain, pricked up her ears and looked away from the book she had not been reading. To realise that two men could apparently be quarrelling almost publicly over a woman in this unchivalrous age sent her on her way with new hope.

The rain had stopped and the sun shone brilliantly as Ianthe and John walked arm-in-arm out of the library. Mervyn, who had decided that this was not the occasion for a packed lunch however delicious, had strode out in front of them and dramatically hailed a taxi, with no clear idea of where he wanted to go. Then he remembered his friend's restaurant in South Kensington and asked to be driven there, leaning forward irritably all the time to make sure that the driver was not taking him a roundabout way.

Ianthe and John were going to an antique shop to buy the engagement ring, for Ianthe had expressed a preference for something 'old-fashioned'.

Supposing he can't afford it, she wondered in a sudden moment of panic, for the scene with Mervyn had shaken her confidence a little. And supposing the man in the shop laughed when he saw a middle-aged woman being bought a ring by a young man.

But the jeweller was more interested in his wares than in the couple trying on the garnet and amethyst rings, and he thought that the amethyst set in a circle of pearls which they eventually chose looked very well on the lady's pale hand. It was such a very pale hand that he found himself humming one of the Indian Love Lyrics as he made out the bill.

Afterwards, when he had slipped the ring on to her finger, John would have liked to go to an expensive restaurant to celebrate, but Ianthe reminded him, gently but firmly, that they must not take too long over lunch, since Shirley was not very good at helping the readers and they didn't know when Mervyn would be back.

So they went into a humbler, nastier place than John would have chosen, which emphasised its lowliness by being in a basement. Ianthe sat down at a table for two, fortunately vacant at that moment, while John went up to the counter and fetched poached eggs, Danish pastries and coffee.

Daisy Pettigrew, also coming away from the counter, did not see John and Ianthe. Whenever she entered a café she always felt obliged to choose a table where a coloured man or woman was already sitting, so that they should not feel slighted in any way. Looking around her now, she saw a table for four with an African already at it. Then she noticed that a clergyman, also bearing a tray, was making for the same table, but she managed to get there before him and put her bag down on the chair next to her to prevent him from sitting down. One never knew – he might be a Roman Catholic or Oxford Group; it did not occur to her that he too might be trying to show the black man that there was no colour bar here.

He gave her a somewhat hostile stare as she crashed her tray down on the table.

'Anyone sitting here?' she asked brightly.

He made a slight movement of his head and went on reading his book which had an abstruse legal title.

That woman looks much too old and fragile to be clearing tables, Daisy thought, noticing a shambling elderly figure gathering up the used dishes and piling them on to a tray, and her legs are bad. 'Bad leg' was an old-fashioned complaint for which one used to see remedies advertised in the cheaper newspapers. Did people not suffer from it now? she wondered.

Daisy put on her reading glasses, examined her welsh rarebit and opened a novel by Angus Wilson, taking a deep breath as if she were about to taste some liquid unfamiliar to her which might not be altogether to her liking. The title, something to do with a zoo, had attracted her, with her great love of animals, but she had not read more than half a page before something made her look up and she saw the blurred image of a woman apparently signalling to her. Exchanging her glasses once more, she saw that it was Ianthe Broome with a young man.

'Miss Pettigrew – Daisy – I want to introduce my fiancé, John Challow,' she said, coming up to the table.

'I think I remember seeing you at the church bazaar,' said John, shaking hands, for indeed she had been unforgettable at her stall behind the piled-up tins of cat food.

What a nice-mannered young man, thought Daisy, and how pleasant it was to see two young people so obviously happy together, especially in these days when it

236

seemed the fashion to make fun of sentiment. And of course Ianthe was not really all that young which made it even nicer that her fiancé should be gazing at her with such obvious devotion.

'Now, let me see, you work at Ianthe's library, don't you,' she said.

'Yes, I do at the moment,' said John. 'But Mervyn Cantrell – he's the librarian – hasn't taken our news too well, so I may have to leave.'

'Oh, what a shame!' said Daisy indignantly. 'I suppose he's jealous. Jealousy is a very powerful emotion,' she declared. 'Of course I've had more experience of it in cats than in human beings. Some cats are of a very jealous disposition. Now take Faustina – Sophia Ainger's cat – she would hate it if Sophia ever thought of getting a companion for her. I have strongly advised her *against* it.'

Ianthe hoped they were not going to have to listen to an account of Faustina's psychological difficulties and was glad when John turned the conversation back to himself.

'I don't see how I'm going to be able to go on working at the library if Mervyn's going to be like this,' he said.

'Oh, you will easily find something else,' said Daisy. 'I suppose you know all about card indexes?'

'Yes.' He laughed. 'And I know the alphabet, too.'

'Very useful,' said Daisy seriously. She had been wondering whether he might like to work for her brother Edwin and help to keep the records of the animals and their treatments. It was an idea worth considering and she decided to speak to her brother about it. 'Will the wedding be at St Basil's?' she asked.

'I'm not sure,' said Ianthe. 'My uncle is a clergyman, so perhaps...' she broke off uncertainly, for she had not yet told Sophia of her engagement and the idea of it embarrassed her a little, especially after their talk in

Italy. 'As a matter of fact, you're the first St Basil's person I've told,' she went on.

'Oh, is it a secret, then?' Daisy looked childishly pleased. 'I won't tell anyone.' All the same, she might sound Edwin about that job.

'We'd better get back, darling,' said John to Ianthe. 'I expect Mervyn will be champing.'

As it happened Mervyn was still out. He had felt he deserved a good lunch and Eric's coq au vin had done a good deal to restore his spirits and heal his wounded pride, if it had been wounded. The restaurant was now beginning to empty and Eric was wandering about talking to his guests, finally coming to Mervyn's table.

'What did you think of it?' he asked.

'Oh, excellent – it's done me a lot of good,' said Mervyn. 'I had a bit of a shock this morning, a sort of a let-down, if you get my meaning. A certain person I'd been thinking rather a lot of – well, it's turned out they prefer somebody else, though they'll soon find out their mistake,' he added ambiguously.

'And there's other good fish in the sea, don't forget,' said Eric, who delighted in culinary metaphors. 'Oh, I knew there was something I had to tell you,' he went on, laying a hand on Mervyn's sleeve. 'I hope your mum's well, by the way?'

'Very well, thank you, the change at Sittingbourne did her good.'

'I'm so glad – I felt awful making that silly mistake. Whatever must you've thought! And now I've just remembered whose mum it *was* that passed on – at least I remembered after you'd gone – it came to me in the middle of the night, like I said it would.'

'Oh – whose, then?'

'Wilf Bason's.'

'Wilf Bason? I don't think I know him,' said Mervyn

238

somewhat testily.

'Oh, you remember Wilf Bason – he had a job at a clergy house and then went to some seaside place to work in a café – home-made cakes and that. Well, now he's back and it's *his* mum. . . .'

How Eric did go on, thought Mervyn wearily. 'I suppose I must be getting back,' he said, standing up.

As he passed an antique shop on his way to the Underground – for the passion that had driven him into a taxi had now cooled – he saw a Pembroke table very much like Ianthe's – that table that would never be his now. On a closer glance, however, he saw that it was an even finer specimen than hers.

22

After some hesitation Ianthe and John decided that it would be proper to announce their engagement in *The Times*. 'What your mother would have wished,' John declared rather piously, and Ianthe agreed with this, though she preferred not to dwell in too much detail on what her mother's feelings might have been.

'It will tell our friends who wouldn't otherwise know,' she said, but a little doubtfully, for it was difficult to imagine that John could number among his friends people who regularly read *The Times*. Yet the announcement did have some results. John received a letter from a former girl friend, which he concealed from Ianthe, while she received three letters from old friends of her parents which it seemed pointless to show to him. A fourth letter was from Basil Branche, delighted to hear her good news, and was her fiancé one of the Berkshire Challows – or was that just a railway station, the sort of place one's host met one at with a car on a Friday evening? Puzzled, Ianthe read on and came to his own news which was that he had 'got a church' of his own – 'St Barbara-in-the-Precinct – a very old, almost moribund church, just off High Holborn, very convenient for Gamages – how would you like to be married *there* – I mean at my church, not Gamages!!!'

For a moment or two Ianthe considered the idea seriously. How nice it would be to slip away quietly, early one morning as Robert Browning and Elizabeth

Barrett had done, and be married at eight o' clock, or whatever was the earliest legal hour, with two witnesses brought in from the street! Then she dismissed the idea as quite impractical. Her uncle and aunt and Mark Ainger would be hurt if she did not choose one of their churches, and, worst of all, it might look as if she was ashamed of John if she did not have a wedding at a conventional time of day with all the St Basil's parishioners at the reception. In any case, it was most unlikely that Basil Branche would be equal to performing a wedding ceremony as early as eight o'clock in the morning. At lunchtime one day she went to look at his church and found it locked. The notice board told her that there were no weekday services earlier than Holy Communion at 10.30 a.m. on Saints' Days – who in all the new blocks of offices would be able to attend a service at *that* time of day, she wondered – and that the Vicar (Rev. B. Branche) lived at an address in Kensington. A paper pinned to the board further informed her that the church would be closed from 27 July to 1 September. Ianthe wondered if he was going abroad again with his elderly ladies, though surely August in Italy would be too hot even for Miss Bede.

She turned away from the church feeling cheated, for she had not even been able to go inside it and say a prayer. She knew that St Barbara was the patron of miners and artillery and though it seemed at first sight unlikely that the saint could have much in common with an Anglican clergyman's daughter, Ianthe remembered that she had decided to visit Miss Grimes that evening to tell her the news, and goodness only knew what help she might need there.

Later that day Ianthe left the library alone and set off for the Finchley Road and the steep side street where Miss Grimes lived in her bed-sitting room. She carried with her a bottle of medium dry Spanish sherry of reasonable but not the best quality. If there was a toast to be drunk – and surely Miss Grimes would insist on it – it would be preferable in a decorous sherry which did not have the raffishness of the Spanish Burgundy, now for ever associated in Ianthe's mind with Miss Grimes.

She reached the house and began looking among the cards under the bells for Miss Grimes's name, but it did not seem to be there. Ianthe was taken aback and slightly alarmed, then stricken with remorse, for perhaps Miss Grimes had died in the months that had gone by since her last visit, or perhaps she had been unable to afford the rent and had to move to somewhere cheaper.

Hesitating on the doorsteps of houses which may have seen better days must be regarded as one of the occupational hazards of being a gentlewoman, but Ianthe felt it had been too much a part of her life lately and she resented Miss Grimes for having moved or even died – she should not have done anything so inconsiderate. What was Ianthe to do now? Who could she ask about Miss Grimes and which of the many bells should she ring for information?

Luckily at that moment a woman came up to the door and Ianthe was able to ask her if Miss Grimes still lived there.

'Miss *Grimes.* . . .' The woman was tall and stooping, encumbered with a heavy shopping basket and out of breath from climbing the hill.

'Yes – I came to see her.'

'Miss Grimes, yes.' She fumbled for her keys, opened the door and then stared at Ianthe with her pale eyes. 'You'd better come in,' she said.

Ianthe followed her rather apprehensively into the hall, where the woman put down her shopping basket with a groan of relief. Ianthe was glad that she did not ask her to go into her room.

'Has something happened to Miss Grimes?' she asked.

I couldn't find her name by any of the bells.'

'No, you wouldn't find it – she isn't here. But nothing has happened to her, at least not in the way you mean.' The woman paused for dramatic effect, or so it seemed when she spoke again. 'Miss Grimes has married Mr Slaski and gone to live in Ealing.'

'Goodness, then something *has* happened,' said Ianthe, taken aback. 'Marrying and going to live in Ealing...' She felt shaken almost as if she were suffering from shock and would have liked to sit down had not the woman put her shopping basket on the only chair.

'Yes, we were surprised too, in a way,' said the woman. 'She met Mr Slaski in a public house – the Four Feathers or whatever the name was where she used to go – they were each alone and got talking. Mr Slaski is Polish. He had just lost his wife. One can see how it came about – life can be very lonely for a man.'

'And for a woman too,' Ianthe murmured.

'Yes, of course. That's why it's better to marry when one has the chance – or perhaps I should say *if* one has the chance.' She laughed rather flutily. 'Well, I'm sorry you've had this journey all in vain – it's quite a walk up from the Finchley Road, isn't it.' Her eyes lighted on the unmistakably wrapped bottle Ianthe was holding. 'And you'd brought a present for her too, what a pity. It looks as if it would be difficult to post. Or perhaps you'll be going to Ealing one of these days – I've got the address somewhere.'

'Thank you, but I shan't be able to go there at the moment. Perhaps....' Ianthe hesitated, changing the position of the bottle in her arms. 'It's quite a good sherry, I believe, if anyone would like it here, I mean, it seems a pity to....'

'Ah, that *is* kind.' The woman's thin face lit up. 'This time of the evening too, just what one needs, and so seldom *has*, something to revive ... though for what

243

one is being revived one sometimes wonders, doesn't one.' She laughed her fluty laugh again and disappeared into a doorway.

Ianthe fled, not wishing to be invited in for a drink. On the way down the hill she realised that she had forgotten to get Miss Grimes's address. Still, no doubt a letter would be forwarded. Miss Grimes married – and to a Pole she had picked up in a pub. Somehow the news disconcerted Ianthe, as did the picture of the other woman drinking sherry alone in her room. At that moment life seemed very dark; Ianthe was perhaps too rigid in her views to reflect that a woman might have worse things to look forward to than the prospect of marriage to a Polish widower and a life in Ealing, or even of a quiet drink in one's own room at the end of a hard day.

It was not until she had seen the announcement in *The Times* that Sophia felt able to call on Ianthe and offer her good wishes and felicitations on the news without the fear of revealing that she had already known about the engagement for some weeks. As she walked the short distance to Ianthe's house she wondered what she should say. 'Of course I have seen *The Times* – as one does – and have come to wish you all happiness', or, 'Mark will be delighted to marry you and I'll arrange the reception in the Parish Hall just to show that there's no ill-feeling.' Yet what 'ill-feeling' could there possibly be? Sophia felt that she must not give the slightest hint of having in any way 'taken umbrage' at not being among the first to be told of the engagement. Perhaps, though, in a curious way which she had not recognised at the time, she *had* been told of it in the conversation in the gardens at Ravello.

Believing that a clergyman's wife should never call at a house empty-handed, even if she brought only the parish magazine, Sophia had hastily picked a bunch of mixed garden flowers and was still trying to arrange them on the doorstep when Ianthe came to the door.

'I've come to offer my congratulations,' said Sophia, 'and to bring you these.'

'Oh, how *lovely*!' exclaimed Ianthe, a little too effusive in her thanks for ordinary garden flowers, Sophia thought, but she may have felt a slight awkwardness at the encounter.

'John is here, so do come in and meet him properly,' Ianthe went on.

Sophia stepped into the hall, realising that she had not been inside the house since the occasion when Rupert Stonebird had so surprisingly answered the door-bell with a hot water bottle in his hand. Inside everything looked as charming as Sophia had remembered it – the water colours of Italian scenes in the hall and the china and books in the white bookshelves. There were summery–looking pink and blue chintz curtains in the sitting room and a copy of the *Church Times* was rustling gently in the breeze from the open window.

'John is putting up some shelves in the kitchen,' Ianthe explained.

There is a certain type of man who is always putting up shelves, Sophia reflected, thinking how full of shelves some houses must be. 'I'm so glad he can do things like that,' she said aloud. 'Mark is hopeless, but luckily our predecessor at the vicarage was rather good at it and left his shelves behind, so we have all we need. Oh, but of course I remember you,' she said, as John climbed down from the stepladder and shook hands. 'You came to the bazaar and bought. . . .' What was it he had bought and did it really matter? It was odd how one found oneself making trivial conversation on important occasions. Perhaps it was because one could not say what was really in one's mind.

'Little did I think then that I should be coming to live here,' said John. 'Isn't it strange the turns life takes.'

Ianthe looked up at him fondly.

'I hope I shall fit into the parish as Ianthe's husband,' said John smoothly.

'Are you a churchgoer?' asked Sophia rather too casually.

'Oh well, not exactly – I mean I haven't been up to now, but I expect I shall come with Ianthe.'

Really, he was very good-looking, Sophia thought, but was he quite the husband for Ianthe? Would it not be wiser to break off the engagement now before it was too late? Yet how was it to be broken? Leaving them together so happy in each other's company, Sophia was shocked to find that she almost wanted something to happen that might expose John as an 'impostor'. She could certainly not have admitted this to Mark – it would not be in his nature to understand such baseness. She wondered if Rupert Stonebird might be a little less noble and if he were at home now so that she could have a talk with him and perhaps explain something of her feelings.

Looking up from reading an offprint of an article entitled 'Steatopygia of the Human Female in the Kalahari', Rupert was surprised to see Sophia coming up to the door. It was a far cry from the protruding posteriors of the Hottentot women to the spare elegance of an English vicar's wife. Of marginal interest to the social anthropologist, he thought, laying the offprint aside, the kind of thing that might give rise to one or two harmless little jokes with his female students, but certainly not relevant to the matter in hand, which was Sophia coming up to his front door.

She seemed almost distressed as she came into the hall and his mind leaped to the various types of restoratives or refreshments he could offer. Leading her into his study he decided on strong tea – it was only ten past four – and murmured something about going to put the kettle on.

Oh, what a haven, Sophia thought, relaxing in an old

comfortable chair, after the un-sympathy and alien air of Ianthe's setting.

'You look as if you'd had a shock or bad news,' he said, coming back into the room with cups and saucers.

'Yes – an accident or a bereavement.'

'I hope tea will be all right,' said Rupert. 'I've got other things.'

'Oh perfectly, thank you – just what I need. We do *not* drink alcohol in the middle of the afternoon,' said Sophia, in the tone she used to reprove Faustina.

'No, but we could.'

'Not unless there's *really* been an accident or a bereavement.'

'And there hasn't?'

'No. I've just been to offer my congratulations to Ianthe and her fiancé.'

'Oh, I see. Will you have a piece of cake? Sister Dew brought me this and it's rather good.'

'Not one of her sponges, I see.'

'No – she evidently thought a man would like something more substantial like this excellent plum cake. Tell me about Ianthe and her fiancé,' said Rupert, taking his cup of tea to his desk and sitting down there.

'Well, there isn't much to tell, really. You know *her*, and he is that good-looking dark young man who was at the Christmas bazaar.'

'Yes, I do remember vaguely. We all had a glass of sherry at her house afterwards – what a long time ago it seems! And now she's going to marry him, or he is going to marry her,' said Rupert rather self-consciously, for he was remembering the little scene in the garden and Ianthe's distress when he had tried to kiss her.

'I never thought of her as getting married – it seems all wrong,' Sophia burst out. 'I wanted her to stay as she was, almost as if I'd created her.'

'No, one had one's own idea of her,' said Rupert

rather stiffly, 'and if one did think of her as getting married it wasn't to somebody like this.' He wondered if Sophia would have felt differently if Ianthe had been going to marry *him*.

'I suppose it's wrong to have preconceived ideas about people – you as an anthropologist must appreciate the value of an open mind.'

'Yes, in field work, certainly. But meeting people in everyday life in north-west London isn't quite the same as studying a primitive community in Africa. Had you a preconceived idea of *me*?' he asked a little nervously.

'A single man probably inspires wider and wilder speculation than a single woman,' Sophia admitted, accepting another cup of tea. 'His unmarried state is in itself more interesting than a woman's unmarriedness, if you see what I mean. We thought of you as somebody who went around measuring skulls, and that was our first wrong assumption,' she said lightly.

Whereas really I go around making nice women cry, thought Rupert, hardly liking to ask what the second wrong assumption could have been. 'This John that Ianthe is going to marry,' he said, seeing a way to turn the conversation away from himself. 'What did you think of him when you saw him just now?'

'Oh, he seems charming and is obviously devoted to her,' said Sophia. 'One wonders whether he can really be as good as he seems to be.'

How understanding Rupert was, she thought, so sympathetic and reliable. It was such a pity that things had not gone as she had hoped between him and Penelope. Perhaps it needed Ianthe's wedding to bring them together. Passing Ianthe's house on her way home she now saw that this marriage was inevitable – it had to be. The lemon leaves had been unwrapped and there were the fragrant raisins at the heart. She imagined John and Ianthe talking happily together and tried to feel glad for them.

23

Rupert had often attended weddings, or 'marriage cere-
monies' as the anthropologists called them, during his
field work in Africa, and although Ianthe's wedding was
not at all like these he was able to observe the proceed-
ings with the same keen detachment as on those other
occasions. Perhaps he was not the person best fitted to
give an account of Ianthe's dress, for as he watched her
moving slowly up the aisle on the arm of her uncle he
had no more than a confused impression of something
blue and silky and a large hat – rather like the one she had
worn at the anthropological garden party, but trimmed
with roses. She did not wear roses for *me*, he reflected
rather sadly. In her hand she carried an ivory prayer
book which he was sure had belonged to her mother.

As for the bridegroom, Rupert looked on him with a
certain amount of prejudice, in the way an only moder-
ately good-looking man will regard one much more
handsome. At least he appeared to be 'devoted to her'
and he had even heard two ladies in the same pew whis-
pering as much to each other, but it seemed to Rupert
only fitting that he should seem to be devoted on this
one day if on no other. He had thought for a time that he
ought to offer to put John up for the wedding and had
seriously considered that it might be his duty. Then he
reflected that there was a certain delicacy about the situation, and while he was reflecting Sister Dew had

offered, 'come to the rescue', as she put it.

The best man was tall and fair, surely the librarian from the library where Ianthe worked, Rupert thought, though he understood that there had been some slight unpleasantness, even a quarrel, over the engagement. There were no bridesmaids or other attendants.

Mark Ainger and Basil Branche were to perform the ceremony and the church was filled with a varied collection of well-wishers and sightseers, among whom Rupert recognised all the usual congregation of St Basil's and some rather unexpected people such as Mrs Grandison, the mother of Sophia and Penelope, and Lady Selvedge, who had opened the Christmas bazaar.

Later, when they were all crowding out of the church into the hall for the reception, Rupert found himself standing by Sophia and Penelope, the tears still glistening in their eyes.

'Weddings always make me cry, no matter *whose* they happen to be,' said Penny fiercely.

She looked up at him and he noticed that her eyes had a curious blundering, half-blind look, as if she could scarcely open them. After a moment he realised that she was wearing false eyelashes, longer, darker and more abundant than her normal ones, and surely there were far too many of them? He wondered if he was supposed to know that they were false and felt embarrassed and somehow mean at having guessed the secret. Quickly he looked away from her face and concentrated on her yellow tulle hat shaped like a soufflé.

'Yes, weddings are very moving,' he said, a little more stiffly than he had intended, 'the whole atmosphere generates emotion.'

'The wedding march, really,' said Sophia, 'don't you think that's what it is, partly? There is something almost sad about Mendelssohn.'

'Not perhaps as music,' said Rupert, 'but the idea of

the Victorian age altogether.'

'Did you think Ianthe looked nice?' asked Sophia.

Rupert hesitated, feeling that Sophia was setting a sort of trap for him and that Penny too was waiting for his answer. 'Oh, brides always look nice,' he said in a cowardly way, 'but of course I'm no judge of the details.'

'That ivory prayer book belonged to her mother,' said Penny.

'Yes, it's strange, that use of ivory,' said Rupert. 'When I was in East Africa I didn't somehow associate the tusks of elephants with covers for Anglican devotional books.'

'Well, if you put it like *that*...' said Penny in a disgusted tone, and turning on her heel she left him and made off towards the tables where the food was spread out.

Rupert looked appealingly towards Sophia for help but she gave him none.

'I must be talking to people,' she said, 'so I'll leave you to observe the scene. After all, you're used to doing that.'

Rupert, feeling that his role had been assigned to him, strolled up to one of the tables and with what he hoped was the right amount of nonchalance took a glass of white wine. A sweet Spanish 'Sauterne', he decided, quite a suitable choice. Noticing that Basil Branche was also sipping it he went up to him and recalled their meeting in Rome in the spring.

'That evening in Trastevere,' said Basil, 'and now this. Do you remember the toast on that occasion?'

'It was to Sister Dew and her sprained ankle, as far as I remember,' said Rupert. 'I suppose this occasion is a happier one.'

'You *suppose* – well that's one way of putting it.'

Rupert felt slightly embarrassed, for he had not meant

his remark literally and he found the young clergyman's cynicism a little shocking.

'I'm sure they will be very happy,' he said reproachfully.

'Imparadised in one another's arms, as Milton put it,' Basil went on. 'Or encasseroled, perhaps – the bay leaf resting on the *boeuf bourgignon*.' He drained his glass with a flourish and took another. 'Entre Deux Mers, would you say?'

'I was thinking Spanish perhaps,' said Rupert.

'Ah, yes, a *dulce* from the land of Ignatius Loyola,' said Basil. 'And the best possible for a mixed gathering like this, though I believe there's champagne for the toasts.'

'I sincerely hope so,' said Mervyn Cantrell, coming up to them. 'This is a little sweet for my liking, but I'm sure it's what Ianthe prefers.'

'Well, women are said to like sweet wines,' said Rupert, 'though I think that's a fallacy.'

'Of course I suppose I know Ianthe better than anyone here,' said Mervyn complacently. 'In fact if it hadn't been for me we shouldn't be here at her wedding today.'

'You "brought them together", as it were,' said Rupert awkwardly.

'Oh, yes. I watched them falling in love in the library – I was very touched when they asked me to be best man, I can tell you. What do you think of these eats?' he asked, lowering his voice.

'Very nice.'

'A bit unimaginative – ham sandwiches and that, but you know what people are. Did you get one of those lobster patties?'

'No, I think I've eaten enough for the moment,' said Rupert, edging away into a corner where he could see Edwin and Daisy Pettigrew. It was restful being with them, for they were quiet like animals. Edwin was

252

watching the time because of his afternoon surgery and Daisy was anxious not to be late for the cats' feeding time.

'You wouldn't believe how long it takes to prepare their meat,' she confided, 'and each animal has its own individual dish. We're very full up at the moment because of the summer holidays. I've even got a cat from Ealing here, a dear old black and white fellow. You know, Mr Stonebird,' she drew him into a corner, 'I hope you don't mind my saying this, but I always used to think that *you* would marry Ianthe Broome. Do you remember that evening at the vicarage in the winter? I felt it then. It only goes to show that feelings aren't always right. Yet the instincts of *animals* are unfailing. . . .'

Rupert now edged quietly away from Daisy, without seeming to do so, he hoped. He had not so far approached Ianthe, for she had been so surrounded by well-wishers that there had been no opportunity to speak to her. Now, when there seemed to be a chance, he did not know what to say, and his being perhaps the last of her friends to wish her well gave the occasion a 'significance' he had not intended. He wished that John would go away, so that he could have a moment alone with her, but John, naturally enough, stood his ground and Rupert remembered that they were married now and must be treated as one.

'You will be near neighbours now,' Rupert brought out, speaking to John rather than to her, 'and I hope you'll come and dine with me when you're settled down.'

A formal and meaningless speech, he reflected, but had his relationship with Ianthe ever been more than that? He had been slow to seize his opportunities, but had he ever really wanted to get anywhere with her? A line of poetry came into his mind, something about a garland of red roses on the habit of a nun – loving her might have been like that. 'Farewell, Ianthe...' he thought and wondered if Landor had ever written such a line.

'John has put up some more shelves in the kitchen,' he heard her saying to another guest, and it seemed suitable for him to move on.

'Rupert...' he realised that the hall was emptying and Sophia was at his side.

'It's all over,' she said. 'Wasn't it dreadful, I almost hoped somebody might stand up at the back of the church and forbid the marriage – like in *Jane Eyre* – and expose John as an impostor. I wanted it to happen, and not only for Ianthe's *good*.' Sophia bowed her head, a little ashamed of having confessed so much to Rupert. John was not an impostor, or no more of one than are most of the men who promise to be something they cannot possibly be.

'Yes, I know how you felt,' said Rupert. 'I think I almost wanted it myself. How dreadful we are basically in our so-called civilised society,' he added complacently.

They walked slowly out of the hall while behind them Faustina stalked towards the table where some eatables still remained. After sniffing critically at several plates she finally picked up the last lobster patty in her mouth and jumped down under the table to devour it at her leisure.

'Oh, you naughty pussy,' said Sister Dew ineffectually, and began collecting together the food that remained and covering it with a cloth.

'There's a cup of tea in the vicarage,' said Sophia. 'Is there ever *not*?'

'Thank you, that would be nice. It will bring us down to earth again. And afterwards, I was wondering if perhaps Penny would have dinner with me?' He looked around, not seeing her anywhere.

'Penny? Oh, but she's gone,' said Sophia. 'She has a date for this evening.'

'Oh, I see,' said Rupert flatly, wondering if Sophia and Penny had contrived the whole thing between them on purpose to spite him. Women were so deceitful that he could well believe it. 'But I wanted to take her out,' he went on almost peevishly. What was he to do with the evening now, he wondered, as he walked home. It was the tradition that one took a girl out on the evening of a wedding day and now here he was left in his study with the prospect of an evening spent alone correcting proofs.

As he sat despondently at his desk, the telephone rang. But it was only Esther Clovis, reminding him that he had promised to give a paper at the first autumn meeting of a certain learned society and asking if he had decided on the subject and title.

'Yes – "The Wiles of Nice Women in a Civilised Society",' he said quickly and hung up before she could exclaim or question.

A few days went by before he could make up his mind to approach Penelope with another invitation. He would make her wait, he decided, but then it occurred to him that if he made her wait too long it might well be too late.

He discovered from Sophia that she was now working in an office near St Paul's Cathedral and he looked forward to calling on her suddenly one day, taking her by surprise so that she could not refuse a casual invitation to lunch. But when, at half-past twelve, he went into her office and asked for her he was told that she had already gone.

Feeling rather dispirited he began to walk up towards the cathedral. On the steps a boys' band was playing the

Pilgrims' Chorus from Tannhäuser, a piece he always found particularly depressing. It was better, though not much, when they changed to 'Land of Hope and Glory'. He went on aimlessly and found himself round at the back of the building among the heaps of broken marble. In the middle of one such pile, as if on rocks at the seaside, sat a woman – middle-aged of course – drinking tea from a plastic cup, the traffic swirling in front of her. If only this could have been Penelope, he thought, what a splendid and unusual place for a love scene!

Coming into the gardens he found himself among the office workers sitting on the iron chairs, some with sandwiches, others with knitting or books, and still others with their eyes closed and faces raised in the mild sunshine. Here, at the end of a row, sat Penelope, a half-eaten sandwich in her hand.

She hasn't seen me, he thought, and I must go carefully and not say anything to annoy or upset her. For the tears that seem romantic and even fitting in Rome on the Spanish Steps at night would be quite otherwise in St Paul's churchyard at lunchtime.

B+T 6-10 ¢